S0-APO-810

The Reluctant Cyprian

Diana Campbell

A SIGNET BOOK

NEW AMERICAN LIBRARY

TIMES MIRROR

NAL BOOKS ARE AVAILABLE AT QUANTITY DISCOUNTS WHEN
USED TO PROMOTE PRODUCTS OR SERVICES. FOR INFORMATION
PLEASE WRITE TO PREMIUM MARKETING DIVISION, THE NEW
AMERICAN LIBRARY, INC., 1633 BROADWAY, NEW YORK,
NEW YORK 10019.

Copyright © 1983 by Diana Campbell

All rights reserved

SIGNET TRADEMARK REG. U.S. PAT. OFF. AND FOREIGN COUNTRIES
REGISTERED TRADEMARK—MARCA REGISTRADA
HECHO EN CHICAGO, U.S.A.

SIGNET, SIGNET CLASSICS, MENTOR, PLUME, MERIDIAN and NAL BOOKS
are published by The New American Library, Inc.,
1633 Broadway, New York, New York 10019

First Printing, June, 1983

1 2 3 4 5 6 7 8 9

PRINTED IN THE UNITED STATES OF AMERICA

It was ok but nothing spectacular
you could take it or leave it

+5

TEACHERS OF TEMPTATION

When Juliet first arrived in London, she had no one to rely on but her distant cousin Louisa—who turned out to have changed from a most proper young lady into a most skillful Cyprian kept by whatever lordly lover was most lavish with his gifts.

When Juliet herself was forced to pretend to be a woman of pleasure, she had no one to teach her that age-old art but the still-captivating Mrs. Fitch—who once had been the toast of London society and had a lifetime of tantalizing tricks and seductive secrets to share.

But when Juliet had to find a way not to fall in love with a man who clearly wished to give her nothing but gold, she had nowhere to look for help—certainly not her own inexperienced heart. : . .

The Reluctant
Cyprian

The Book Nook
Paperbacks ½ price
7904 E. Harry (at Rock Rd.)
Buy - Sell - Trade

PAPERBACK EXCHANGE
322 N. West St.
Wichita, Ks. 67203
945-7202

SIGNET Regency Romances You'll Enjoy

(0451)

☐ THE AMERICAN DUCHESS by Joan Wolf. (119185—$2.25)*

☑ A DIFFICULT TRUCE by Joan Wolf. (099737—$1.95)*

☒ HIS LORDSHIP'S MISTRESS by Joan Wolf. (114590—$2.25)*

☐ A KIND OF HONOR by Joan Wolf. (092961—$1.75)*

☒ MARGARITA by Joan Wolf. (115562—$2.25)*

☐ THE SCOTTISH LORD by Joan Wolf. (112733—$2.25)*

☐ THE RELUCTANT CYPRIAN by Diana Campbell.
(123387—$2.25)*

☐ A MARRIGE OF INCONVENIENCE by Diana Campbell.
(118677—$2.25)*

☐ LORD MARGRAVE'S DECEPTION by Diana Campbell.
(114604—$2.25)*

☐ COME BY MY LOVE by Diana Brown. (121309—$2.50)*

☐ A DEBT OF HONOR by Diana Brown. (114175—$2.25)*

☒ ST. MARTIN'S SUMMER by Diana Brown. (116240—$2.25)*

*Prices slightly higher in Canada

Buy them at your local bookstore or use this convenient coupon for ordering.

THE NEW AMERICAN LIBRARY, INC.,
P.O. Box 999, Bergenfield, New Jersey 07621

Please send me the books I have checked above. I am enclosing $_____
(please add $1.00 to this order to cover postage and handling). Send check
or money order—no cash or C.O.D.'s. Prices and numbers are subject to change
without notice.

Name_____

Address_____

City _____ State _____ Zip Code _____

Allow 4-6 weeks for delivery.
This offer is subject to withdrawal without notice.

Chapter 1

When Juliet learned that the coach journey from North-ampton to London would require just above eight hours, she marveled at the astonishing efficiency of modern transportation. However, she had not previously been confined in a carriage for longer than *two* hours, and at the end of that period, the remainder of the day loomed before her like a veritable eternity. She decided she must find some sort of diversion, and as generally happened when she grew bored, she felt a keen desire to draw. Consequently, during the change of horses at Newport, she retrieved her portmanteau, removed her sketch pad and pencil, and—when the stage got under way again—began to draw the party in the facing seat. The group, consisting of a woman and two small children, made an interesting study; and when they left the coach in southern Bedfordshire, some two hours later, Julie immodestly judged that she had captured the mother's harried expression, the children's devilish little faces, quite successfully indeed.

Fortunately, the departing family's places were assumed by an entirely dissimilar but equally intriguing party: a country clergyman and, Julie surmised, his wife and mother. All three wore identical and apparently permanent frowns, all pursed their lips in the same prim, disapproving fashion; and when Julie finished the sketch, she could not suppress a grin of triumph. Her smile elicited a glower of intense displeasure from the black-clad cleric, and Julie hastily dashed off a second rendering of him alone.

The clergyman and his female companions exited the stage at Watford, at which point a rather plump man of middle years appropriated the whole of the facing seat. His appearance was most distinguished, Julie thought, sketching his longish, graying hair, his lavishly starched shirt-points, his immaculate neck-cloth. But unlike the groups that had preceded him, he was not an *unusual* figure, and she soon grew bored again and laid her pad aside.

"Am I not to be permitted to see it?" he asked.

"See—see what?"

Julie belatedly attempted to cover the sketch pad with the frayed muslin skirt of her dress, but, in the process, she knocked the pad off the seat, and her drawings fluttered to the floor of the carriage. The man, now her only fellow passenger, bent and scooped them up.

"It's an excellent likeness," he said, examining the sketch of himself. He leafed through the other drawings, and a grin tickled the corners of his mouth. "Indeed, they are all excellent, Miss—Miss . . ."

"Brandon," Julie murmured. "Juliet Brandon."

"Well, you are a young lady of considerable talent, Miss Brandon." He studied each of the sketches once more, then passed them back. "Are you traveling to London to pursue a career in the world of art?"

"Heavens, no." Julie's voice was shrill with embarrassment, for she had kept her "talent" (if, in fact, she possessed any) a secret even from Aunt Sophia. "No, I regard my drawing merely as an amusement, sir."

"My name is Compton," he supplied. "Reginald Compton." He leaned back and laced his fingers over his generous belly. "I am sorry to learn that you view your ability so lightly, Miss Brandon. But I daresay you needn't concern yourself with the odd shilling; you're no doubt going to town to be wed."

Wed, wed, wed, Julie thought irritably; was she

never to escape that suggestion? It had been Grand-aunt Sophia's primary topic of conversation—one which, toward the end, she had addressed at least once per day.

"You are already two and twenty, Juliet," Aunt Sophia would dolefully remind her. "Past your prime and not likely to grow any younger." Since this was Aunt Sophia's notion of a jest, she would flash her skeletal smile, then sober again. "And though I shall, of course, leave my entire estate to you, you must not fancy my resources sufficient to see you through your declining years."

Julie, even in her most pessimistic moments, could hardly regard two and twenty as the beginning of her "declining years," but she would dutifully nod. "Yes, Aunt. That is, no; I do not think to survive on any funds you may see fit to leave me." This was quite true, for if Aunt Sophia's clutchfistedness was indicative of her financial situation, Julie could only collect that her grandaunt subsisted at the very edge of poverty.

"Then perhaps you might be a trifle more encouraging to Mr. Howe," Aunt Sophia would snap. "You cannot expect to do better, Juliet; you've no dowry at all, and you certainly are not a *handsome* girl."

As soon as Aunt Sophia dismissed her, Julie would rush to her bedchamber and peer into the ancient cheval glass, anxiously pondering her grandaunt's observation. She was not beautiful, that much was true: she was too short, too thin, and her auburn hair tumbled about her face in wild, uncontrollable curls. Her eyes were a peculiar hue, a rusty brown; as Aunt Sophia frequently, unkindly pointed out, they were precisely the same color as Julie's numerous freckles.

On the other hand, her odd eyes were enormous and luxuriantly lashed, and she had splendid high cheek-bones, a lovely, straight nose, and excellent teeth. So while she might not be classically "handsome," surely she wasn't odious, and she *could* do better than Mr. Howe.

Julie had been gazing sightlessly into her lap, but she now saw that her drawing of the clergyman lay atop the pile Mr. Compton had returned. Mr. Howe was a merchant-banker rather than a cleric, but she nevertheless detected a sharp resemblance between him and her anonymous subject. Mr. Howe also wore a perennial frown and pursed his thin lips in that same grim, forbidding way. If she had had any doubts about leaving Northampton, they were quite resolved, and she heaved a sigh and looked back at Mr. Compton.

"No," she said, "I am not going up to London to be married. I plan to reside with my cousin while I search for . . . for . . ." But Julie had no idea what she was looking for, what she might find. She quelled a surge of panic and stared determinedly back at her drawing.

"Have you been to London before?" Mr. Compton inquired.

"Yes." Her eyes flew up again. "Yes, Papa took me when I was twelve, and we visited all the attractions. Astley's and the Botanical Gardens and Hampton Court . . ." She realized how dreadfully unsophisticated she must sound, and her voice trailed off. "Papa died a few years later," she continued, "and when I was seventeen, Mama died as well. So I went to live with Papa's aunt—my Grandaunt Sophia—in Northampton, and I remained with her until *she* died. That was just above a month ago . . ." She lapsed once more into silence.

"I am sorry," Mr. Compton said.

Julie nodded, suspecting that she herself wasn't nearly so sorry as she should be. She had served Aunt Sophia for five years; there was no other word to describe her existence. She had been an unpaid companion, unpaid abigail, unpaid maid of all work. And when Aunt Sophia had, at last, passed to her reward (at the ripe age of six and eighty), her "entire estate" had proved to comprise a crumbling house, mortgaged to the very hilt, and a few dilapidated sticks of furniture. After paying Aunt Sophia's debts, Julie had been left with enough money to finance her transportation to London and establish a contingency fund of five scant pounds. She did not count herself an avaricious person, but—in light of all she had endured— she could not but feel that her remuneration had been a bit inadequate.

But she could not, of course, reveal these rather shocking sentiments to a perfect stranger. "Thank you," she said.

"So you are to reside with your cousin," Mr. Compton repeated. "In what portion of the city is he located?"

"She," Julie corrected. "Cousin Louisa lives in Grosvenor Street."

"An excellent address." Mr. Compton nodded approvingly. "Her husband must be quite well-fixed."

"Louisa is not married," Julie said, "but her father did leave her a good deal of money. He—my Uncle John—was Mama's elder brother and a naval officer. Indeed, that is why I did not join Louisa when Mama died. Uncle John was abroad and, as he was a widower, he had placed Louisa in the charge of a housekeeper. Naturally, Mrs. Skinner could not be expected to assume responsibility for me as well."

"I collect that your cousin is but little older than you yourself," Mr. Compton remarked.

His tone was noncommittal, but he had raised his thick gray eyebrows, and Julie guessed that he found the situation a trifle irregular. Indeed, she had pondered that very matter at considerable length; Louisa was just five and twenty, and it *was* somewhat improper for two young women to live together with only an elderly servant as chaperon. But Louisa was Julie's last living relative, and, with five pounds in all the world, she could not afford to fret unduly about convention. However, she did not wish to discuss these circumstances with Mr. Compton either, and, in any event, she realized that she had talked far too much about herself.

"Louisa is some years older than I," she dissembled. 'But what of *you*, Mr. Compton; do you conduct business in town?"

He was a barrister, Mr. Compton replied, and he proceeded to regale her with tales of several recent fascinating cases. Julie suspected that their familiarity was another impropriety, but it did serve a useful purpose, for very shortly, it seemed, the coach stopped, and Mr. Compton announced that they had reached London.

Mr. Compton assisted Julie out of the stage, and she gazed with awe at the seething yard of the Swan with Two Necks. A maroon-and-black mail coach had pulled in just behind them, another was leaving, and some half a dozen other stages stood about in various phases of loading or unloading. Their own luggage was swiftly brought down, and Julie began to look for Louisa.

"Is your cousin to meet you, Miss Brandon?" Mr. Compton had evidently read her thoughts.

His inquiry touched a subject of nagging concern for, in point of fact, Louisa had not responded to Julie's letter. Letters, she amended. She had written her cousin a few days after Aunt Sophia's death, stating her intention to travel to the city and proposing a date and time for her arrival. When several weeks had passed without a reply, Julie had dashed off a second note to remind Louisa of her itinerary. She had received no answer to that communication either, but— Aunt Sophia's house sold, the new owner scheduled to move in at once—she had been compelled to proceed.

"If not," Mr. Compton said, "I should be delighted to take you up in my carriage." He indicated a handsome barouche near the exit of the innyard, and a liveried coachman swept a bow of recognition.

But that would be tempting fate too far, Julie decided, recalling Aunt Sophia's incessant warnings that she must *never,* under any conditions, occupy the conveyance of a stranger. "Thank you, Mr. Compton," she said brightly. "As it happens, Louisa *is* to meet me, but she is invariably late." Julie essayed a sigh. "I daresay she will be along at any moment."

"Very well." Mr. Compton clapped on his beaver hat. "Good-bye then, Miss Brandon. If you should require any assistance during your residence in London, I do hope you will advise me." He strode to the barouche and clambered inside, and his coachman closed the door behind him and mounted the box. The carriage clattered out of the yard, and Julie glanced around again.

It was another fact, she owned grimly, that she did not know whether Louisa was "invariably late" at all, for she was but remotely acquainted with her cousin. They had played together as children during the rare periods when Captain John Linley was posted ashore, but she had not even *seen* Louisa since Mama's funeral, five years before. Surely, Julie thought desperately, surely Louisa would have written if Julie were *not* welcome in London . . .

A mail guard crashed into her, growled an apology, and hurried on to a loaded mail coach, obviously ready to depart. Julie glanced anxiously upward and realized that it was twilight; within half an hour, it would be fully dark. She could not continue to mill about the innyard, she decided; she must proceed to Louisa's on her own and hope she would not pass her cousin en route. She spotted a hackney coach just drawing up to the exit, its driver peering into the yard in search of a fare, and she raised her hand and called out to him. He inclined his head but allowed her to struggle unaided to his vehicle, whereupon he grudgingly crashed her portmanteau onto the floor of the coach. Julie gave him Louisa's address and wearily laid her head against the seat.

Julie collected that she had dozed, for she remembered nothing of the drive, and it *was* fully dark when she felt the carriage come to a halt. "We're here, miss," the driver announced gratuitously.

He sounded rather dubious, and when Julie peered

at the house, she experienced a sinking sensation. It was not pitch-black—there was the dim, distant glow of a lamp within—but it certainly did not appear a place where guests were imminently expected.

"If you will but wait a moment," Julie said nervously, "I shall see whether my cousin is in."

"Aye, miss," the driver agreed. "Just be aware that my waiting will cost ye."

With this dire admonition echoing in her ears, Julie dashed up the shallow front steps and rang the bell. Its peal seemed ominously hollow, and when it died away, Julie rang again and, for good measure, knocked sharply on the heavy door. Her exertions appeared fruitless, and she had nearly given up when she glimpsed a shadow behind one of the windows. She stood, literally holding her breath, and eventually the door creaked open.

"Yes?"

The woman who intoned the question was a formidable figure indeed: though no taller than Julie, she weighed at least twelve stone, and the white hair sprouting from beneath her nightcap lent her a positively ferocious aspect. She was scrutinizing the intruder on the doorstep with small, suspicious gray eyes, and Julie licked her lips and swallowed.

"Is Miss Linley at home?" she managed to croak.

"No, she is not." The door, which had been, at best, half open, began to ease shut.

"She does live here though." Julie's voice was ragged with relief because it had occurred to her, as she stood on the porch, that Louisa might have moved to another part of London, another shire, another continent.

"Miss Linley lives here, but, as I believe I just informed you, she is away from home."

The door started to creep to again, and Julie determinedly planted her foot in the crack. "Miss Linley must have advised you of my arrival," she said. "I am her cousin, Juliet Brandon." The forbidding doorkeeper scowled, and Julie tried another tack. "And I fancy you are Mrs. Skinner," she added, in as friendly a tone as she could muster.

"Yes; yes, I am." Julie thought the fierce expression moderated a bit. "And I now recollect that Miss Linley *does* have a cousin. They used to visit in Northamptonshire—she and Captain Linley. He always allowed me a holiday when they went."

Mrs. Skinner scowled again, and Julie surmised that Louisa had not been so generous with holidays since Uncle John's death. She elected to strike while the iron was yet lukewarm. "Well, I am that very cousin, Mrs. Skinner, and I shall instruct my driver to bring in my bag—"

"However," Mrs. Skinner interrupted severely, "Miss Linley did *not* advise me that her cousin was coming to visit, and as she is out, I certainly cannot admit you. If you will leave a card, I shall have her get in touch with you in the next day or so."

A card? Julie thought wildly. Get in touch with her where? Mrs. Skinner was attempting to close the door again, and Julie winced as her foot was squeezed between it and the jamb. She envisioned an imaginary clock in the hackney coach, ticking off her few precious pounds. She did not have the time to argue, and she groped desperately about for an alternative.

"There has clearly been a misunderstanding, Mrs. Skinner," she said at last. "If you can tell me where Louisa is, I shall find her, and I am sure she will write a note attesting to my identity."

Mrs. Skinner mulled this suggestion over at excruciating length but ultimately nodded. "Very well," she agreed. "Miss Linley is attending an assembly at the Argyle Rooms."

"The Argyle Rooms." Julie hastily, mentally recorded the name. "I shall leave my bag here then . . ."

But Mrs. Skinner would have none of *that,* she snapped, and, to Julie's dismay, an argument did ensue. She eventually persuaded the fearsome housekeeper

that her battered portmanteau hardly posed a threat.
Quite the contrary: her meager belongings might well
be viewed as hostages to her good behavior. After an
endless debate, Mrs. Skinner grudgingly acquiesced,
and Julie prevailed upon the hackney driver to carry
her bag into the foyer, a task he performed with
exceedingly poor grace. As they returned to the coach,
Julie started to advise him of her new destination and
belatedly recalled that Mrs. Skinner had not given
her the address.

"Oh, dear." She looked back at the front door, now
firmly closed again, and shuddered to contemplate
Mrs. Skinner's reaction if she were to be disturbed a
second time in the same evening. "I am to go to the
Argyle Rooms, but I do not know precisely where that
is."

"Never mind, miss: *I* know."

Julie thought the driver smirked a bit as he spoke,
but it might have been a trick of the wavering
streetlamp. In any case, she was far too tired to care;
she fairly stumbled into the coach and collapsed once
more against the seat.

She was drifting into and out of sleep during this
leg of her journey, Julie surmised, for she occasionally
noted a brightly lighted house or a carriage passing in
the opposite direction. However, she had no notion of
how much time had elapsed when the hackney coach
stopped again and the driver, evidently suffering a
sudden attack of helpfulness, came down from the box
and opened her door.

Julie gazed around and immediately recognized the
enormity of her task: the street was a sea of carriages,
and a veritable roar of conversation emanated from
the building. It was clear that this was no small country ball, such as those Aunt Sophia had insisted she
attend with Mr. Howe. There were no doubt several
hundred guests inside, and it might require considerable time for her to locate Louisa. And she could ill
afford to expend the bulk of her contingency fund on a

single hackney ride during her very first evening in London.

"You may leave me here," she said to the coachman, hoping she sounded more confident than she felt. "I daresay I can arrange for other transportation when I am ready to depart."

"Oh, I daresay you can, miss."

In the glow of light splashing from the Argyle rooms into the street, his smirk was now unmistakable, but Julie was too distracted to puzzle over his reaction. She opened her reticule and narrowly suppressed a gasp of horror when he demanded half a crown as his fare. She added a tip of sixpence, but he apparently found this entirely inadequate, for his last look, as the coach rattled off, was one of extreme displeasure.

Julie sighed, squared her shoulders, and ventured into the building. She had initially thought to ask for the hostess and present herself, apologize for her intrusion and explain her mission. But the sight that met her eyes rendered her literally paralyzed, and she stood at the entry of the ballroom and frankly gaped.

The room itself was like nothing she had ever seen: an enormous chamber lined with great marble statues, whose feet rested perhaps three yards above the floor. The orchestra sat on a raised platform at one end, and the floor was so jammed with dancers that Julie wondered how they could possibly maneuver through the crush. The dancers! Julie caught her breath in awe. The men were clearly the cream of the *ton*, variously and elegantly clad in small clothes, in pantaloons, in military uniforms. The women were not to be outdone, of course: Julie had never glimpsed, had never *imagined*, such a splendid assortment of muslin and silk and satin gowns, of glittering jewels, of plumed headdresses waving gracefully in the air.

Julie overcame her paralysis sufficiently to finger the skirt of her own muslin dress, and she felt her cheeks color with humiliation. She was forced to concede that even her one evening gown—a graying white crepe—was not fit to darken the door of the Argyle Rooms. But at least, in evening garb, she would have been *properly* attired; as it was, she was dressed shabbily and inappropriately as well.

Julie sighed again, returned her attention to the throng in the ballroom, and entertained a sudden, peculiar notion that something was amiss. Were the women not rigged out a bit *too* brilliantly? Julie was certainly no expert in matters of fashion, but it did seem that the gowns were colorful to the point of garishness, the skirts daringly short, the corsages cut shockingly low in the front. She was frowning over a particular gown of emerald satin, the bodice of which exposed its wearer's bosom most provocatively, when she became aware of a presence at her side.

"Good evening, miss. Dare I hope that you are alone?"

He attempted to sweep a courtly bow, an effort that suffered considerably in execution when he swayed, nearly lost his balance, and sloshed half a glass of champagne on his highly polished shoes. He straightened, and Julie collected, from the odor of spirits which wafted toward her, that the spilled wine was far from being his first portion. He was classically dressed in knee breeches, a wasp-waisted coat, and white silk stockings, and Julie could not but wish that he had elected to wear pantaloons instead, for he was perhaps two stone too plump, and his heavy calves threatened fairly to burst through his hose.

"Yes, I am alone," she responded coolly. "However, I am searching for someone."

"Well, I am happy to say"—it came out "shay"—"that you have succeeded in your quest. I am Sir Lucius North."

"Sir Lucius," Julie murmured. She had expected to be accosted by the hostess long since, had anticipated a demand that she display her card of invitation. But when she glanced nervously over Sir Lucius' shoulder, she detected no avenging angel bearing down upon them, and she essayed a polite smile. "As it happens, though, I am looking for my cousin."

"Then I shall assist you." It was a noble sentiment, somewhat marred when Sir Lucius altogether dropped his glass. Fortunately, it was empty; even more fortunately, it landed in a nearby chair and came harmlessly to rest on the striped-silk upholstery.

"That is very kind of you," Julie said, "but I daresay I shall spot her soon enough. Good evening, Sir Lucius."

"You will *never* find her if she is dancing," he protested. ("Danshing.") "Not from here. No, you must go onto the floor yourself, and I shall stand up with you."

Before Julie realized what he was at, he had seized her elbow in a most commanding grip and begun to drag her on into the ballroom. She was so startled that they were, in fact, well inside the main chamber when she dug in her heels and wrenched her arm furiously away.

"I do not wish to dance, Sir Lucius!" She had intended to hiss her refusal very discreetly, but her voice sounded alarmingly shrill. "Good evening."

"Do not play coy with me." His fleshy face was flushed, and his bloodshot blue eyes had narrowed to angry slits. Julie sensed that the situation had altered—instantaneously and dramatically—from one of mere embarrassment to one of genuine hazard. "You would not be here had you not desired to meet new friends, and that is my desire as well. Come now."

His swollen fingers snaked round her wrist, and he jerked her forward again. His dissipated appearance notwithstanding, he was exceedingly strong; and Julie was wondering how she could possibly extricate herself from this dreadful contretemps when Sir Lucius abruptly dropped her arm. Julie staggered, recovered herself, and saw that Sir Lucius' own wrist was firmly imprisoned in a spare, gloved masculine hand.

"I believe the lady stated that she did not wish to stand up with you." The voice was smooth and frigid,

and its owner towered well over Sir Lucius; he was a
tall man and as lean as his graceful fingers.

"Lady!" Sir Lucius sniffed. "She is far from that,
Stafford, and in any event, you've no right to meddle
in my affairs."

"Nor should I," Mr. Stafford rejoined, "if you were
able to conduct yourself with somewhat more finesse
than that of a rampaging Hun. Be that as it may—
and I again quote the *lady*—'Good evening,' Sir Lucius."

The gloved hand released the plump wrist, and Sir
Lucius marched indignantly away, pausing—when he
had attained a safe distance—to cast a baleful backward glare. Julie was hard put to quell a giggle, and
she feared that exhaustion was well in the way of
unhinging her mind.

"Thank—thank you," she stammered at last. "Thank
you very much indeed, Mr. Stafford."

"Captain," he corrected. "Captain Nicholas Stafford."

Julie studied him with full concentration for the
first time and noted at once that he was not wearing a
uniform. He was dressed in immaculately tailored black
pantaloons, a frock coat of charcoal Bath, a dove-gray
waistcoat, and an ivory neckcloth tied in such intricate fashion that it quite defied her comprehension.
She further observed that his skin was burned dark
by the sun, his brown hair shot through with streaks
of blond, and his eyes so pale a brown as to be lighter
than amber. Almost golden, she decided; nearly yellow.

"I should have said that I was *lately* a captain." He
coughed, as though she had caught him up in a bla-
tant distortion of fact. "I retired from the navy two
years ago, but I daresay my rank will accompany me
to the grave. I descend from a naval family, you see;
my father was an admiral and my grandfather before
him."

He flashed a smile, and Julie debated whether or
not he was handsome. Not exactly, she concluded; his
countenance could better be described as arresting.
His thin face—like hers—was all eyes, all bones . . .

"But I fancy I do not have the pleasure of *your* acquaintance." Captain Stafford interrupted her appraisal, and, for some inexplicable reason, Julie felt the onset of a blush.

"Juliet Brandon," she mumbled. "And I wish to thank you again for your assistance."

"Do not give it another thought." In her avid perusal of his face, Julie had not seen him remove his gloves, but he now waved one bare, brown, slender hand. "I collect you have but recently come up from the country, Miss Brandon."

His strange yellow eyes swept over her, obviously assessing her wretched dress, her limp straw bonnet. But his smile, when he flashed it again, was warm, in no way disdainful; and Julie could not take offense.

"Very recently," she responded dryly. "Only today, in fact."

"Then I hope you will derive comfort from the knowledge that Sir Lucius' lamentable conduct is not confined to this sort of occasion." Captain Stafford tossed his brown-gold head toward the dancers, who were whirling, as best they could, to the strains of a waltz. "Indeed, *on dit* that his behavior has so incensed Lady Jersey that she has expelled him from Almack's. If that rumor is true, we can hardly be surprised by his disgraceful comportment at the Cyprians' Ball."

The Cyprians' Ball! Everything became suddenly, horribly clear: the sneers of the hackney driver, the garish gowns in the ballroom, Sir Lucius' slurs upon her honor. Julie had somehow blundered into the annual assembly of London's expensive barques of frailty. The glittering women on the dance floor were—if they were lucky—the mistresses of the *ton;* if not, they served as casual, paid companions. How such an error could have occurred, she could only guess: she must have misunderstood Mrs. Skinner's information. The how of it did not signify; the important point was that she must escape at once.

"There has been a fearful mistake, Captain Stafford."
She scarcely recognized her voice; it was something
between a whimper and a wail. "Obviously I have
been misdirected. I am searching for my cousin, a
Miss Louisa Linley. I shouldn't suppose you would
know her . . ." Julie stopped, glanced at the brilliant
birds of paradise on the floor, and strove to suppress a
shudder.

"But of course I know Miss Linley!" Captain Stafford snapped his long brown fingers. "She is called the
Red Fawn, and I ought to have detected your resemblance at once, particularly since I saw Miss Linley
not an hour ago. She was, as I recall, in the company
of Lord Romney."

The Red Fawn! Captain Stafford had begun to peer
eagerly about, but Julie was so distraught that she
scarcely noticed. The truth was abundantly, appallingly clear: Julie had not been misdirected, for Louisa
was, in fact, a Cyprian. Julie's mind was fairly
churning, but eventually one thought struggled to the
fore. If she could leave the ball unnoticed (noticed no
further, she amended grimly), she might be able to
keep her connection with Louisa a secret. She whirled
around, intending literally to run into the street, but
it was too late.

"Yes, there she is!"

Captain Stafford raised one hand, helpfully tapping
Julie's shoulder with the other, and she abandoned
any hope of flight. She turned reluctantly back round
and watched as Louisa, wearing a frown of puzzlement,
approached them. She could well understand why her
cousin was known as the Red Fawn, Julie thought
distantly. Louisa was as thin as Julie herself but far
taller, with endless long legs and a slender, graceful
neck. Her eyes were untinged with the rust of Julie's—
were, indeed, the warm brown eyes of a deer—and her
hair was not auburn but vividly, uncompromisingly
red.

"You wanted to speak with me, Captain Stafford?"

Louisa was panting a bit from the exertion of traversing the crowded dance floor. Her dark eyes flickered casually to Julie, started to flicker away, widened. "Juliet?" she gasped. "*Julie?*"

"Yes, it is I." Julie entertained a horrid notion that everyone in the ballroom was staring at them, prayed this was merely a figment of her overwrought imagination.

"But whatever are you doing in London?" Louisa demanded. "Oh, do forgive me." She rattled on without awaiting a response. "I fear I have neglected to present Viscount Romney. This, Godfrey, is my cousin, Juliet Brandon, and I fancy you are acquainted with Captain Stafford."

Lord Romney negotiated a brief bow, and Julie noted that he bore a keen similarity to Sir Lucius. Though the Viscount was considerably taller than the baronet, he possessed the same dissolute look, the same unhealthy plumpness, the same red-rimmed eyes. "Lord Romney," she murmured.

"But what are you doing in London?" Louisa repeated.

"I wrote you that I was coming." It was only with the greatest effort that Julie managed to hold her voice below a shriek, for she was utterly furious with Louisa for having drawn her into this horrifying situation. "I wrote you nearly a month since, just after Aunt Sophia died, and I wrote again early last week."

"Oh, dear." Louisa sighed. "Mrs. Skinner has been pinching at me to read my mail, but my circumstances are most confused just now. The fact is, Julie, that I am to move very shortly; Godfrey has leased a lovely little house in South Audley Street."

If Julie had retained the slightest shred of doubt as to her cousin's mode of life, it would have been quite dispelled by the flirtatious glance Louisa now directed at the Viscount. It was apparent that Louisa had ensnared a permanent protector; whether he was the first, Julie neither knew nor cared.

"It was Mrs. Skinner who sent me." Julie again

commended herself on the moderate timbre of her voice. "Since she had not been advised of my arrival, she refused to admit me to the house. I am to obtain a message of permission from you."

"Mrs. Skinner." Louisa fondly smacked her tongue against her teeth. "The dear woman is *so* protective." Julie wondered—if this was true—how Mrs. Skinner could possibly have allowed her charge to sink to such an abysmal level of existence. "I should be happy to write a note, Julie, but I daresay, now you're here, you would prefer to enjoy the festivities for a time. At the end of the assembly, Godfrey and I shall drop you by—"

"I do not wish to remain at the ball," Julie interjected frostily. "I want to leave at once."

"Oh, very well." Louisa's tone was peevish, but when she turned to the Viscount, her lush, red lips turned up in a winsome smile. "If you've a pencil, Godfrey, and some paper . . ."

Lord Romney shook his massive, graying head, and Julie reflected that she would not be at all surprised to learn that he could neither write nor read. Indeed, in view of the fact that he had not uttered a single word, she would not have been astonished to discover that he was incapable of speech as well.

"Umm." Louisa frowned, tapped her teeth with one long fingernail, then brightened. "I shall send a token then." She stripped off a ring—one of many, Julie observed—and shoved it into Julie's hand. "When Mrs. Skinner sees this, she will have no further objection, for it is my most *prized* possession."

Louisa favored the Viscount with another seductive smile, and Julie could not resist a glance at the ring. It was composed of diamonds and emeralds, and she calculated that it was worth many times the price she had obtained for Aunt Sophia's house.

"Good evening, Julie. And good evening to you, Captain Stafford." Louisa bobbed her bright red head, dipping her plumes most gracefully, and led Lord Romney back to the dance floor.

Julie examined the ring again, then dropped it gingerly in her reticule. "I must bid you good evening as well, Captain Stafford," she said. It occurred to her that he had not spoken during the conversation either, but she suspected that—unlike the Viscount—he had registered every distressing syllable. "I shall hire a hackney coach—"

"A hackney coach?" His eyebrows darted into the fringes of his hair, and Julie observed that they were quite blond, almost white. His coloring was very arresting indeed. "Even had we not discussed the matter, Miss Brandon, I should collect at once that you are new to London. You cannot go disporting about in a hackney coach at this time of night, especially not with an item of such value on your person." He nodded toward her reticule. "No, *I* shall drive you home."

He took her elbow and guided her into the foyer, and Julie remembered every one of Aunt Sophia's sinister warnings. But she was terribly, achingly tired, far too tired to protest; and, in any event, she had already been compromised beyond Aunt Sophia's wildest fears. They reached the street, and she sagged against Captain Stafford as they waited for his carriage, noting—if dimly—that his body was very hard, very strong. She took only distant note of his vehicle as well; she thought it was a fine new curricle, but she could not be certain.

He somehow maneuvered her into the seat and climbed up beside her. He clucked his team to a start, and Julie's head fell against his shoulder. He was hard there, too, in a way, but, in another way, astonishingly soft. She burrowed into his frock coat and tumbled into a deep, dreamless sleep.

Chapter 2

When Julie woke, she realized at once that she was in a bed, and she closed her eyes again, attempting to reconstruct the final events of the evening. She vaguely recollected Captain Stafford lifting her out of his carriage and propelling her up a shallow flight of steps. He had then conducted a conversation with someone—Mrs. Skinner, no doubt—and had eventually reached for Julie's reticule. He must have given Mrs. Skinner Louisa's ring, and Mrs. Skinner must have been satisfied, for Julie next recalled Captain Stafford nudging her into the house and carrying her up the stairs.

Carrying her up the stairs! Julie's eyes flew open, and she bolted upright and gazed down at herself in horror. She nearly collapsed with relief when she discovered that she was fully dressed; apparently the ever-helpful Captain had stopped short of removing her wretched muslin frock.

Julie tugged a pillow up behind her and leaned against it, but her relief was short-lived. The memory of Louisa's ring had inevitably brought to mind her cousin's shocking circumstances, and Julie was sorry to own that she was not as surprised as she should have been. No, Louisa had always been a trifle wild; at least that had been Mama's word.

"We must not condemn her, Juliet," Mama had once said. Louisa had perpetrated some particularly appalling prank, the nature of which Julie could no longer recollect. "We must remember that Louisa lost her mother when she was but two years of age. I am sure John has tried his best to give her a proper upbringing, but, as you know, he is away a great deal. And a housekeeper, though with the best will in the world, can hardly substitute for a mother's guidance. So Louisa is naturally a bit wild, but I daresay she will outgrow it."

Obviously Mama had been wrong on one count alone: maturity had not improved Louisa's conduct. But to become a Cyprian! Julie shook her head, then reflected that she could ill afford to dwell on her cousin's dismaying profession. If such it could be termed. The longer Julie remained under Louisa's roof, the greater the likelihood that her own good name, by association, would also be ruined. On the other hand, she *must* stay with Louisa until she found some means of support. Therefore, her first requirement was to locate a suitable post.

Julie leaped out of bed and tugged the bell rope just above it. Her best approach, she decided, as she awaited the arrival of a servant, was to study the notices in *The Times*. Surely there were any number of elderly women seeking a companion, and *that* was a position for which Julie was abundantly qualified. She recalled Mr. Compton's words and entertained a new and optimistic notion: she might, indeed, be able to pursue a career in art. She did not fancy herself sufficiently talented to paint portraits, but she could certainly teach young ladies to draw a line or two upon a sketch pad.

Julie was impatient, eager to proceed, and when the expected maid failed to appear, she elected not to ring again. She dearly wished a bath, but she could scarcely draw it herself, so she went to the washstand and shook the pitcher. She was delighted to discover it half full, and she declined to consider who the last occupant of the room might have been. She poured the water into the basin, stripped off her clothes, and

sponged herself off as best she could. Her portmanteau was lying on the carpet, and she suspected Captain Stafford had brought it up as well. She opened
the trunk and donned her other day dress: an apple-
green percale which was, if possible, in even worse
condition than the muslin. She proceeded to the dressing table, attempted, rather vainly, to repair her unruly hair, then hurried down the stairs.

Julie had not visited Louisa's house before, and she
was hesitating in the foyer, examining the various
doors which issued from it, when Mrs. Skinner emerged
from one of the doors and gave her a cool nod.

"Good morning, Miss Brandon. There is a bit of
breakfast for you."

The housekeeper turned, nodded, and Julie followed
her into what was clearly the dining room. "A bit of
breakfast" was an extremely accurate description, she
thought grimly; a single rasher of cold bacon, a dry
slice of toast, and a scant cup of coffee remained on
the sideboard. Julie helped herself to this miserable
fare, sat at the table, and, as she had not eaten for
nearly four and twenty hours, wolfed down every inadequate morsel. Her mind was still whirling, and she
determined, while she ate, that she must advise Louisa at once of her intention to seek a post and depart.
The discussion would be a delicate one, but surely
Louisa had not fallen so far that she would fail to
understand her cousin's position.

Julie licked a final crumb of toast from her finger
and noted that Mrs. Skinner was stationed at the
dining room doorway. The forbidding housekeeper—
clad in black bombazine and resembling a great, dark
balloon—wore a deep frown, and Julie guessed that
her "bit of breakfast" was, in fact, the remnants of
Mrs. Skinner's own meal. Julie collected that Louisa's
household was ill prepared for a houseguest—an unin-
vited *female* houseguest, at any rate—and this surmise hardened her resolve.

"I should like to speak with my cousin," Julie said. "Is she awake?"

"Miss Linley is not at home."

The housekeeper's tone was altogether expressionless, and Julie suspected that Mrs. Skinner was compelled to deliver this message numerous times each day.

"She is already gone?" Julie was genuinely amazed; she did not know the precise time, but she reckoned it shortly after noon. "She must have had very little sleep then, for I believe she planned to stay quite late at the ball."

Mrs. Skinner's small gray eyes had gone stony, and Julie felt herself flush with embarrassment. Louisa had not come home, of course; indeed, Julie now recalled that her cousin had offered to "drop her by."

"Not that it signifies." Julie had hoped to sound very sophisticated, very airy, but her voice was undeniably strangled round the edges. "I merely wished to ask Louisa if she had any recent copies of *The Times*. If I might read them."

"If Miss Linley does have any newspapers, they will be in the parlor." Mrs. Skinner tossed her fierce gray head, indicating the room behind her. "I suppose she would have no objection if you were to take a look."

Mrs. Skinner's sniff suggested that she herself had very grave objections indeed, and Julie decided to move before the terrible woman changed her mind. "Thank you, Mrs. Skinner." She abandoned her chair so quickly that it nearly toppled over and fled through the dining room door, across the entry hall, and into the room beyond.

The housekeeper had called it a parlor, but Julie was initially inclined to pronounce it a storage room, for it was crammed with paper boxes, perilously stacked one atop another. However, she soon recalled Louisa's announcement that she was shortly to move, and she guessed that the multitudinous boxes contained those items her cousin had already packed. She glanced about, and her eyes fell on a massive Sheraton writing table, heaped with papers. She hurried to it, dodging the boxes in her path, and began to paw through the clutter on the surface.

She was not *spying,* Julie persuaded herself, but she could not but observe that Louisa had accumulated an astonishing number of bills. The statement of one mantua-maker fairly took Julie's breath away, and there were invoices from other dressmakers, several milliners, a greengrocer, a butcher. To say nothing of the many unopened pieces of correspondence, amongst which Julie spotted her own two letters. She wondered if Lord Romney knew just how dearly Louisa's company would cost him.

In any event, there was no sign of a newspaper, and Julie realized that if she pressed her search, she *would* be spying. She threaded her way back through the boxes and paused at the parlor door, speculating how far she might have to walk before she located a newsboy.

The doorbell pealed, and Mrs. Skinner's heavy footfalls sounded in the foyer. Julie stepped back and shrank against the parlor wall, for it was just this sort of encounter she wished to avoid: a chance meeting with one of Louisa's admirers. She heard the front door open, heard a mumble of conversation, heard the door close. She moved cautiously away from the wall, and the housekeeper loomed up in the doorway.

"It is a caller for you, Miss Brandon," she announced. "Captain Stafford." Mrs. Skinner's scowl allowed for no doubt that her brief acquaintance with the Captain had proved most unsatisfactory.

"Captain Stafford?" Julie hissed.

She had not expected to see him again. Furthermore, though she had found him most attractive, she had not *wanted* to see him again, for she judged Captain Stafford the only man in London capable of threatening her fragile reputation. Sir Lucius had learned neither Julie's name nor that of her cousin, and Lord Romney appeared totally lacking in sense.

"Tell him I am away, Mrs. Skinner." Julie continued to whisper. "Tell him I have gone to—"

"Ah, *here* you are, Miss Brandon."

The Captain had materialized behind Mrs. Skinner, and Julie managed a weak smile. "Good—good afternoon," she stammered.

"Good afternoon to you." He negotiated a bow. "If it would not be too inconvenient, perhaps I might prevail upon you for a cup of tea?"

Mrs. Skinner's glower indicated that tea would be *exceedingly* inconvenient, but Captain Stafford flashed his own winning smile and peered over Julie's shoulder. "The—er—parlor appears a trifle disordered," he remarked. "Perhaps we might venture up to the drawing room?"

"The drawing room is disordered as well," Mrs. Skinner snapped. "Miss Linley is engaged in preparations to move." If she had hoped to set the Captain down, she was doomed to disappointment, for he merely smiled again. "Oh, very well," she grumbled. "If you *must* have tea, I daresay the dining room is in the best condition."

The enormous housekeeper stalked across the entry hall, and Captain Stafford beckoned Julie ahead of him. When they reached the dining room, he seated her at the table and watched as Mrs. Skinner stormed out the door on the opposite side. The Captain took the chair directly across from Julie's and feigned a wince as Mrs. Skinner began to pound down the stairs to the kitchen.

"I fear she is most overset with me," he said in a stage whisper. "I doubt she will *ever* forgive me for rousting her from bed in the middle of the night."

He leaned back in his chair, and his change of position placed him in a shaft of sunlight spilling through the dining room window. He was dressed all in brown today, Julie observed: in dark-brown pantaloons, a coat of rusty superfine, a biscuit waistcoat edged in almond, an ecru neckcloth. His choice of

attire enhanced his peculiar coloring, and Julie suddenly thought that she would like to paint him. She
had had scant experience with oils; she had done
only a few landscapes and a portrait of Mama just
prior to her death. But Julie had been unable to afford
such expensive supplies on the occasional shilling Aunt
Sophia had grudgingly tossed her way, and she now
wondered whether she would remember the technique.
She continued to study Captain Stafford, attempting
to visualize him on canvas, and noted that he did not
look as weather-beaten as his naval career would have
led her to expect. His skin was dark, and there were
fine, light lines about his eyes, but he did not have the
leathery appearance which so often marked a sailor.

"Is something amiss, Miss Brandon?" he asked. "Have
my shirt-points begun to wilt? I do hope my neckcloth
is not coming undone, for my man spent *hours* in the
tying."

His grin was wry, and there was absolutely no reason for Julie to blush. But blush she did, and she felt
compelled to offer a response.

"No. No, I was but remarking that you do not resemble a navy man. Uncle John, for instance, was excessively wrinkled at a very early age. Whereas you . . ."
She detected the onset of another flush, and her voice
trailed off.

"I own myself most fortunate in that regard, Miss
Brandon, for I am told that a naturally dark complexion protects one from the effects of sun and wind. I
was in service a full ten years—from the age of eighteen to that of eight and twenty—but I do not appear
to have suffered any permanent mark of my career.
Indeed, I fancy that if I were to resume the indoor
life, my skin would turn respectably pale again, and
my hair would darken to a proper shade. Perhaps my
brows might even revert to brown; who can say?"

But his eyes, Julie thought, would surely remain
golden . . . Her cheeks were oddly warm, and she cleared

her throat. "I collect, however, that you prefer the *outdoor* life," she said.

"Indeed I do, and there is too little of it in England to suit me. The outdoor life, that is. I consequently travel to North America at least twice in the year. I am familiar with that area of the world, for my final tour of duty was during the recent American war. When that conflict ended, I resigned my commission."

Julie calculated that he must, then, be thirty years of age, and she inexplicably recalled that Papa had been thirty when he married Mama.

"But that is neither here nor there." The Captain laced his lean brown fingers behind his head, and though Julie could not see them, she suspected he had extended his long legs beneath the table. "I wished to call so as to ascertain that you arrived home safely from the assembly."

"You know I did," Julie said, "because you brought me."

"So I did."

He coughed as he had the night before, and Julie felt her eyes narrowing. It was clear that his excuse for visiting was patently that—an excuse—and Julie's heart bounded into her throat. She had never had a *parti,* unless one counted Mr. Howe, which Julie chose not to do. She had never had a suitor, and she hardly dared imagine that this arresting, sophisticated gentleman judged her sufficiently appealing to initiate a courtship.

"So I did," Captain Stafford repeated, coughing once more. "So let me not hide my teeth, Miss Brandon." He straightened, leaned forward, crashed his elbows on the table, and Julie's heart hammered so painfully that she feared he must hear it. "The fact is that I came to present a proposition."

"A proposition?" Julie's heart momentarily ceased to beat, then tumbled back into her chest. "I thought, Captain, that you quite understood my situation." She had not thought this at all, so perhaps it was disap-

pointment that turned her voice to ice. "As you yourself perceived, I am just up from the country—"

"A factor which, in my view, adds immensely to
your charm." His strange yellow eyes darted from her
impossible hair to her rather pointed chin, down the
bodice of her disgraceful dress; and Julie feared, for
one awful moment, that he would peer under the table
so as to examine her shoes. But he did not; he smiled
again. "Immensely," he reiterated.

Julie willed herself not to succumb to *his* charm.
"You have made a grave error, Captain Stafford," she
said severely. "A very grave error indeed. I admit that
the circumstances of our meeting were somewhat—ah—
unusual, but I am not what you may fancy. I am *not* a
Cyprian—"

"You may call yourself whatever you like," he
interjected soothingly. "I should have supposed, however, that you and the Red Fawn would elect to capitalize on your relationship. One cannot but be reminded of the fascinating Wilson sisters: Harriette,
Amy—"

"Captain Stafford!" Julie was fairly shrieking.

"But," he continued mildly, "ranks and titles are
exceedingly unimportant. I believe I mentioned that I
myself shall no doubt be known as 'Captain' through
the remainder of my days."

"It has nothing to do with ranks and titles," Julie
hissed. "I am *not* a Cyprian—"

She was interrupted by a clatter, and she mutely
watched as Mrs. Skinner panted into the room and
slammed a tea tray on the table. The housekeeper
poured two cups, sloshing a good deal of tea into both
saucers, whirled around, and marched out again.
Julie— whose mouth had gone quite dry—swilled greed-
ily at her cup, belatedly fearing that she might scald
her mouth. As it happened, there was no such danger:
the tea was lukewarm and entirely too weak.

"I do wish you would listen a moment, Miss Brandon."
Captain Stafford sipped his own tea, then pushed the

cup gingerly away. "I fancy my proposition could benefit the both of us, for I am prepared to confess that I
am in a bit of a hobble."

Julie did not want to listen, even for a moment, but
her mouth was full of tepid tea, and she was finding it
peculiarly difficult to swallow.

"I might begin by saying," the Captain went on,
"that I am the nephew of the Earl of Arlington."

Julie had managed to swallow by now, but she was
forced to own that he had captured her attention.
Though she could hardly claim an intimate familiarity with the *ton* (Papa had been an obscure, impover-
ished baronet), she vaguely recollected that Lord
Arlington was deemed one of the wealthiest men in
England.

"His nephew by marriage, at any rate," Captain
Stafford amended. "My Aunt Dorothea, Papa's elder
sister, was Uncle Edmund's first wife. I might add
that he has no closer male relative; no sons, no blood
nephews, not so much as a blood cousin."

"You are Lord Arlington's heir then," Julie said.
She could scarcely define this as a "hobble."

"Not exactly." The Captain drew his cup forward,
stared into it. "There is another nephew by marriage,
connected to Uncle Edmund through his *second* wife,
whom he married after Aunt Dorothea's death. The
second Lady Arlington is also deceased, by the by."
Julie was growing confused. "His name is Sir Oliver
Crane. My cousin, that is. I call him cousin though
there is no actual relationship." Very confused. "Oliver
is several years younger than I."

Julie was very confused indeed, and she attempted,
aloud, to sort out Captain Stafford's complex connec-
tions. "It would seem to me that as you are the elder
nephew, as well as the nephew of the first wife"—did
she have it right?—"you would be the logical heir."

"So it would seem to me." The Captain nodded.
"However, since there is no question of entailment,

Uncle Edmund has a notion that he should select his heir on merit."

"Merit?" Julie echoed. His "hobble" continued to elude her. "I daresay, as you are a veteran, you have rather more to recommend you than a young baronet."

"Ahem." Captain Stafford took refuge in his now familiar cough. "The fact is, Miss Brandon, that Uncle Edmund is a rather—rather *prim* fellow, and he attaches a great deal of importance to a nebulous factor which he terms 'good character.' "

"And?" Julie pressed.

"Ahem." Captain Stafford tugged at his elaborately tied neckcloth. "Uncle Edmund has somehow conceived a notion that my behavior is on the rackety side. I do—it is true—engage in a bit of high-stakes gaming at White's . . ."

And you attend the Cyprians' Ball, Julie silently added, and God knows what other vices you may indulge. She felt her eyes narrowing again, and the Captain abruptly ceased his explanations.

"In any event," he said, "*Oliver's* character is appallingly 'good'; indeed, he is quite the dullest chap I have ever encountered."

A grin tickled the corners of Julie's mouth, but, on principle, she suppressed it. Captain Nicholas Stafford was certainly the most amusing "chap" *she* had ever encountered, she reflected; so amusing that she had momentarily forgotten the origins of their discussion. At length it came to her, and she strove to arrange her face in a serious expression.

"What is the point, Captain?" she asked. "How could your situation possibly involve me?"

"Oh, that is very simple, Miss Brandon." He leaned back in his chair again and, this time, clasped his fingers over his lean ribs. "I ventured to the Cyprians' Ball last evening with a specific objective in mind: I am in need of a woman to compromise my cousin."

"Compromise!" Julie screeched.

"I have not yet figured the particulars." He went on

as though he had not heard her. "However, in light of
Uncle Edmund's strict opinions, I fancy there will be
no need for an actual seduction." Julie's cheeks were
positively flaming, but she could not respond, for he
had rendered her literally speechless. "It should,
therefore, prove an easy assignment. And one for which
you, Miss Brandon—with your wonderful country look
and your ingenuous ways—are splendidly suited."

"I am not interested in your '*proposition*,' Captain
Stafford." Julie had found her voice at last, but it was
trembling so violently that she hardly recognized it.
She wanted to shout to the very skies that she was *not*
a Cyprian, but she was certain her protest, as before,
would fall on deaf ears. "Indeed, I find your suggestion shocking, annoying, disgusting . . ." She groped
for another scathing adjective or two, but none came
immediately to mind, and she leaped up, tipping the
chair over behind her. "In any case, I do not intend to
discuss it any further, so I shall bid you good day."

"I am sorry to have overset you, Miss Brandon."
The Captain came lazily to his own feet. "I shall leave
my card in the event you change your mind—"

"I shall *not* change my mind," Julie said frigidly.

"Nevertheless I shall leave a card." He reached into
a pocket of his frock coat and laid a small white
rectangle on the table. "Perhaps it would be best if I
were to show myself out. Good afternoon, Miss Brandon."

He strode around the table, paused to right her
chair, flashed a final, pleasant smile, and continued
into the foyer. Julie heard the front door open and
waited—her fingernails jammed most painfully into
her palms—for it to close. Instead, she detected an
indecipherable murmur of conversation from the porch,
and at length she ventured a glance into the entry
hall. Louisa sailed through the door and pulled it to
behind her.

"Well, Julie," Louisa's tone, her expression, were

those of grudging admiration. "You are not one to let
the grass grow under your feet, are you?"

Julie was in no frame of mind to conduct a difficult
discussion with her cousin, but she could not permit
Louisa's assumption to pass unchallenged. "I must
speak with you, Louisa," she said. "I intended to do so
earlier, but you were . . ." To Julie's dismay, her cheeks
grew warm again. "You were otherwise occupied," she
muttered.

"And I am *still* occupied," Louisa said crisply.
"Godfrey and I are to attend the opera this evening,
and I anticipate my coiffeur at any moment. Consequently, you will have to excuse me; we shall talk
later."

Louisa proceeded toward the stairs, and Julie trailed
desperately after her. "Please, Louisa, it will only
take a moment."

"Oh, very well," Louisa snapped. "But we shall have
to converse in my bedchamber, for I must prepare for
M. Jacques."

Louisa hurried on up the stairs, and Julie followed,
entertaining an unkind notion that M. Jacques—unlike
her cousin's unpaid mantua-makers and milliners and
greengrocers—exacted his fee in trade. Louisa threw
open a door just off the landing and beckoned Julie
inside. Her cousin's bedchamber was exceedingly disordered as well, Julie observed. She suspected that
the surface of the rosewood dressing table was always
buried beneath a clutter of jewelry and hairpins and
cosmetic jars, but there were boxes stacked all about
this room, too, and the bed had been stripped to the
mattress. Louisa began to remove her gown (the same
daring blue net she had worn to the ball), and Julie
perched on the edge of the bare bed.

"Well, what is it?" Louisa demanded impatiently.
"What is it you wanted to discuss?"

Julie cast about for a tactful approach and fortunately perceived one almost at once. "I realize that my
visit is somewhat inconvenient," she said, "and I there-

fore plan to depart as quickly as I can. Indeed, I hope
to leave in the very near future."

"An excellent decision." Louisa nodded approvingly
and donned a lace dressing gown, so revealing as to
bring another flush to Julie's face. "I should like, in
fact, to commend you upon your choice of a protector. I
have always judged Captain Stafford most attractive;
had I not been previously involved with Godfrey, I
might well have gone on the catch for him myself."

Louisa had treated the matter so casually that it
was a moment before Julie registered her cousin's
words. When she did, she felt her eyes widen with
horror. "Protector?" she gasped. "Good God, Louisa,
you have quite misinterpreted my intentions. I certainly do not propose to follow in *your* footsteps."

So much for tact, Julie thought grimly; her ill-chosen
remark was the very essence of discourtesy. She gazed
at Louisa, fumbling for an apology, but she was suddenly overwhelmed by two and twenty years of training.
"How could you?" she whispered. "How could you,
Louisa?"

"It happened quite by accident," Louisa replied
briskly. She went to the dressing table, sank into the
chair, and started to unpin her hair, which had been
none too tidy to begin with. "You no doubt fancied
that Papa was quite well-fixed; I know I did. It
transpired, however, that he had borrowed heavily so
as to finance some rather risky investments, investments which came to naught. I learned of the situation a few weeks after Papa's death when an exceedingly proper banker came to call. He advised me
of his intention to foreclose on the house, then made it
clear that there was another alternative. Am *I* making it clear, Julie?"

"Yes," Julie mumbled. The circumstances were so
similar to her awful bumblebath that she was hard
put to repress a shudder.

"That was the beginning," Louisa continued. "I soon
discovered that there are a great number of men

about—men possessing more money than sense—who are eager to pay for female companionship. And that, I fancy, is the end: a very short story, eh, Julie?"

"Yes," Julie murmured. In view of her own distressing experience, she could not but pity her cousin, and she lowered her eyes.

"It is not such a bad life." Louisa went on as if she had read Julie's thoughts. "I do sometimes long for respectability; for a husband and children . . ." Louisa stopped a moment, then slammed her hairbrush on the dressing table. "But, as they say, I have made my bed"—she laughed rather shrilly—"and I must lie in it. And, at any rate, *my* life is not the one you wished to discuss." Louisa turned the chair around and looked directly at her cousin. "If you will not accept a protector, Julie, what course *do* you propose to follow?"

"Course." Julie's voice was far too loud—a symptom of relief, no doubt, for she did not believe she could have borne another instant of Louisa's horrifying revelations. "I propose to secure a post, and immediately thereafter I shall locate accommodations—"

"In three days?" Louisa interrupted dubiously.

"Three days?" Julie echoed.

"Did I not tell you I was to move?" Louisa frowned.

"Yes. Yes, you did, but you did not say precisely when—"

"Is this Friday?" Louisa's frown deepened.

"Yes; yes, it is."

"I thought so." Louisa nodded triumphantly and turned her chair back round, retrieved her brush and attacked her long red hair. "This is Friday, and the moving wagon is to come on Monday. That is three days, but the new owner will not move in till Tuesday, so I can actually grant you *four* days."

"Four days," Julie repeated weakly. With the greatest of good luck, she might receive an offer within that space of time. But her prospective employer would then wish to check her references, and she would have to search for suitable quarters . . . Her stomach fairly knotted with panic, and she shook her head.

"I shouldn't wish you to feel that you are not welcome to live with Godfrey and me," Louisa said kindly.

It was an extremely distasteful prospect—residence with Louisa's dissipated, obtuse viscount—but Julie could ill afford to be choosy. "Thank—thank you," she stammered.

"However, in point of fact, you would *not* be welcome," Louisa continued. She smiled; she did not appear to detect the slightest contradiction in her remarks. "Godfrey is generous to a fault; he has already agreed to pension off Mrs. Skinner. To pension her off most handsomely, I should add, so I am sure you understand that I cannot request another favor."

"No, indeed," Julie choked.

"Consequently, as I stated, you must arrange to be out of the house by Tuesday morning. I suppose, *legally,* you should vacate by Monday midnight, but I doubt the new owner will discover the difference."

Julie distantly wondered where, with all the furniture removed, she was to sleep past "Monday midnight." More importantly, she wondered whether she should, *could* abase herself sufficiently to beg Louisa—indirectly beg Lord Romney—for a brief period of grace. She was still engaged in agonizing debate when the door opened and Mrs. Skinner thrust her fearsome head inside.

"M. Jacques has arrived, Miss Linley," the housekeeper intoned.

"Please send him up, Mrs. Skinner."

The great, amorphous black form disappeared, and Louisa's eyes met Julie's in the mirror above the dressing table. "You really *must* excuse me now," Louisa said. "I wish you good fortune in your quest for a post." She knitted her vivid red brows again. "If you like, I shall ask Godfrey if any of his friends require a—a . . ."

But Louisa was apparently unable to conceive a

single position for which Julie might qualify, and Julie, for her part, wanted nothing to do with Lord Romney's "friends."

"Thank you," she muttered. "Thank you, but I daresay I shall find something."

She rose and went to the door, which Mrs. Skinner had left ajar. She turned and nodded at Louisa, but her cousin had begun to fuss with her hair again. Julie left the room, started down the stairs, and met, halfway, a very small, very elderly man panting his way upward. She collected, from the malodorous cloud which seemed to surround him, that M. Jacques had not bathed for months—possibly years—and owned her nasty notion wrong: Louisa couldn't be tumbling *this* lamentable creature. He smiled at her—displaying a mouth full of blackened teeth—and she smiled nervously back and scurried past him.

Julie lingered in the foyer until M. Jacques had disappeared, then peered guiltily about for the huge black shape of Mrs. Skinner. But there was no sign of the housekeeper, and Julie dodged into the dining room and—with a final glance over her shoulder—snatched Captain Stafford's card off the table.

Chapter 3

Julie did not wish to arouse Mrs. Skinner's curiosity by hailing a hackney coach within view of Louisa's house. Consequently, she turned right at the footpath and proceeded toward the nearest intersection, intending to engage the first coach that happened by. However, an address marker on the corner house identified the cross street as Davies, and since this was the street name printed on Captain Stafford's card, Julie reckoned that she could be but a few blocks from his residence. She checked the pattern of the house numbers and struck off in the indicated direction.

Julie walked very fast, so fast that within the space of a dozen houses she had begun to pant for breath. Her unseemly haste was prompted by an emotion which had grown all too familiar within the past six and thirty hours: panic. She had recognized—after half a day's deliberation and a largely sleepless night—that she must accept Captain Stafford's proposition; and she was fairly limp with the terror that her agreement might come too late, that the Captain might have found a *true* bird of paradise to carry out his distasteful scheme.

When Julie reached Captain Stafford's home—a Palladian-fronted house much like Louisa's—she paused on the footpath to regain her breath and assessed her alternatives one final time. Had she been in better humor, she might have chuckled at the realization that she, a most reluctant Cyprian, was compelled to identify her options as the men of her acquaintance.

Mr. Howe was first; as soon as she had recovered from the shock of Louisa's ultimatum, it had occurred to Julie that she could return to Northampton and accept his vague but standing offer of marriage. However, she had rapidly judged this prospect the proverbial fate worse than death and put it out of her mind.

Mr. Compton had initially appeared a far more promising possibility. He had not—it was true—given Julie a card, but his interest had seemed quite genuine, and there could not be *that* many barristers named Compton even in London. She could surely locate her fellow passenger within the required four days, could stay with him and his wife until she secured a post . . . But she did not know whether Mr. Compton *had* a wife, did not know, upon reflection, just what sort of "assistance" he was prepared to render. Julie recollected the "exceedingly proper" banker who had led Louisa down the primrose path of destruction and shuddered.

And that, of course, left Captain Stafford. He, at least, had promised that no "actual seduction" would be required. Well, he had not exactly *promised* . . .

Julie's stomach rumbled with hunger, and she could not but regard the sound as a signal from heaven. Mrs. Skinner had provided her a few slivers of chicken and a spoonful of beans last night, another desiccated slice of toast this morning. Her present discomfort was but a foretaste, Julie thought grimly, the merest hint of the starvation literally nipping at her heels. She squared her shoulders, marched up the front steps, and rang Captain Stafford's doorbell.

The peal of the bell resounded through the house, then died away, and Julie's shoulders drooped. Apparently she *was* too late. Captain Stafford was out, probably negotiating with one of London's numerous

Fashionable Impures, who would no doubt be delighted
to undertake such an "easy assignment . . ."

"Yes?"

Julie had been so absorbed in her unhappy specula-
tion that she had failed to hear the door open. She
started, and her eyes flew to the man on the other side
of the threshold.

"Is—is Captain Stafford at home?" she stammered.

"Yes, he is. He is not yet dressed, however, so I
shall have to ask you to wait. This way, please."

He stepped aside, beckoned Julie into the house,
and led her up the flight of stairs issuing from the
center of the foyer. Julie noted that the Captain's man
did not appear at all surprised to discover a young
woman on his doorstep at this early hour of the
morning.

"You may wait in the drawing room," he said, nodding her through a doorway. "I shall advise Captain
Stafford that you're here, Miss—Miss . . ."

"Miss Brandon," Julie supplied through stiff lips.

"Miss Brandon." He nodded again and continued up
another staircase to the second story.

Julie was far too nervous to sit, and she lingered in
the doorway, gazing about the room. Captain Stafford's
furniture was quite ordinary, she observed—expensive
and in excellent taste but in no way unusual. His
accessories, on the other hand, were clearly the souve-
nirs of his travels, and they were beautiful and unusual indeed. The rug before the couch, for example,
obviously came from the Middle East, and the great
brass bowl on the sofa table had surely been made in
India. There was a bow-fronted commode against one
wall, and the pottery arrayed upon it was so intriguing that Julie crept across the room for a closer
look. The pieces were like nothing she had previously
seen: imperfect in form but exquisitely painted in
earthen tones—

"It is lovely in its own way; do you not agree?"

Julie whirled around and spied the Captain in the

doorway, lounging against the jamb. She could not determine whether he was "dressed" or not, for above his light-brown pantaloons he wore a loose, soft shirt, open at the neck. It vaguely reminded Julie of the sort of garment one normally associated with pirates, and she wryly decided that it might be very suitable attire for Captain Stafford.

"It is Indian." He straightened, crossed the room to Julie's side, and picked up a small bowl. He evidently read her frown of puzzlement, for he shook his brown-gold head. "*American* Indian, I should have said. Altogether different from our Wedgwood or Spode, but I personally prefer it."

"It is lovely," Julie agreed.

"But you did not come to admire my pottery, did you, Miss Brandon?" He set the bowl back on the commode, and his disconcerting yellow eyes swept her face. "You came to advise me that you *did* change your mind after all, and I am delighted by your decision."

As much as the Captain's statement relieved her, Julie found his cool confidence exceedingly annoying. "I have not changed my mind," she lied primly. "I have merely elected to discuss your—er—proposition a bit further."

"Romney won't have you, eh?" There was a twitch at one corner of his mouth, and Julie flushed and bit her lip. "I can't profess to be surprised; the 'lovely little house' your cousin described so glowingly is scarcely more than a city cottage. Hardly sufficient for two, much less three. But come, let us sit. I have instructed Wyatt to bring up some tea."

Captain Stafford strode toward the Grecian couch, and Julie trailed miserably after him and perched on the very edge of the satin cushion. He had put her at a severe disadvantage, she realized, and it was critically important that she should have the next word.

"It is true that circumstances compel me to consider your proposal," she said, with as much dignity as she could muster. "However, I certainly shan't consent until I know the full particulars."

"My dear Miss Brandon." The Captain occupied the other end of the couch and shook his head once more. "I thought I had explained yesterday that I *myself* do not know the full particulars. My *idea* is very simple: I wish to persuade Uncle Arlington that my cousin's character is no better than my own." Julie decided that this topic—Captain Stafford's character—was best left unexplored. "I believe I also pointed out that in light of Uncle Edmund's strict views, it should not be difficult to maneuver Oliver into a situation which he—my uncle—will judge a compromising one. Beyond that, however, I have formulated no details: I propose to introduce a comely young woman into the household and play the score by ear."

Whatever his character, Julie thought Captain Stafford was stating the truth. She could demand no conditions, exact no promises, and she gazed down at her hands.

"You are no doubt wondering what sort of remuneration I have in mind," the Captain said, evidently misreading her silence. "Naturally I should furnish room and board for the duration of the assignment. I further feel that you will require several new gowns, which I shall provide." Julie looked defensively up, but—as had been the case the night before—his odd, golden eyes were not unkind. "Insofar as actual money is concerned," he continued, "I shall operate our venture like a ship. Your uncle was in the navy, Miss Brandon, so you must know that naval officers are compensated with a share of their prizes. If Uncle Edmund names me his heir, you will be paid accordingly. If not . . ." He stopped and shrugged.

If not, Julie mentally finished, she would have a roof above her head and food in her belly for weeks, possibly months, to come.

"I might add," Captain Stafford went on, "that you will be free to seek a permanent protector while you are in my employ. As long as your search does not interfere with the task at hand, I shall have no objection."

Julie started to bristle, then reckoned it quite useless to reiterate her insistence that she was not the barque of frailty for which the Captain had mistaken her.

"If you do not find a protector, I shall bring you back to London, regardless of the outcome—"

"Back to London?" Julie interrupted sharply. "I was not aware that I was to *leave* London."

"No? Apparently I neglected to mention that Uncle Edmund—with faithful Oliver at his side—is presently in Bath. Where we shall repair as soon as possible after you accept my offer." He hesitated so fractionally that Julie fancied she might have imagined it. "You *do* accept, I trust; surely you find my arrangements satisfactory."

His arrangements were far from satisfactory, of course, but Julie had long since resigned herself to agreement. And during his discourse, she had glimpsed an avenue of escape which even the clever Captain had evidently failed to see. She could accept his proposition, journey to Bath, and, if his demands grew unbearable, she could leave. She still possessed nearly four and a half pounds, and at that juncture, she would also have a full stomach, a new wardrobe . . .

"Eminently satisfactory, Captain Stafford," she cooed.

"Splendid. Indeed, Miss Brandon, I must own myself relieved." He did, in fact, emit a small sigh, and Julie suspected that a genuine Cyprian could have struck a far better bargain than the one to which she had so readily acquiesced. "I am relieved because there is considerably more at stake than Uncle Edmund's fortune alone—"

He was interrupted by a discreet cough from the doorway, and, at the Captain's nod, Wyatt entered the drawing room, deposited a silver tray on the sofa table, and started to pour. Julie had earlier been too

overset to remark his appearance; she now observed
that he was a large, muscular man of perhaps forty
and had the weather-beaten look of the sailor which
Captain Stafford himself had avoided. Despite his
thoroughly masculine aspect, Wyatt filled the delicate
cups with a good deal more grace than Mrs. Skinner
had displayed, and when Julie sipped from hers, she
was forced to concede that the Captain's brawny man
also brewed a far superior grade of tea. Wyatt straightened and, with a rather awkward bow, left the room.

"As I was saying, Miss Brandon, there are factors
besides Uncle Edmund's financial resources which you
should be aware of. There is, to begin with, the question of a title."

"A title," Julie echoed weakly. She was so hungry
that she was beginning to grow lightheaded, and she
desperately wished that Wyatt had brought some
muffins, some small cakes . . .

"Naturally you are confused, for you no doubt realize that my uncle cannot pass *his* title to any but a
blood relative. However, Uncle Arlington is quite close
to the Regent, and he has every expectation of secur-
ing a viscountcy for his designated heir."

Julie wondered if Captain Stafford, after receiving
the anticipated viscountcy, would be known as Captain Lord Something-or-Other. Probably not since he
was not precisely a captain.

"Do you want a title?" she asked. It was a foolish
question, but she was trying to overcome her dizziness,
to ignore her painfully empty stomach.

"Not especially, for I find many of the peers of my
acquaintance excessively silly." Julie—recollecting
Louisa's inane viscount—was compelled to concur.
"Lord Carlon, however, views the matter quite dif-
ferently: he endows titles with an almost supernatural significance."

"Lord Carlon?" Julie was becoming confused again,
but perhaps this was a symptom of her physical debility.

"That is the other factor I wished to bring to your

attention, Miss Brandon. Viscount Carlon, or, more accurately, his daughter Georgina." Captain Stafford sighed once more, this time rather heavily. "Had we conducted this discussion six months since, I should have described Georgina as my fiancée. We were never formally engaged, but we had reached a private understanding . . ."

The Captain rattled on, but Julie scarcely heard him. A fiancée! She vaguely registered the information that Lord Carlon and his daughter, Miss Georgina Vernon, were the Earl of Arlington's Norfolk neighbors, that Captain Stafford had courted Miss Vernon for some years. Julie was entirely at a loss to explain her feelings: a rush of bitter disappointment and a notion that she had been deceived, betrayed. But these *were* her feelings, and she crashed her cup into her saucer.

"Forgive my digression." The Captain had obviously (and fortunately) misinterpreted Julie's reaction. "The point is that Georgina represents Lord Carlon's last hope: he has nearly dissipated his own fortune, and his elder daughters entered into most unfortunate marriages. The eldest married a naval officer who failed to return to his ship after a shore leave in the Mediterranean. I am sure I needn't add that this circumstance has hardly enhanced my own suit. The middle daughter wed a baronet who—if he ever had sixpence to scratch with—has lost every groat at Brooks's—"

"You were attempting to get to the point, Captain," Julie snapped.

"Ah, yes. The point is that Lord Carlon is desperate for Georgina, his youngest daughter, to make the best possible marriage. As I believe I mentioned yesterday, I am frequently abroad, and during the course of my most recent journey, Carlon shoved Georgina and Oliver together—"

"The point!" Julie hissed.

"The point." Captain Stafford coughed. "The point is

that my cousin seems quite taken with Georgina, and Lord Carlon has indicated that Uncle Edmund's heir will be awarded her hand. So you perceive, Miss Brandon, that *everything* is at stake: Uncle Edmund's riches, a title, and the object of my affections."

Julie perceived his situation very well indeed, but she had yet to figure why it distressed her so. Captain Stafford meant nothing to her, nothing personally, yet, if she could, she would have risen and marched out of his drawing room. But she could not; she had debated every other alternative for endless hours before.

"I understand," she said. She congratulated herself on the level, sensible tone of her voice.

"Excellent." The Captain drained his teacup and refilled it. "Then we must next devise a suitable pretext under which to bring you into Uncle Edmund's household. I can hardly introduce you as a Cyprian, engaged for the express purpose of compromising Oliver." Captain Stafford flashed his winsome grin, and Julie gritted her teeth. "No, I have to contrive a credible excuse for your presence. Perhaps you could assist me, Miss Brandon; do you possess any particular abilities? Any *other* abilities, that is?"

Julie started to bristle again, then realized that she could not continue to take offense at the Captain's every word. He assumed she was a barque of frailty, and if she were not to drive herself mad, she must live with that assumption.

"I do draw," she replied hesitantly. "Rather well, I'm told, and I have toyed with oils a bit—"

"But that is marvelous!" Captain Stafford interjected. "Perfect! Uncle Edmund has been talking for months of having a final portrait done."

"A final portrait?" Julie repeated. "Is he dying then?"

"My uncle has been dying for the past twenty years," the Captain said dryly. "I am persuaded that his multitudinous ailments exist primarily in his imagination, but *he* is persuaded that he could succumb at any moment. Indeed, that is why he is in Bath: he spends the better part of every year there, hoping to restore his health. In any event, it will appear most thoughtful of me to have engaged a young artist to paint him."

"But I am not sure I *can* paint him," Julie protested. "I have not worked with oils for some time—"

"Do not tease yourself about it." Captain Stafford waved one slender brown hand. "We shall procure canvases and paints before we depart, and you can practice. That leaves only the matter of a chaperon. Though it may not have occurred to you, Miss Brandon, a *respectable* young woman would not travel about, unaccompanied, with an unrelated gentleman."

Another furious rejoinder tickled Julie's tongue, but she reminded herself of her recent decision and bit it back.

"Fortunately, I am acquainted with a splendid candidate," the Captain continued. "Mrs. Emily Fitch—a charming woman of middle years. But perhaps you know her, Miss Brandon; prior to her retirement, Mrs. Fitch was a *most* Fashionable Impure."

"I do not know her," Julie choked.

"I am sure the two of you will get on famously," Captain Stafford said. "Does that complete the preliminary details?"

Julie suspected his question was rhetorical, but there was, in fact, one detail she had overlooked. "My portmanteau," she said. She did not care a whit for her wretched clothes, but she did want her sketch pad. "I left it at Louisa's."

"I shall drive you over then—"

"No!" She could not face Mrs. Skinner again. "No, if it would not pose too much difficulty, perhaps you could send Wyatt to retrieve it."

"It would pose no trouble at all," the Captain said. "However, I doubt Miss Linley's formidable housekeeper will let it go without some sort of instruction from you. Do you, too, possess a king's ransom in jewels, Miss Brandon?"

Julie, quite beyond blushes by now, shook her head

and requested pencil and paper, which Captain Stafford produced from the center drawer of a *bonheur du
jour* desk on the opposite side of the drawing room.
She composed a one-line note to Mrs. Skinner—"Please
allow Mr. Wyatt to take my portmanteau"—then decided she really should dispatch a message to Louisa
as well. And the simplest thing . . .

"Louisa," she scrawled, "I have elected to follow
your advice about Captain Stafford. I wish you much
happiness in your new home."

Julie added her signature to both missives, addressed
two envelopes, and handed them to the Captain. He
strode out of the drawing room, and Julie laid her
head against the back of the Grecian couch. Her fate
was sealed as surely as the envelopes, and—perhaps
she was beyond shame as well—Julie could not quell
a great flood of relief.

"Wyatt is on his way," Captain Stafford reported,
stepping back into the room. "I desired him to deliver
your trunk to Mrs. Fitch's, so I daresay we should be
off as well. Though I do believe, Miss Brandon, that
we have time to stop en route for a bite of lunch."

Julie's stomach growled concurrence, and she guessed
this might be the *only* subject on which she and Captain Nicholas Stafford would ever agree.

Chapter 4

"Nick Stafford! Is it really you, dear boy, or do my old eyes deceive me?"

Insofar as Julie could determine, there was nothing about Mrs. Emily Fitch that could accurately be described as "old." She was above the average in height, but her shoulders were quite unbent, and she retained the willowy figure of a girl. The lines about her eyes and at the corners of her rather wide mouth were so tiny as to be almost indiscernible, and the eyes themselves were a deep, piercing blue. Julie decided that only Mrs. Fitch's hair betrayed her as a woman of "middle years"; apparently she had once been blond, and her stylish Sappho was now a soft blend of gold and silver intermixed.

"You look wonderful!" Mrs. Fitch continued. "Not a day older than when last I saw you, and that was—what?—three years since?"

"Nearer to four, I should guess." Captain Stafford sounded a trifle guilty.

"Do not tease yourself about it, dear." Evidently Mrs. Fitch had perceived his tone as well. "I shan't claim that your letters have been an adequate substitute for your charming person, but I enjoyed them immensely. Enjoy, I should have said: I have saved every one of them, and I often read them over."

Julie entertained a sudden, and horribly embarrassing, notion that Mrs. Fitch had introduced an adoles-

cent Captain Stafford to the realities of life. She was
well aware that many English fathers regarded such
a liaison as a critical form of education, considerably
more important than a course of study at Oxford or
Cambridge.

"I thought to respond to the one letter," Mrs. Fitch
added, "but at the time, I did not know your direction.
So I shall tell you now that you must not dwell on
your resignation from the navy. I daresay your father
would have been disappointed, but I advised you years
ago that you cannot live your life as Henry would
have had it." She shook her gold-and-silver head.
"Henry," she sighed. "I still miss him, Nick."

Julie collected that Mrs. Fitch's relationship had
been with the late Admiral Stafford rather than his
son. She could not but regard it as odd that the Captain would perpetuate a friendship with his father's
chère amie, but this was so vastly preferable to the
alternative circumstance that she narrowly repressed
a sigh of relief.

"I miss him, too, Emily," Captain Stafford said gently.

"But I have been exceedingly rude, I fear." Mrs.
Fitch flashed a tremulous smile and turned to Julie.
"I'm prattling on of times long past, and I've given
you no opportunity to present your—your friend."

"This is Miss Brandon," the Captain supplied. "Juliet
Brandon."

"Mrs. Fitch," Julie murmured.

"Miss Brandon." The former Fashionable Impure
stepped slightly back, and Julie surmised that age
had rendered her a trifle farsighted. "Well," Mrs. Fitch
went on briskly, "I fancy Miss Brandon finds herself
in a bit of trouble. And that you, naughty boy, have
come to solicit my assistance—"

"No!" the Captain yelped. To Julie's astonishment,
he had flushed a deep brick-red. "No, you have quite
misconstrued the situation, Emily. In point of fact,
I've come to tender a proposition."

"I'm much too old for propositions, dear," Mrs. Fitch protested wryly.

"Not *that* sort of proposition. Though, as I think on it, I daresay you're not too old at all."

"I shall be fifty on my next birthday, but I appreciate your gallantry."

"Enough sparring, Emily." Captain Stafford frowned with mock severity. "Surely you can allow me a moment or two to elucidate my proposal. A moment or two in a *chair*, I might add."

Mrs. Fitch briefly raised her brows, then beckoned them on into the foyer and through a door at their left. Julie had noted from the street that the house had only two stories above the ground, and she guessed this was the drawing room; the bedchambers must be upstairs. She observed that Mrs. Fitch's furniture, while of excellent quality, was decidedly worn; and, upon close inspection, the retired Cyprian's clothes showed similar symptoms of long use. Mrs. Fitch's walking dress, of peach jaconet, had obviously been fashioned by a mantua-maker of considerable talent, but the rouleau round the hem was frayed, and there was a visible patch on one sleeve of the white lutestring spencer. Mrs. Fitch moved past them and plumped the once-fat cushions of an ancient Adam sofa.

"Please do sit down," she instructed, nodding them toward the sofa, which did not appear to have been improved by her ministrations.

Julie and the Captain took opposite sides of the couch, and Mrs. Fitch sank into a matching and equally dilapidated chair on the other side of the sofa table. Julie noticed that she did not suggest refreshments and recollected that she had opened her own door; apparently the faded bird of paradise had no full-time servants.

"I'm sorry I can't offer tea." Mrs. Fitch spoke as if she had read Julie's thoughts. "However, my girl comes only in the morning, and she left several hours since."

"It's quite all right, Mrs. Fitch," Julie said soothingly. "We just had an enormous lunch." This was true; though Julie would not have believed it possible, her stomach was stuffed fairly to bursting. She smiled and looked at Captain Stafford for concurrence, but he was frowning again.

"Are you comfortable, Emily?" he demanded sternly.

"Quite comfortable, dear. As I said, Abby comes every morning in ample time to prepare my breakfast. She then tidies up, and before she departs, she prepares my dinner as well. She leaves it in the kitchen, and I've only to heat it. I've really no need for butlers and footmen and those sorts of people, for I no longer entertain. And when I wish to go out, I borrow Mr. Foster's carriage and coachman. Mr. Foster lives just across the street," she explained, "and he has been *most* accommodating."

"You should not be compelled to borrow a carriage." The Captain's frown had deepened.

"We have covered that ground before, Nick." Mrs. Fitch sighed once more. "I have informed you repeatedly, and I remind you now, that I shall not accept a farthing from you."

"Not even in wages?"

"Wages?" Mrs. Fitch lifted her brows again, and Julie noted that they were still entirely blond. "Wages for what?"

"*That* is what I came to discuss." Captain Stafford sat forward on the sofa and clasped his long tanned hands between his knees. "Miss Brandon and I are prepared to embark upon a most interesting venture . . ."

Julie bitterly resented the implication that *she* had somehow helped to devise his shameless scheme. Nevertheless, since the plot had been presented to her only in bits and pieces, she followed his every word; and when he had finished, she found herself, no less than Mrs. Fitch, perched quite literally on the edge of her seat.

"It *could* succeed." Mrs. Fitch sat back, tapped her

fingernails on the arms of her chair, narrowed her bright blue eyes. "It could succeed, Nick, though you will have to concoct some means of slipping past Miss Crane."

"*Miss* Crane?" Julie echoed sharply. Was the cast of characters never to end?

"Ah, yes, I fancy I neglected to mention her," the Captain said. "Hester is Oliver's elder sister."

"Though one might well guess her to be his mother," Mrs. Fitch added disapprovingly. "Henry always found her *most* irritating, and I should suppose she is worse now that she's a spinster of advanced age."

"I can hardly term two and thirty an advanced age," Captain Stafford said dryly.

"You know quite well what I mean, Nick. Miss Crane is as protective as a mother hen, and she'll not readily permit Miss Brandon to form a friendship with Sir Oliver."

"She permitted *Georgina* to form such a friendship," the Captain pointed out darkly.

"Perhaps she believes that Lord Arlington wants the match. Miss Crane is well aware on which side her bread is buttered." Mrs. Fitch paused a moment, and when she continued, Julie thought it was with some hesitation. "Speaking of Miss Vernon, dear, I collect—since you seem determined to marry her—that you see no resemblance between her and the remainder of her family."

"There is no resemblance whatever. The older daughters look astonishingly like Lord Carlon, but Georgina evidently favors her mother, whom I never met—"

"I was not referring to her physical appearance, Nick; I am concerned about her character. I was acquainted with Viscount Carlon before you were born, and I should be hard put to identify a greater scoundrel. Insofar as the girls are concerned, I am told—by those in a position to know—that the eldest son-in-law would have sold his soul to the devil to escape his wife, so the poor man no doubt viewed desertion as a very

moderate course. I am given to understand that the
second son-in-law took up gaming in an attempt to
satisfy *his* wife's impossible demands. And how Lord
Carlon can be so hypocritical as to criticize either of
them quite defies my imagination, for *he* did not spend
above two weeks in the year with Lady Carlon. This
was before his rakeshame conduct drove her to an
early grave—"

"We are wasting time, Emily," Captain Stafford
snapped. Julie thought he appeared unduly overset by
Mrs. Fitch's *on-dits,* but perhaps he was merely
impatient. "I assure you that we shall find a way to
breach Hester's defenses. We shall, at any rate, if you
agree to pose as Miss Brandon's chaperon."

Mrs. Fitch clasped her hands together, and Julie
observed that she wore several splendid rings, quite
undimmed by age or wear.

"Come now," the Captain coaxed, "what have you to
lose? It should prove most amusing, and you will, at
the least, have a holiday in Bath."

Mrs. Fitch studied one of her rings—an enormous
burst of rubies and sapphires—but before she could
answer, the doorbell rang. She leaped out of her chair
with visible relief, hurried into the foyer, and returned with Wyatt in tow.

"Miss Brandon's case is in the hall, sir," the Captain's
man reported. "Miss Linley herself was not at home,
so I left the other note with that—that woman."

Wyatt shuddered a bit, and Julie surmised he had
had no easy time with Mrs. Skinner. She wished her
message could have been delivered directly into Louisa's
hands, but, on second thought, it didn't seem to signify.
Julie doubted she would see her cousin again, and she
did not find this prospect in the least distressing.

"Very good, Wyatt," Captain Stafford said. "Please
carry Miss Brandon's trunk to one of the guest
bedchambers. Which of them would be most convenient,
Emily?"

"The one to the left of the stairs, I suppose."

Wyatt nodded and disappeared, and Julie soon heard his footfalls on the staircase. Mrs. Fitch was glaring at the Captain, but Julie noticed a telltale twitch at one corner of her generous mouth.

"Apparently you took my cooperation quite for granted," she said. "It seems I must either accept your proposition or put poor Miss Brandon into the street. Very well, I do accept, but I shan't take any money. A holiday in Bath will be ample payment."

"You're a stubborn woman, Emily, but I shan't argue. However, you must permit me to pay Miss Brandon's room and board for the period prior to our departure." He had donned a proper shirt and a lemon-colored frock coat before they left his house, and he now rose and dug in a pocket of the latter. He extracted a very large roll of bank notes, peeled off the outer two, and passed them to Mrs. Fitch.

"Just how long is our departure to be delayed?" Mrs. Fitch asked wryly, studying the bills.

"A week at the minimum, I should say, for I have instructed Miss Brandon to procure several new gowns. I should appreciate it if you would take her to your mantua-maker, Emily, and assist her in making her selections. While you are there, please order half a dozen dresses for yourself."

"Nick!"

"I am not offering charity," he said blandly. "It is imperative that both of you be appropriately attired if we are to persuade Uncle Edmund that Miss Brandon is a respectable young woman traveling with her . . . What do you think? Her aunt? Yes, I daresay 'Aunt Emily' will do very nicely. In any case, for the clothes . . ." He counted off four more bills and shoved them into Mrs. Fitch's hand. "I shall send Wyatt by for you early Monday morning, and he will drive you to the mantua-maker. Have I overlooked anything?"

"The art supplies," Julie said.

"Ah, yes." He passed another bank note to Mrs. Fitch, and Julie collected that he did not entirely

trust the strange country "Cyprian" he had employed.
"I fancy that does it then. I shall return on Tuesday so
as to evaluate our progress."

Captain Stafford briefly bowed to Julie, and Mrs.
Fitch escorted him into the foyer. Evidently Wyatt
departed with him, or had left already, for when Mrs.
Fitch returned, she suggested that Julie might wish
to repair to her bedchamber. Julie—hard pressed to
quell a notion that she had stumbled into a very vivid,
exceedingly peculiar dream—mutely nodded and trailed
her unlikely hostess up the stairs and through a door
just beside the landing.

"It certainly isn't elaborate." Mrs. Fitch bustled
about—smoothing the worn counterpane, fussing with
the tattered curtains, running one finger along a crack
in the cheval glass. "But it will have to suffice, and I
do hope you'll be comfortable."

"I'm sure I shall be very comfortable, Mrs. Fitch,"
Julie said politely.

"I do believe, dear, that we had best assume our
roles at once so the novelty will have worn off by the
time we reach Bath. You must begin calling me Aunt
Emily. And do you go by Juliet or have you a nick-
name?"

"Julie," she mumbled.

"Julie."

Mrs. Fitch inclined her head and peered critically
around the room, and Julie fervently prayed that she
was about to take her leave. But it was not to be;
"Aunt Emily" sat on the edge of the counterpane and
began to pluck at the loose threads of her rouleau.

"I collect," she said at last, "that your present situation has rendered you a trifle overset."

This was an understatement of such historic magnitude that Julie nearly burst into a peal of hysterical
laughter.

"I can well understand your feelings," Aunt Emily
continued kindly. "You met Nick only two nights ago,

and your previous experience was obviously not a happy one."

Mrs. Fitch's eyes rested for a moment on Julie's dress (she was wearing the wretched muslin again), then fled discreetly to the scarred mahogany wardrobe. Julie did not at once perceive her meaning; when she did, she discovered that she was not beyond blushes after all. She was briefly tempted to relate her true "situation," but she immediately reconsidered. Captain Stafford had described the circumstances of their initial encounter in excruciating detail, and Julie doubted Aunt Emily would believe her protests any more than had the Captain himself.

"I wish to assure you that Nick will not mistreat you," Mrs. Fitch said. "I know you are thinking that men make promises only to break them; your last protector was clearly typical in that regard." Julie bit her lip. "But Nick is different; as you have recently observed for yourself, he is generous to a fault." Aunt Emily patted a pocket of her skirt—the one in which she had deposited Captain Stafford's sheaf of bank notes—and fondly shook her head. "He is much like his father in that respect."

Julie frowned and glanced around the shabby little bedchamber, gazed at Mrs. Fitch's fine, worn clothes. She caught herself almost at once and smiled into Aunt Emily's bright blue eyes, but it was too late.

"I can imagine your thoughts now as well, dear, but you are mistaken. Henry provided for me very handsomely; unfortunately, he could not foresee the dismal economic conditions which have plagued us since the end of the war. Nick is forever attempting to compensate, but I don't allow it. Since he inherited very few *assets* from Henry, he certainly should not be compelled to inherit the liability of a doddering mistress."

Julie wondered where—if he had not inherited it— Captain Stafford had come by his impressive bundle of bank notes. Prize money, even cleverly invested, could hardly last forever. So perhaps the Captain's "high-stakes gaming" returned a consistent profit.

"But I digress," Aunt Emily said briskly. "I was saying that Nick is excessively generous and that you need have no fears on that account." She knitted her blond brows. "Though, now that I think on it, it occurs to me that Miss Vernon—if she *does* resemble her father and her sisters—could fritter away even Lord Arlington's fortune in a matter of months." She heaved a great sigh. "I *do* wish the dear boy would direct his attentions elsewhere, but what more can I say?"

"What more?" Julie repeated. Her voice was inexplicably harsh, and she wondered why the subject of Miss Georgina Vernon distressed her so. "He appears to be very much in love with her—"

"Love?" Aunt Emily shook her head again. "Nick is kind and generous and thoughtful, but I have always reckoned him incapable of developing a great *tendre*. And if he *should* fall in love, it won't be with the likes of Georgina Vernon. No, my suspicion is that he grew infatuated with her years ago and that she has since become a habit. Which, I am sorry to say, is a common motive for marriage, and I daresay he'll wed her in the end. Perhaps she *is* unlike her sisters and won't ruin him after all."

"Perhaps so," Julie miserably agreed.

"In any event, it all goes to emphasize the wisdom of your course, doesn't it, my dear?"

Julie personally thought her most recent "course" had been *un*wise in the extreme. But she was starting to feel the effects of two difficult days, the effects of incipient starvation followed by a surfeit of food. "What course?" she asked sleepily.

"Though one may find the seemingly perfect protector, one *never knows* precisely what may happen," Aunt Emily replied. "So it is very clever of you to have cultivated a second skill. When you are old, as I am, and there is no man pounding at your door, you can paint portraits for a living. Very clever indeed."

Julie was far too tired to talk about tomorrow, much less her old age, and she did not respond. Nor did she object when Aunt Emily stood, turned down the counterpane, and led her to the bed.

"Nap awhile, Julie, and I shall wake you in time for dinner. Abby always makes far too much for me alone, so I daresay you won't go hungry . . ."

Julie tucked the pillow beneath her cheek, and Aunt Emily was still talking, still crooning, when she fell asleep.

Chapter 5

As Captain Stafford had promised, Wyatt returned early Monday morning. The Captain's man was driving a splendid landau which Julie had not previously seen and now registered as another sign of Captain Stafford's mysterious (and no doubt misbegotten) wealth. Wyatt assisted the two women into the carriage, and Mrs. Fitch gave him an address in Leicester Square.

"I shall tender but one bit of advice, dear," she said, as the vehicle got under way. "Whatever your *personal* taste, I must counsel you not to order anything too—too bold. Keep in mind that we are striving to project an image of the utmost respectability."

"Yes, Aunt Emily," Julie sighed.

The "Aunt Emily" came quite naturally, for over the past six and thirty hours, Julie and Mrs. Fitch had conducted several lengthy, intimate conversations. During the course of which the sigh had grown habitual as well, for at some point Julie had recognized the depth of her entrapment. What if she *did* confess the truth to Aunt Emily? What if Aunt Emily believed her and persuaded Captain Stafford of his dreadful error? The questions were rhetorical, the answers clear. If the Captain possessed a shred of honor—and Aunt Emily had convinced Julie that he did—he would refuse to permit an innocent country girl to participate in his plot. He would give her a few pounds to see her back to Northampton, where Mr. Howe would greet her with a disapproving frown of forgiveness. In short, as Julie had calculated long since, Captain Stafford was by far the best of her wretched alternatives; and she dared not disabuse him of his notion that she was a green-headed Cyprian, eager to abet his scheme.

So Julie had told Mrs. Fitch the basic facts about her life, omitting only those details that would enable her clever new "aunt" to divine the truth. When, for example, she described her parents' deaths and her residence with Aunt Sophia, she managed to avoid any mention of the times involved. She didn't actually *lie,* but Aunt Emily naturally inferred that Julie had been alone, plying her mythical trade, for some years. Nor did she lie about the Cyprians' Ball; she confirmed the Captain's report that she had gone to the Argyle Rooms to find her cousin. Julie could hardly be blamed if Aunt Emily, like Captain Stafford himself, had leaped to the obvious conclusion.

Aunt Emily, for her part, revealed that she had become a Fashionable Impure entirely by accident. Her father, too, had been an out-at-heels baronet and had jumped at the chance to marry his daughter to a prosperous, middle-aged merchant. Sir Philip had died a few weeks after the wedding, and, within the year, Robert Fitch was dead as well.

"His prosperity proved to be a puff of smoke, my dear." Aunt Emily shook her gold-and-silver head. "He left me a pile of notes beyond my wildest nightmares—debtor's notes, not the better sort. As I was pondering what to do, where to turn, Robert's dearest friend offered to take me under his wing. In fact, he was seeking to satisfy an altogether *different* portion of his anatomy; need I say more? In any case, one thing led to another . . ."

Julie could not but reflect that Aunt Emily's history was much like Louisa's. And, far more horrifying, much like her own. She regarded her employment by

Captain Stafford as simply that—employment—but
perhaps escape would not be as easy as she fancied.
Perhaps she, thirty years hence, would be justifying
her situation as one that had occurred quite by accident.

Julie's unhappy reverie was interrupted by the halt-
ing of the landau. Wyatt clambered down from the
box and handed his charges into the street, and Aunt
Emily led the way into a small but elegant shop. As
Julie took note of the tall cheval glasses, the delicate
gilt chairs, the glittering crystal chandeliers, the pro-
prietress bounded forward to greet them and fairly
screeched to a stop when she recognized her customer.

"Mrs. Fitch!" she gasped. "What a surprise! It has
been an age since I have seen you."

"It has been some time," Aunt Emily agreed briskly,
"but I trust the surprise is a pleasant one, Miss
Howard."

"Of course it is." The mantua-maker's dark eyes
darted between them, and Julie surmised that she
was pondering the peculiar nature of the man who
had extended his protection to *two* barques of frailty
of such widely divergent ages. "A very pleasant surprise indeed, Mrs. Fitch, but I daresay I can make up
just the thing for the both of you."

Julie had not visited a dressmaker since Mama's
death, and she willingly submitted to Aunt Emily's
guidance. If Miss Howard was further surprised by
the conservative walking dresses the notorious Mrs.
Fitch selected for herself and her young friend, she
gave no sign as she busily jotted down the order.

"I fancy that does it for the daytime attire," Aunt
Emily said at last, "so we shall now consider evening
gowns."

"Evening gowns!" Julie protested. She had been unable precisely to follow Aunt Emily's complex instructions, but she calculated that the order already approached a dozen garments. "I do believe we've purchased enough, enough for me, at any rate—"

"Nonsense," Mrs. Fitch interjected crisply. "Unless

Miss Howard's prices have risen *most* precipitously"
—this with a sharp tilt of one blond eyebrow—"we
can well afford another dress or two on Nick's allot-
ment."

Julie listened with amazement as Aunt Emily and
Miss Howard debated the relative merits of crepe and
satin, of net and lace, of blue versus green for Julie's
distinctive coloring. She thought "another dress or
two" had swelled to eight or nine before Aunt Emily
was finished, and she was nearly in a daze by the time
Miss Howard recorded the specifications of the final
gown and took Julie's measurements.

"When will the order be ready?" Aunt Emily inquired,
after the mantua-maker had completed her volumi-
nous paperwork.

"With this number of garments"—Miss Howard
frowned at her note pad—"I shall require at least
three weeks . . ." Aunt Emily fixed her with a paralyz-
ing stare, and the dressmaker's voice trailed off. "That
is," she hastily amended, "it *would* take three weeks
for any but a favored client. For you, Mrs. Fitch, I
shall have the order ready next Tuesday."

Aunt Emily regally nodded, propelled Julie through
the door, and, when they were safely outside, flashed
her "niece" a triumphant smile. They proceeded to the
milliner, just next door, then purchased shoes and
gloves at neighboring shops across the street. At last
Aunt Emily pronounced their wardrobes complete, and
they returned to the carriage, where Wyatt relieved
them of their numerous parcels and assisted them
into their places. He remained in the street, gazing up
at Julie.

"Captain Stafford desired me to remind you about
the art supplies, Miss Brandon," he said. "He suggested a place in Fitzroy Square."

"Yes," Julie murmured; "yes, that would be fine."

The landau clattered to a start again, and Julie—
her head swimming—collapsed against the seat. It
would be fearfully easy to become a Cyprian, she

admitted. Hideously easy—if one had the right protector—to ride to the mantua-maker and the milliner
in his handsome carriage, to buy a dozen gowns and
every accessory to match. Julie had always fancied
herself an exceedingly moral person, moral nearly to
the point of intolerance. But after a few hours in
Leicester Square, she could well understand how Mrs.
Fitch, Louisa, a thousand other girls, might stumble
into the demimonde and succumb to its undeniable
advantages. Julie closed her eyes, and Aunt Emily
patted her knee, almost as if she had discerned the
drift of her young friend's thoughts.

The landau halted once more, and Wyatt dutifully
left the box and opened Julie's door.

"We are here," Aunt Emily announced gratuitously.
She dug in her reticule and extracted a bank note.
"This is the amount Nick set aside for your supplies,
but if it isn't sufficient, I can give you a bit more."

Not sufficient? Julie stared down at a ten-pound
bill, more money than she had ever before held in her
entire life. "I believe it will be sufficient, Aunt Emily,"
she said dryly.

The establishment was a gallery-cum-shop and suitably shabby for London's artists' quarter: the windows
were so grimy as to be nearly opaque, and the floor
did not appear to have been swept within the year.
The proprietor, an effeminate man of middle years,
immediately ascertained that Julie did not intend to
purchase any of the overpriced paintings he had on
display and lost any desultory interest he might have
had in such an unprepossessing client. Consequently,
Julie poked about the dusty shelves alone, selecting
the proper canvases, several brushes, an easel, a palette,
fifteen containers of paint. Fifteen? She examined the
Captain's bank note again and, to be perfectly safe,
snatched up another ten colors.

"An artist, are you?" The proprietor had permitted
Julie to lug her purchases quite unassisted to the
front of the store, but the magnitude of her bill had

evidently recaptured his attention. "I'd be happy to take your work, miss. On consignment, of course."

Julie glanced at the landscapes, the still lifes, haphazardly hung on the cracked and peeling walls. "Thank you," she said sweetly. "I shall keep that in mind."

Wyatt loaded Julie's purchases into the unoccupied seat of the carriage and clucked the horses ahead again. Julie felt honor bound to return her change to Aunt Emily, who shoved the notes and coins back into her reticule.

"With so much equipment, I daresay you will need a separate room for your artwork," she said. "Fortunately, the bedchamber across from your own is not in use; perhaps it will suffice."

As it turned out, the room was a bedchamber only in Aunt Emily's imagination, empty except for an ancient dining table and a rickety shield-back chair. But it was situated in a corner of the house and therefore fairly flooded with light, and its very barrenness enhanced Julie's impression that it could be a genuine studio. She instructed Wyatt to place her easel beneath the rear windows and watched as he stacked her canvases against one wall and laid her paints and palette and brushes on the scarred surface of the table. When the Captain's man had finished, Aunt Emily escorted him downstairs, and Julie began arranging her paints by color. She felt a quiver of anticipation, a stir of excitement, but she decided to start with something simple. A still life maybe; she had observed a silver bowl of fruit and a rather unusual candelabrum in Aunt Emily's dining room. She had just set the first canvas on her easel when Mrs. Fitch sailed back into the room.

"I was hoping you might defer your painting for a time, dear," Aunt Emily said. "There is something else I should like you to do this afternoon."

"Something else?" Julie attempted to keep the disappointment out of her voice.

"Yes. I permit myself but a single luxury: I have a

coiffeur in once a week, and he is due at any moment. I trust you will not take it amiss when I say that your hair is badly in need of attention. I am sure Nick would not object if we were to use the change from your supplies to finance a new hairstyle."

"Is M. Jacques by any chance your coiffeur?" Julie asked nervously.

"Indeed not," Aunt Emily sniffed. "That horrid little man is the most expensive hairdresser in London and not worth half his fee." She gazed at Julie's unruly tresses with dawning shock. "M. Jacques did not do *your* hair, did he?"

"No," Julie said wryly. "No, he didn't."

"Well, I am certain you will be far more satisfied with Mr. Paul than the—the charlatan who has coiffed you in the past."

"I am certain I shall," Julie agreed, choking back a laugh.

Mr. Paul—an attractive, sweet-smelling man scarcely older than Julie—studied her hair with visible displeasure and pushed her quite unceremoniously into the chair in front of Aunt Emily's dressing table. Julie had planned to supervise his every snip, his every twist, but, to her dismay, Mr. Paul turned her away from the mirror. He then began wielding his scissors and combs and brushes with an enthusiasm bordering on ferocity, and Julie could only wince as one auburn tendril after another tumbled to the worn Aubusson carpet. Aunt Emily issued frequent suggestions, mostly consisting of the word "shorter," and when Mr. Paul at last turned Julie back around, she peered fearfully at her reflection.

Peered, then frankly gaped, for she hardly recognized the arresting countenance which stared back at her from the glass. Mr. Paul had, indeed, cut her hair very short in the front, creating a profusion of soft curls about her face, but he had left the back just long enough to form a curly knot àt the crown of her head.

He had somehow made her eyes look even larger, her
cheekbones even higher, and the effect was so astonishing that Julie was almost able to overlook her
multitudinous freckles.

"You look *very* handsome, dear," Aunt Emily pronounced. "I suspected there was a beauty lurking beneath that awful clutter of hair, and I am seldom
wrong about such matters. Off with you now; it will
take Mr. Paul considerably longer to make something
of an old woman."

Julie surrendered the chair and hurried to the dining room to borrow the bowl and candelabrum she
wished to paint. She returned to her studio and arranged the objects on the table, but when she stepped
back to gain the proper perspective, she discovered
that her vision was a trifle blurred. She reached up
and found her cheeks damp, and she was initially
inclined to attribute her tears to the strain of the
preceding days. But she soon realized that she was
responding to a warmth she had not experienced since
Mama's death. Mrs. Fitch, in six and thirty hours, had
shown Julie more real kindness than Aunt Sophia
had displayed during five long years; and the situation was another threat to Julie's sense of order, her
perceptions of right and wrong.

But those were dangerous notions indeed, she advised herself sternly. She brushed her tears furiously
away, fussed with the apple and the orange, the grapes
and the pear in the silver bowl and began to open her
paints.

Julie scurried back to her studio immediately after
breakfast the following morning and critically examined her half-completed still life. She didn't plan to
finish it (the Earl of Arlington certainly wouldn't ask
her to paint his fruit and his candlesticks), but she
wanted to be sure she could still put oils on canvas
without embarrassing herself. She stood away, trying

to be as objective as she could, and felt a tremor of triumph. It was not bad; it really wasn't bad at all. In fact, there was but one obvious flaw: the pear was entirely the wrong color, and color was everything. Julie mixed a yellow with a green and began to repair the offending fruit.

"Have you scheduled a showing at Somerset House or must I wait a bit longer?"

Julie whirled around and spotted Captain Stafford, lounging—as was his wont—in the doorway.

"It's nothing," she said quickly. "Nothing; just some practice."

She reached out, intending to take the canvas off the easel, but the Captain strode across the room and snatched her hand away. He studied the painting for a long, agonizing moment, and Julie realized that she attached a great deal of importance to his opinion.

"It's actually quite good," he said at last. He stepped back as well and frowned. "Quite good except that the pear isn't the proper shade. It looks rather—rather green."

"The pear I am painting *is* rather green," Julie said defensively, pointing to the silver bowl on the table. "If anything, my pear is still too yellow."

"Ah, you paint what you see then."

"I know no other way *to* paint," Julie said stiffly.

"No? I am told that society artists often flatter their subjects. Though, now that I think on it, Uncle Edmund is not an unhandsome man, not in view of his lingering, terminal illness." Captain Stafford flashed a mischievous grin. "So perhaps your technique will suffice."

"Thank you," Julie murmured absently. She was determined to get the pear exactly right, and she added another dot of green to her mixture and dabbed at the canvas again.

"Have you not done something to your hair?" the Captain demanded. "Yes, you have; you no longer

look like a country girl. But I daresay that will be all
to the good."

He fell silent, and Julie carefully stroked a final
touch of green on the canvas. The pear was perfect
now, absolutely perfect.

"In fact," Captain Stafford continued, "your hair is
most becoming. _Very_ becoming."

"Thank you, Nick."

Julie was still gazing at the pear, and it was a
moment before she registered the liberty she had taken.
When she did, she whirled around again.

"I'm sorry," she said. "I intended no familiarity.
Aunt Emily always calls you that, and it simply slipped
out."

"I should not mind in the least if you wish to use my
Christian name. Not so long as we remember our
roles when we reach Bath. Not in the least." His
golden eyes were narrowed, speculative, yet oddly
distant. "Your hair is _exceedingly_ becoming," he concluded somewhat lamely.

"Thank you." Julie's face was warm, and to her
vague astonishment, she observed that Nick appeared
a bit discomfited as well. "Thank you very much."

"Well." He coughed. "In any event, we haven't the
time to debate about pears. You will be painting Uncle Arlington, and I therefore suggest you concentrate
on a human subject. I daresay Emily will be delighted
to sit for you—"

"No!" Julie blurted out. Her protest had emerged
entirely unbidden, but she now recollected her desire
to paint Captain Stafford. Nick, she amended. "No,"
she repeated, "since I am to paint a man, I believe I
should experiment on a man. And as you are the only
man here, I fear I must impress you into service."

To Julie's further amazement, the Captain seemed
to suffer a sudden attack of modesty—insisting that
he did not have the time to sit for a portrait, would
not sit if he _did_ have the time ... But Julie eventu-

ally moved the sagging shield-back chair to a position near the side windows and maneuvered her reluctant subject into the chair. She did not suppose she could keep him captive for long, so she hastily brushed his outline, his features, on a blank canvas. She then started mixing a new batch of colors, noting, as she had before, that he was all yellows and golds and browns—brown and golden hair, pale brown skin, yellow eyes, a cinnamon frock coat, a saffron waistcoat.

"Must I sit perfectly still in this damnable chair," Nick grumbled, "or may I talk?"

"You may talk if you move nothing but your mouth," Julie replied.

"Excellent." He pursed his lips in exaggerated fashion, and Julie could not repress a grin. "I was wondering how you came to be in this situation."

Julie's smile abruptly faded. Much as her sense of morality had been distorted by recent events, she did not wish—if she could avoid it—to tell an outright lie. "What set you to wondering that?" she dissembled.

"Emily and I had a brief chat when I arrived, and she related a bit about your background. I am given to understand that your father was a baronet and that after his death you lived with his aunt in Northampton."

"That is true," Julie said.

"I assume that when your grandaunt died, you found a local protector. One in Northamptonshire, that is."

"Please do not move!" Julie admonished sharply.

In fact, he had moved only his arm, which she was not yet painting, but she hoped her digression would serve to distract him. Her ploy appeared to be successful, for after he had resumed his original posture, he plunged ahead in time.

"And when that—that liaison ended, you came to London to join forces with your cousin."

"I did come to London to live with Louisa," Julie agreed. She desperately wanted to put an end to his inquiries, and it occurred to her that she was free to interpret "this situation" in any manner she chose. "Let us simply say," she added, "that my present circumstances result from a long series of accidents."

"Not an uncommon story," the Captain mused.

"Not uncommon at all," Julie concurred wryly. "I believe Aunt Emily and Louisa experienced similar twists of fate."

"That is not what I meant." Nick's tone was uncharacteristically serious, and when Julie glanced up, she observed that his eyes had narrowed again. "I daresay *everyone's* life is a series of accidents. I know that I myself am embroiled in circumstances I could never have envisioned."

"No, indeed," Julie said. "If you *had* envisioned them, you would not be compelled to go to such drastic lengths to compromise your cousin, would you?"

She had intended it as a jest, and she waited for an appreciative chuckle. But the Captain remained silent, and when Julie looked up again, she found him gazing over her shoulder, gazing into space.

"But that is not what you meant either, is it?" she said. She recollected one of Aunt Emily's comments. "Perhaps you were referring to your courtship of Miss Vernon."

Julie immediately wanted to retract her words, but it was, of course, too late. And, to her relief, Nick did not seem annoyed by her prying; his expression was more nearly one of bemusement.

"As it happens, I was not referring to Georgina," he said. "However, now you mention it, our courtship *was* in the way of an accident. I believe I explained that Lord Carlon lives near Uncle Arlington in Norfolk, and I have known Georgina all my life. All *her* life, I should have said; Georgina is some years younger than I. For a short time, we were both children, playing together as children do. Then I became an adolescent, and Georgina was still a child, and I suppose I regarded her as a little sister. By the time Georgina herself reached adolescence, I was a man grown and already in the navy. Naturally I continued to encounter her during my leaves, and at some juncture I recognized that she, too, had become an adult."

Julie began to regret her ill-chosen remark most bitterly, for, as always, she found the subject of Miss Vernon inexplicably oversetting. She attempted to shut her ears to the Captain's interminable accounting and suddenly remembered Wyatt's calm acceptance of her presence on his master's doorstep.

"I suppose you will next try to tell me that you have been true to Miss Vernon from that moment to this," she snapped.

"That would depend upon your definition of 'true,' " he said mildly. "I shan't deny that there have been other women in my life, but none have challenged Georgina's place in my affections. I am sure you recognize the difference between affection and casual amusement."

Julie thought he had stressed the "you" very slightly, but it might have been her imagination. In any event, emphasis or no, his message was clear: the woman he fancied Julie to be was vastly different from the innocent girl he had chosen to be his wife. If Julie had entertained any wild notion of competing with Georgina Vernon—and she had *not,* she assured herself quickly—Nick's words had set her quite straight. The Captain thought her a demimondaine, literally the inhabitant of another world, and she reminded herself that she must live with that perception.

"Why have you not married Miss Vernon long since?" she asked, eager to shift the discussion away from herself.

"Georgina was exceedingly reluctant to wed a naval officer," he said. "A position I can well understand in view of her sister's distressing history."

"Is that why you resigned your commission?" Julie

was pleased to note that she could converse and paint at the same time: she had already brushed in the outlines of his hair, captured the color of his eyes, his skin, his clothes, recorded the slant of his cheekbones and the distinctive angle of his rather prominent chin.

"In part it was. In greater part, I belatedly discovered myself unsuited to a military career."

At which point, Julie thought, he had embarked upon a career as a rake. But she dared not tempt Nick's good humor any further, and she hastily stroked his rather thin lips on the canvas.

"That was two years ago," she said. "One might have expected you to marry since then."

"Indeed, one might." His voice seemed a trifle sharp, but when Julie peered over the canvas, his lean, bony face was bland. "However, as I fancy I also explained, I travel extensively, and Georgina judges my present circumstances little improved over the former."

"Surely she could accompany you." Julie outlined his ears, barely visible beneath his hair, which was straight and perhaps a shade too long.

"Georgina has no interest in travel. To be more specific, she refuses to venture to North America. She regards the entire continent as the merest outpost of civilization, infested by insects and savages and all manner of other dreadful creatures."

"Perhaps you should show her your pottery," Julie said. "She would recognize at once that it wasn't created by 'savages.'"

He was silent for so long that Julie glanced up again and took the opportunity to paint in the complicated folds of his neckcloth.

"In point of fact, I *gave* Georgina a piece of Indian pottery," he said at last. "She didn't care for it at all; as I recall, she termed it 'crude.'"

"Well, we each have our personal tastes," Julie murmured.

She had captured all but one detail: the Captain's

nose. It presented an interesting contrast to the rest of his stark features; it was a trifle too short and incongruously tip-tilted. She brushed it in very carefully, backed away from the canvas, and immodestly owned herself satisfied. Though she had produced only a sketch in oils, she thought it astonishingly good in light of her inexperience, and she returned her full attention to Nick.

"We have our own tastes," she reiterated, "and I daresay you are prepared to alter your life substantially when you *do* wed Miss Vernon."

"I have sat long enough," the Captain said abruptly. "You may poke fun at society artists, but they do, at least, work speedily. A skill you must learn."

Julie did not believe she had uttered a single word about "society artists," and she wondered what she *had* said to irritate him so.

"You cannot insist that Uncle Edmund pose for hours on end."

Julie calculated that Nick had posed for under forty-five minutes, but he gave her no opportunity to protest. He leaped out of his chair, and it rocked alarmingly for a moment before he smashed it onto the bare floor.

"You will have to finish without me, and I'm sure I needn't remind you that time is of the essence. I want to leave for Bath as soon as possible though I daresay we shall have to wait until your clothes are finished. When is that to be?"

"Tu—Tuesday," Julie stammered. She was utterly taken aback by his sudden, vicious attack. "Miss Howard said the order would be completed by Tuesday."

"We shall depart on Wednesday then; I shall write Uncle Edmund and advise him of our arrival. Perhaps I'll return later in the week to ensure there have been no difficulties."

The Captain bowed and stalked out, and Julie's shock gave way to anger. She stared at the portrait, her fingers childishly itching to add a black goatee, a

thin mustache, and a commanding pair of horns.
However, before she could succumb to her whim, the
studio went dark, and there was a great crash of
thunder followed by a furious drum of rain. Julie
decided to content herself with the knowledge that
Nick, in his curricle, was growing thoroughly soaked,
and, with a final glare at the portrait, she laid her
palette and brush aside.

Chapter 6

When Julie returned to her studio the following morning, she fully intended to paint the canvas over and ask Aunt Emily to sit for her after all. However, she soon realized that her mercurial subject did not care a whit about his portrait and that any such gesture would serve to punish only herself. It was *she* who must paint the Earl of Arlington, *she* who would be humiliated if she dashed off the merest sketch and found herself unable to continue. Consequently, she labored over the canvas for the better part of six days, and when she reviewed her effort on Tuesday morning, she was reasonably pleased.

It was far from perfect, of course, she admitted objectively. She had captured Nick's essence prior to his abrupt departure, and she had an excellent memory, but she nevertheless feared she had missed many details. She thought, for example, that she had failed to streak enough blond into his hair, and she suspected that the shape of his earlobes was entirely wrong. And she had neglected to make any note of his buttons; the Captain looked as though he had magically been sewn into his waistcoat. This, at least, she could remedy, she decided: brown buttons would look very well against the saffron of the fabric. She closed her eyes, attempting to envision just how many buttons a waistcoat normally had, and was interrupted by a cough from the doorway.

"Good morning, Julie."

She recognized his voice at once and willed herself not to turn around. "Good morning," she said frigidly.

"Where do you wish me to leave this?"

Since Julie had no idea what "this" might be, she was forced to cast a cool, cursory glance over her shoulder. As she did so, Nick set an enormous trunk on the floor, and even from some feet away, Julie saw that it had been fashioned by a splendid craftsman, using the finest leather.

"If I am to believe Emily, you have ordered *hundreds* of new gowns." The Captain flashed his mischievous grin. "I shouldn't suppose they could possibly fit in your old case."

Nor was her old case suitable for such a respectable young woman of means, Julie thought dryly. She was not sure whether Nick's failure to mention this aspect of their scheme could best be attributed to tactfulness or deviousness, but one thing was certain: he could have purchased a new trunk for considerably less than the amount he had obviously expended. Julie chose to interpret his gratuitous generosity as a peace offering, and she managed a thin smile.

"Thank you," she said. "You may leave it in my bedchamber."

"Yes, I shall take it over shortly. In the meantime . . ." His gaze flew past her and alighted on the canvas. "In the meantime, I should like to see the portrait."

"Well, you cannot," Julie said firmly. She had never planned to show it to him; good, bad, or merely indifferent, she had not intended to display it to anyone. "You well know that it was simply an experiment."

She was again unsure whether he had failed to hear her or had elected to ignore her protest. In any event, he started across the room, and before Julie could gather her wits sufficiently to reach for the canvas, he had seized her elbow in a most commanding grip. He drew her away from the easel and stared at the portrait,

and Julie was too unnerved to look at him, too unnerved to attempt to gauge his reaction.

"You have told me you paint what you see," he
said at last. "Is this how you see me?"

"You cannot expect perfection," Julie snapped. "Had
you come back for another sitting, I should probably
have got the colors right, and your ears, and I should
definitely have put buttons on your waistcoat. I assure
you I shall do much better when I paint Lord Arlington."

"Better?" he echoed. "I'm afraid you're rather too
good as it is. I was in hopes no one else had noticed
my lines."

He dropped Julie's arm, and she peered cautiously
up at him. He was gingerly touching the tiny sun-
bursts at his temples, but he did not seem annoyed;
indeed, he gave her a rueful grin.

"Everyone has lines," she said. It had never occurred to her that men might be as vain as women,
and she stifled a smile of her own. "You yourself once
pointed out that you're fortunate not to be altogether
weather-beaten, like Uncle John or Wyatt."

"Perhaps so." He frowned and continued to study
the canvas. "But surely you've mistaken my eyes. I
always fancied them a very fetching shade of amber.
Not—not yellow."

"But they *are* yellow," Julie insisted. "In certain
lights, at any rate. And you shouldn't tease yourself
about that either because it's a very arresting color."

"I shall defer to you in that regard," the Captain
said gravely, "for you must be quite expert in the
matter of arresting eyes. Yours are red, you know."

"Red-brown," Julie corrected. He was gazing unwa-
veringly down at her, and she was helpless to tear her
eyes—whatever their hue—away. "Aunt Sophia often
pointed out that they are exactly the same color as my
freckles."

"I collect that disturbs you. Your freckles, that is." He
took her chin in his long brown fingers and tilted her

face toward the side windows, toward the sunlight. "Permit me to assure you that they are most becoming."

His touch was light—the brush of a butterfly—but Julie's heart was crashing against her ribs, and her knees had grown alarmingly weak. His eyes darkened to gold, then to the amber he himself preferred, and, with his other hand, he gently pushed a wayward curl away from her face.

"Ah, here you are, dear boy!"

Aunt Emily bounded into the room, nearly tripping over the trunk, and Nick hastily dropped his hands and stepped forward to meet her.

"I was just across the street, bidding Mr. Foster farewell. I presume you still intend us to depart tomorrow?"

"Yes." The Captain sounded a trifle hoarse, and he cleared his throat. "Yes, I drove over to bring Julie a trunk. We shall leave tomorrow if your clothes arrive on schedule."

"But they *have* arrived," Mrs. Fitch announced happily. "Miss Howard's man was just pulling up as I left Mr. Foster's, and I instructed him to deposit the boxes in the foyer. I do hope I can prevail on you to carry them upstairs."

Of course she could, Nick responded, and he trailed Aunt Emily out of the studio without a backward glance. Julie gazed in their wake, wondering what might have transpired had they not been interrupted. She further wondered whether she was regretful or relieved that she would never know.

The two-day journey to Bath was, in Julie's view, exceedingly uncomfortable.

To begin with, her physical circumstances were wretched in the extreme, for Nick decreed that Julie, as the smallest member of the party, must share the rear-facing seat of the landau with her art supplies. Consequently, she was confined to the merest speck of upholstery, one of her canvases precariously balanced against her arm, while the Captain and Mrs. Fitch fairly sprawled in the seat across. When Wyatt turned the first corner, the canvas tumbled into Julie's lap, a painful assault that was to recur approximately a thousand times during the ensuing hours.

In the second place, Nick seemed determined to ignore her presence altogether, electing, instead, to engage Aunt Emily in endless reminiscenses about people and places and events Julie had never seen or heard of. Mrs. Fitch occasionally attempted to include Julie in the conversation by pointing out a particularly pleasant bit of passing scenery. However, since Julie could see said scenery only as a backward blur, these attempts were not notably successful.

And, finally, Julie was simply, purely, and intensely frightened. It had been all very well to agree to paint Lord Arlington, to prattle of cleverly compromising Sir Oliver Crane. All very well in the safety of London, but she would soon be compelled to deliver on her promises, and the prospect rendered her almost physically unwell.

They stopped for the night in Reading, where Julie—so tired and sore she could scarcely walk—chose to dine alone in her room. She hoped that a night's sleep would restore her natural good spirits, but she tossed and turned on the lumpy hotel mattress, and morning found her, if possible, stiffer and more exhausted than she had been before retiring. She then began to hope that her first view of Bath, said to be one of the loveliest cities in England, would supply the needed restorative. But from her dreadful vantage point, Bath was a confusing blur of white buildings, of carriages and pedestrians and sedan chairs spilling in every direction; and by the time they reached Lord Arlington's palatial home in Queen Square, she was in very poor humor indeed.

The Captain bestirred himself sufficiently to assist her out of the landau, and Julie gazed down at her skirt with dismay. She had initially derived some enjoyment from her new clothes, but the two walking dresses she had thus far worn had been quite crushed by the long drive. She jerked her elbow out of Nick's grasp, tugged despairingly at the black-crepe flounce round her hem, and stalked behind him up the front steps.

"Good afternoon, Captain Stafford."

The butler—or so Julie assumed him to be—looked as though he could well profit from a regular regimen of Bath's fabled waters. To her admittedly jaundiced eye, he appeared to be at least eighty years of age, and his thin, pale face much resembled a skull.

"Good afternoon, Baxter," Nick rejoined. "I should like to present Mrs. Fitch and her niece, Miss Brandon. I believe you were expecting us."

"Yes," the butler confirmed dolefully, "his lordship received your letter."

"And?"

The Captain peered over Baxter's shoulder. The entry hall was extremely dark—almost sepulchral, Julie thought—but insofar as she could ascertain, it was empty.

"I regret to report that Lord Arlington is most unwell," Baxter whispered. "Most unwell indeed, and he is resting in his bedchamber. He plans to join you for dinner this evening, but one never knows."

Julie could not suppress a wonderful, awful notion that the Earl of Arlington might expire before she could lay brush to canvas.

"One never does," Nick agreed solemnly. "In any event, it is already half past five, and, as I recollect, dinner is served at seven. So, with the fervent hope that Uncle Edmund *will* be able to join us, I daresay we should freshen up. Perhaps you might summon a footboy to assist my man . . ."

In fact, Baxter summoned two footboys and a maid, and the latter escorted Julie and Aunt Emily up two flights of stairs and into enormous adjoining bedchambers on the second story. Julie's room was exquisitely decorated in shades of rose and pink, and she stopped on the threshold, breathlessly absorbing the magnificent Brussels carpet and the heavy drapes at the windows. She observed that the drapery fabric matched the cushions of the two Sheraton armchairs, matched the counterpane, curtains, and canopy of the oversized bed. She had just turned her attention to the mahogany wardrobe and chest of drawers, the rosewood washstand and dressing table, when one of the footboys panted in and deposited her new trunk on the bed. The footboy rushed out, and the maid scurried through the door connecting to Aunt Emily's room; Julie, in a daze, vaguely recalled that her name was Lucy.

"I do trust you'll forgive me, Miss Brandon, but I'm to attend you and your aunt as well, and Mr. Baxter suggested that I unpack Mrs. Fitch first. I reckoned you'd both be wishing a bath, so I've made the arrangements, and I daresay the tub will be here before I'm finished. If you wouldn't mind then, I'll be getting back to Mrs. Fitch."

Lucy bobbed a curtsy and fled back through the connecting door, and Julie shook her head. Mind? She had never had a personal servant in all her two and twenty years. She crossed the room very tentatively, as though even her new black chamois shoes might damage the rug, and opened the wardrobe. She could not quell an impression that she was dreaming again, and she carefully removed her black crepe bonnet and set it on one of the shelves.

There was a clock somewhere in the upper corridor, and by the time it struck a quarter to seven, Julie felt immeasurably better. She had had a long, hot bath, following which Lucy had returned to help her dress and to tidy up her hair. Julie studied her image in the mirror above the dressing table and immodestly owned herself pleased. She had elected to wear the simplest of her new evening gowns: a net frock of the palest green over a satin slip in a slightly darker hue. The bodice was cut exceedingly low, and Julie uttered a silent prayer of thanks that her freckles ended at her chin; her exposed chest and shoulders were gratifyingly smooth and creamy. She briefly fussed with her toque and straightened the lace flounce round the bottom of her skirt, then turned away from the glass.

Julie gazed around the room as she had for the past hour and more, but she continued to marvel at its luxurious appointments. The wardrobe doors were open, and she glimpsed her new dresses inside, all except those she had worn during the journey, which Lucy had borne away to be pressed. So easy, she reflected again. So easy to grow accustomed to beautiful clothes and elegant surroundings and servants scampering all about . . .

Fortunately, these dangerous thoughts were interrupted by the chime of the hall clock, and before the last peal had sounded, Aunt Emily appeared at the connecting door and suggested they repair to the dining room.

"You look *very* handsome, dear," she said approvingly as they descended the stairs. "Miss Howard wished to put you in blue, but I *insisted* on green, and I do believe I was right."

Mrs. Fitch looked extremely handsome as well, Julie observed. She had been too miserable during the interminable drive to take note of Aunt Emily's new daytime attire, but now—clad in a square-necked gown of black crepe, with glittering jewels at her ears and throat—the former Cyprian cut an imposing figure indeed.

"You look lovely, too, Aunt Emily," she murmured.

"And I daresay we appear quite as *respectable* as any two women in England."

Aunt Emily chuckled, affectionately squeezed Julie's hand, and tugged her across the foyer to the dining room.

For the second time that day, Julie stumbled to a halt at the threshold, staring at the marble hearth, the intricate murals, the gigantic crystal chandelier.

She estimated that the dining table could accommodate at least twenty, but only six places were set along the upper half. She took some dim, perverse satisfaction in the awareness that Lord Arlington's staff had made an error: though the place at the head of the table was set, there was no chair drawn up before it. Julie was wondering whether she should say something, discreetly mention the oversight to one of the footmen, when Nick leaped out of his chair.

"And here they are now," he said brightly. "Mrs. Fitch, Miss Brandon, pray permit me to introduce my dear cousins. Sir Oliver Crane."

Sir Oliver, who occupied the chair directly across from Nick, came to his feet, and Julie narrowly repressed a start of surprise. She had fancied from the Captain's description that his "dull" cousin was no doubt a rather homely fellow, but, in fact, Sir Oliver Crane was quite attractive. He was almost as tall as Nick and built along the same lean lines, and, by any classical definition, his symmetrical features were handsomer perhaps than the Captain's own.

"And Miss Hester Crane," Nick continued, indicating the woman seated next to Sir Oliver.

Miss Crane's chilly nod coincided with her brother's stiff bow, and Julie noted their astonishing similarity. Indeed, had she not known otherwise, she might have presumed them twins, for they had the same blond hair, the same gray eyes, the same fair complexions. They were undeniably attractive, but as Julie glanced back and forth between them, her artist's eye sensed a defect. They were *colorless*, she decided at last; they looked as if they'd been painted from a palette too diluted, a palette of bland, neutral shades.

"Mrs. Fitch," Miss Crane snapped. "Miss Brandon. I was just telling Nicholas how delighted we are that he was able to find time in his busy schedule to pay a visit to poor Uncle Edmund. Was I not, Oliver?"

"Yes, Hester."

Sir Oliver's chair was too close to the table, and,

with a grimace, he bent his knees. He smiled weakly
at Julie, at Aunt Emily, clearly wondering whether
he could now properly resume his seat.

"Sit down, Oliver," Miss Crane commanded.

"Yes, Hester."

He collapsed back into his chair with an audible
sigh of relief. Nick seated Julie and Aunt Emily on
either side of himself and reclaimed his own place.

"I am given to understand that you are an artist,
Miss Brandon." Miss Crane seemed to be snapping
again, but maybe that was merely her way. "Nicholas
did not have an opportunity to explain whether you
are a *professional* artist."

"A professional artist," Julie echoed. This was a
detail she and the Captain had not discussed, and she
kicked his ankle under the table.

"A professional artist." Nick was gasping with pain. "I
believe Miss Brandon, were she not too modest to do
so, would describe herself as an extremely accomplished amateur. Naturally she does not accept monetary recompense for her work, but she has nevertheless
done a number of portraits. Have you not, Miss
Brandon?"

"A number of portraits," Julie agreed. Two was a
number, was it not?

"Well, I hope she will not disappoint Uncle Edmund,"
Miss Crane said. "Assuming, that is, that the poor
man is able to sit for her at all. He has deteriorated to
a shocking degree; not that *you* were here to see it,
Nicholas . . ."

Miss Crane's voice trailed off, and she emitted a
great sniff, and Julie uncharitably thought she was
trying to spill a single, perfect tear from either eye. In
any case, her dramatic display was interrupted by a
bark from the entry hall.

"*Will* you be careful, Baxter? I am quite ill enough
without being subjected to this eternal jostling."

Nick and Sir Oliver simultaneously jumped up—the
latter carefully easing his chair away from the table—

and Julie peered as discreetly as she could over her shoulder. She at once perceived the reason for the empty spot at the head of the table: Baxter pushed a Bath chair through the door, propelled it behind Julie and Nick and Aunt Emily, and eased it carefully to a stop in the vacant space.

"That will be all!" Lord Arlington roared. "I dragged myself from bed, hoping to enjoy a meal with my family, but you have dislocated my intestines to such an extent that I doubt I can digest a single morsel. That will be all, Baxter," he repeated; "you have wreaked sufficient harm."

The butler bowed and slunk out the rear door of the dining room, and the Earl of Arlington glared at his guests.

"Sit down, for God's sake! I do not require the two of you to remind me I'm an invalid. I quite recognize my situation; you needn't be forever towering over my head."

Sir Oliver resumed his chair with such alacrity that he nearly tipped it over, and Nick sat as well, though somewhat more slowly.

"If I may be permitted an observation, Uncle Edmund," the Captain said politely, "I believe you look astonishingly well."

Julie studied Lord Arlington as unobtrusively as possible and found herself compelled to concur in Nick's opinion. She reckoned the Earl to be a man of perhaps five and sixty, but his skin was ruddy and remarkably unlined, he possessed a full head of white hair, and his pale blue eyes seemed exceedingly sharp. She thought he was tall, though it was difficult to tell, and his body appeared quite unravaged by his long illness: his shoulders and chest were broad, his arms thick and strong. She recollected that Nick had once described his uncle as "not unhandsome"; and though his nose was a bit too long, his mouth a bit too full for Julie's taste, she was forced to agree with this as well.

"Indeed," the Captain continued, "I must say that I am agreeably surprised."

"Agreeably surprised or merely surprised?" his lordship snorted. "I can only suppose that, having neglected me for well above six months, you traveled down in hopes of witnessing my demise."

"I believe Nicholas has neglected you for above *eight* months," Miss Crane corrected. "How fortunate that *Oliver* has been with you during your time of need. Have you not, Oliver?"

"Yes, Hester."

"What the devil is amiss?" Lord Arlington bellowed. Julie started, but the Earl was glowering at the footmen arrayed along the walls. "Am I to starve to death in my own dining room? Bring the soup!"

The footmen jumped as well, then seized bowls from a silver tray on the sideboard and galloped forward to distribute them about the table. The soup was a broth of some sort, and when Julie sampled hers, she calculated that it consisted of water, celery, and carrots. Whatever its composition, it was quite the most tasteless concoction she had ever eaten, and she surreptitiously dipped it, spoonful by spoonful, out of the bowl and trickled it, spoonful by spoonful, back in.

"I have engaged a new physician," Lord Arlington said, wolfing down his own wretched soup. "He has recommended a stringent diet as one means of restoring my health. One of the *last* means," he added heavily. "However, we were discussing you, Nicholas, and I daresay it little signifies whether your absence has extended to six months or eight."

"I am sorry if you interpret my absence as neglect, Uncle," the Captain said mildly. "I was abroad for some time, and I have been in town the past few weeks, attending to matters of business."

"The business of mischief, no doubt." The Earl snorted again. "It is entirely clear to me that you abandoned a promising military career so as to become a full-time wastrel." His lordship's assessment was so close to

Julie's own that she was hard put to stifle a smile.
"But we have discussed your rakeshame habits in the
past, and as you have obviously elected to defy me, I
shan't discuss your odious conduct any further."

"How very generous of you, Uncle Edmund," Miss
Crane said. "I hope you derive *some* comfort from the
knowledge that *Oliver's* conduct is beyond reproach."

"Umm," Lord Arlington growled.

He slurped down the last of his broth and signaled
the footmen. Julie prayed that her attendant would
remove her still-brimming bowl, and he did; but the
entrée he delivered in its stead represented scant
improvement. Julie examined the dry, overdone fish,
the limp green beans, the soggy boiled potato, and
wryly reflected that she might well succumb to starvation after all.

"In any event, my sojourn in London was not without its compensations," Nick said. "I encountered Mrs.
Fitch and Miss Brandon, whom, I fear, I have not yet
properly presented."

The Captain made the introductions, and Lord
Arlington's keen blue eyes darted back and forth between Julie and Aunt Emily. "Which one of you is the
artist?" he demanded, by way of greeting.

"I—I am," Julie coughed.

She had been valiantly attempting to swallow a
minuscule bite of fish, but it was now lodged in her
throat, and she feared she would choke to death long
before starvation could set in. She groped for her glass,
but it was empty (apparently the Earl's "stringent diet"
did not permit wine), and she gulped the fish on down.

"I am," she croaked.

"I must caution you, then, Miss Brandon, that I
shall be unable to sit for extended periods of time. My
new doctor has counseled me to avoid all forms of
stress, to eschew any potential annoyance. Indeed, I
daresay that if I were to consult him on the matter, he
would refuse to allow me to sit at all."

"That is precisely what I told Miss Brandon earlier,"

Miss Crane said. "I warned her that your delicate health might not permit you to sit at all, and I do wish you would reconsider, Uncle Edmund."

"Umm." His lordship stared at his empty plate and, unbelievably, signaled for a second portion. "Perhaps you are right, Hester."

"Oh, I do hope not." Aunt Emily spoke for the first time. "My niece was thrilled by the prospect of painting your portrait even before she met you, Lord Arlington, and now she *has* met you, I am sure her enthusiasm has immeasurably increased. You cannot be unaware that you are a *splendid* subject."

"Indeed?" His lordship visibly preened. "I fancy you are right, Mrs. Fitch, and I *shall* sit, even if my physical condition dictates a limited schedule." He gobbled down three great chunks of fish and a forkful of sodden beans.

"Excellent," Nick said. "You can begin tomorrow then—"

"No, tomorrow is out of the question," the Earl interjected. "I have planned a long drive in the country, for my new physician has also advised frequent exposure to fresh air."

"Tomorrow?" Miss Crane said sharply. "I had hoped to use the carriage myself, Uncle Edmund; I am to take lunch with Lady Dartmouth in Laura Place."

"Perhaps Oliver could drive you over in Uncle Edmund's curricle," the Captain suggested.

"Oliver does not drive," Miss Crane snapped. "We view curricles and phaetons as exceedingly dangerous vehicles, do we not, Oliver?"

"Yes, Hester."

"Allow me to offer my landau and coachman then." There was a wayward twitch at one corner of Nick's mouth, and Julie sternly bit back a grin of her own. "Wyatt will take you to Laura Place and anywhere else you might fancy."

"Very well."

Miss Crane was unmistakably displeased, and Julie

realized that the clever Captain had scored a modest victory. Lord Arlington had agreed to sit for the artist Nick had brought to Bath, and the black-sheep nephew must inevitably appear a trifle grayer.

"Splendid," the Earl said.

He tossed his napkin on the table, and Julie dismally surmised that there was to be no dessert. Upon the instruction of his lordship's marvelous new doctor, no doubt.

"Indeed," Lord Arlington continued, "it has worked out very well. I am certain, in light of their long journey, that Mrs. Fitch and Miss Brandon will want to rest tomorrow."

Evidently the Earl assumed that the entire world shared his precarious state of health, Julie thought dryly. His piercing blue eyes swept down the table, rested on Julie and Aunt Emily in turn, drifted back to his empty wineglass.

"Consequently," he went on, "we shall go our separate ways during the day, and tomorrow night we shall all attend the assembly at the Lower Rooms."

"The assembly?" Miss Crane's mouth fell open. "You have not been to a ball in years, Uncle Edmund."

"Nevertheless I *shall* be at the one tomorrow evening. Baxter?" he shouted. "I am ready to retire, Baxter."

The butler crept back into the room and wheeled the Bath chair away from the table. He had nearly maneuvered it through the doorway when Lord Arlington reached up and jerked commandingly at the sleeve of his frock coat. Baxter eased the chair to a careful halt.

"Since Hester mentioned transportation," his lordship said, "it does occur to me that we should consider our arrangements for the evening as well. I daresay we shall require my barouche and your landau as well, Nicholas, to accommodate the eight of us."

Julie's eyes flew round the table, but she again counted six places, and she surmised that the Earl's illness had rendered him a trifle confused.

"Eight?" the Captain repeated.

"Did I fail to mention that other travelers reached Bath today? Lord Carlon has leased a house just down the street, and I trust he and Georgina will be comfortable. *I* shall certainly make every effort to ensure their stay is a pleasant one."

Lord Arlington plucked Baxter's sleeve again, and the butler guided the Bath chair into the foyer and out of sight.

Chapter 7

When he returned from his drive in the country, Lord
Arlington sent word, via Lucy, that Julie and Aunt
Emily must be ready to depart for the assembly
promptly at nine. Julie, wishing to allow herself ample time for preparation, began her toilette at seven,
as a result of which she was entirely dressed and
coiffed by half past eight. And that, she thought glumly,
gave her a full half hour to dwell on her upcoming
introduction to Miss Georgina Vernon.

Julie wondered, as she had repeatedly throughout
the day, whether Nick had known of Lord Carlon's
intention to bring his daughter to Bath. She thought
not, for the Captain had gone quite pale following his
uncle's announcement; and though Julie had developed considerable respect for his Thespian talents, she
could not suppose that even the devious Captain was
capable of regulating his blood supply. Nor did Nick's
knowledge or lack of it much signify, she realized; the
painful fact was that she could not avoid a meeting
with Miss Vernon. Like it or not (and she did not like
it a whit), she would have to confront Nick's intended
this evening and probably on many occasions thereafter.

Julie sighed and critically examined her reflection
in the mirror above the dressing table. She had selected a gown of white lace over satin, surmounted by
a low-cut corsage of lime-green satin and trimmed
with matching puffs around the skirt. Her white satin

toque, ornamented by a diadem of roses, left visible only the auburn curls about her face; and these—she was pleased to note—Lucy had arranged to perfection. In short, Julie could find no specific flaw, but she vaguely sensed something amiss. She sighed again and turned away from the mirror.

"Are you ready, dear?" Aunt Emily trilled.

She peered round the connecting door, which Lucy had left ajar, then opened it and stepped into the room. Fond as she was of Mrs. Fitch, Julie could not quell a stab of irritation, for Aunt Emily's appearance was flawless indeed. She was clad in a conservatively cut gown of black and white crepe, trimmed very simply with black velvet Vandykes, but she managed to project an aura of elegance far beyond Julie's wildest aspirations.

"Yes, I am ready." She sounded a trifle sharp, and Aunt Emily's keen blue eyes swept over her.

"Not quite, dear," she said at last. "If you will but wait a moment . . ."

Mrs. Fitch hurried back to her own bedchamber, and when she returned, she rotated Julie toward the mirror again. Before Julie could guess what she was at, Aunt Emily had fastened a great emerald necklace about her throat and long matching earrings in either lobe.

"Much better," she pronounced, tugging on her black chamois gloves.

It was, indeed, "much better," the precise touch that had previousy been lacking, but Julie reluctantly shook her head. "Thank you, Aunt Emily, but I couldn't possibly borrow your jewelry—"

"Whyever not?" Mrs. Fitch interjected crisply. "*I* certainly have no need of it." Julie—observing her diamond necklace and earrings, her jet brooch and armlet—could not but concur. "And if you are to be my niece, I should like you to look as well as you can." The hall clock struck the hour, and Aunt Emily briefly fussed with her own toque. "It's too late to discuss it now, at any rate; come along, dear."

She sailed into the corridor, and Julie trailed after her, reaching up from time to time to make sure the emeralds had not fallen from her ears.

Julie and Mrs. Fitch were the last to reach the foyer, and when they did, they found a bitter argument in progress. Julie soon collected that the quarrel concerned the distribution of the party between the two available carriages. Evidently there was agreement on but a single point: Lord Arlington was to travel in Nick's landau because that vehicle offered easier accommodation of his Bath chair.

"I see no problem!" the Earl roared. Julie suspected that he had voiced, nay, *shouted,* this opinion several times prior to their appearance on the scene. "Nicholas will accompany me in his carriage, and we shall naturally take Mrs. Fitch and Miss Brandon as well." This with a courtly nod to acknowledge the new arrivals.

"I have explained," the Captain snapped, "that I told Georgina *I* should escort her and Lord Carlon to the ball."

It was clear that Nick had visited Miss Vernon earlier in the day. Clear and certainly a matter of no surprise, but Julie bit her lip and gazed down at her white satin slippers.

"Consequently," the Captain continued, "I shall once more suggest that *Oliver* go in the landau with you and Mrs. Fitch and Miss Brandon. Hester and I shall drive by for Georgina and Viscount Carlon."

"Absolutely not!" It was Miss Crane's turn to snap. "Uncle Edmund's solution is obviously the best." She gave his lordship one of her chilly smiles. "However, if you are determined to defy his wishes, Nicholas—which you invariably *are*--you and Oliver may fetch Lord Carlon and Georgina, and *I* shall go in the landau."

Miss Crane's proposal prompted a good deal of glaring and foot shuffling, but the consensus seemed to be that she had devised a reasonable compromise. They

all proceeded into the drive, where the two carriages—
unaware of the ferocious controversy they'd sparked—
were patiently waiting. Wyatt began handing his female passengers into the landau, and before he was
finishèd, the barouche—with Nick and Sir Oliver
inside—clattered toward the street.

Julie had idly wondered whether Lord Arlington
was entirely immobilized by his illness, and she now
noted that he was not. Wyatt assisted the Earl out of
his chair, and the latter, with astonishing agility,
clambered into the carriage and took the place next to
Aunt Emily. Wyatt struggled at considerable length
with the chair and eventually managed to fasten it to
the roof. None too securely, Julie feared, and she tried
to ignore the constant *thump-thump, rattle-rattle* as
Wyatt clucked the horses to a start and the landau got
under way. Lord Arlington, for his part, appeared
quite oblivious to the alarming creaks and thuds just
above their heads; he politely pointed out the sights of
Bath as they passed them.

"Though I daresay you can see little in the dark,"
he said at last. Julie, in fact, could see nothing.
"Perhaps you'll permit me to guide you about in the
light one day, Mrs. Fitch. And you, too, Miss Brandon,"
he added quickly.

When they reached the assembly rooms, Wyatt was
compelled to wrest the Earl's chair *off* the roof of the
carriage, and a full five minutes elapsed before they
actually entered the building. Julie peered nervously
about, but it appeared, their delays notwithstanding,
that they had preceded the remainder of the party. If
she could locate the ladies' withdrawing room, she
could at least *postpone* her ordeal, Julie thought
optimistically. She studied the various doorways issuing from the main hall and eventually glimpsed two
young women hurrying toward an exit in the rear.
She turned around, preparing to excuse herself, but
the entrance was now in her line of vision, and she
saw that she was too late.

Miss Vernon had stationed herself impartially between her two suitors, one gloved hand on the Captain's arm, the other on Sir Oliver's. As they approached, however, it became evident that she and Nick were engaged in animated conversation while Sir Oliver was engaged in a penetrating examination of his shoes. Despite this intense scrutiny, the baronet managed to set one foot nearly atop the other and stumbled to a sudden halt. His companions stopped as well, and Miss Vernon, with a scowl, sharply jerked his arm. Sir Oliver's faux pas allowed the fourth member of the advancing group, who had been panting along well behind the rest, to draw alongside, and they closed the distance in a neat, formidable row.

"Lord Arlington!" "Lord Carlon!" "Hester!" "Georgina!" The confused babble of greetings was followed by a brief silence, and Nick hastened to fill the breach.

"And may I present our guests from London? Mrs. Fitch, Miss Brandon; Viscount Carlon and his daughter, Miss Vernon."

Julie was sure she muttered an appropriate response, but she could not have said what it was, for she was staring, with perverse fascination, at Miss Vernon. Her complexion was exceedingly pale, unhealthily pale until one noticed the vivid slashes of rose on either cheekbone. In startling, stunning contrast, her hair and eyes, her brows and lashes were black, and the latter—her lashes—were so thick as to shadow the fair skin beneath her eyes. Miss Vernon did initially seem to suffer one defect: she was excessively tall, only a few inches shorter than the Captain himself. But, on second look, she carried her height magnificently, and her clinging muslin gown had obviously been designed to emphasize her willowy grace.

"Have I not encountered you before, Mrs. Fitch?" Lord Carlon's question jolted Julie from her reverie, and as she transferred her attention to him, he raised a quizzing glass to one eye. "You look extremely familiar."

"I daresay we *could* have met," Aunt Emily said dubiously. "I fancy not though, for I don't recollect it, and you would not be an easy man to forget, Lord Carlon."

"No, *that* is true."

The Viscount somehow swaggered and lowered his glass at the same time, and Julie choked back a laugh. She recalled that Nick had once mentioned the dissimilarity between Lord Carlon and his youngest daughter, and she now judged this a monumental understatement. The Viscount resembled nothing so much as a toad: he was fully a head shorter than Miss Vernon and nearly as broad as he was tall. His complexion might once have been fair, but decades of high living had burst a hundred tiny veins in his face, leaving him with a red bulb of a nose and a permanent flush in his cheeks. His small, watery eyes were a pale shade of blue, and the fringe of hair surrounding his bald crown was a dark, dirty blond. If the elder Vernon daughters did, in fact, favor their father, Julie could only pity their wretched husbands.

"Well, Arlington." Lord Carlon exposed his yellow teeth in an expression Julie assumed to be a smile. "I must say that you look—look . . ." Evidently the Viscount was unsure how Lord Arlington *wanted* to look, and his voice trailed off.

"I am feeling astonishingly well," the Earl supplied. "I have engaged a new physician, and I do believe his strict program has produced some improvement. Some *slight* improvement," he added hastily.

"I was just at the point of saying that." Lord Carlon nodded. "I was just at the point of saying that you look astonishingly well and seem to have experienced a slight improvement."

As Julie stifled another laugh, the orchestra struck up a waltz, and Miss Vernon glanced archly from Nick to Sir Oliver.

"Now which of you," she said coyly, "shall I permit to stand up with me for the first set?"

It might have been a harmless—albeit heavy-handed—bit of coquetry, but Julie detected a dangerous spark in Miss Vernon's dark eyes. She truly hoped to foment trouble between the cousins, Julie realized. She suspected that Miss Vernon would thoroughly have enjoyed life in a less civilized age, would have adored the sight of two churlish Saxon swains hacking one another half to death for the pleasure of her company.

"I daresay Oliver will agree that in all fairness it should be I," the Captain said smoothly. "Since I have been deprived of your companionship for so many months."

"You would not be deprived of my companionship did you not feel it necessary to be forever rushing off to the edges of the world," Miss Vernon said coolly. "I should punish you for your neglect, should I not, Nick?"

The Captain's eyes narrowed so fractionally that Julie thought she might have imagined it. But apparently she had not, for Miss Vernon flashed a gay smile, as if to say that she had only been jesting after all.

"But I shall not punish you. You shall have the first dance, and perhaps, if Oliver behaves himself, I shall give him the next."

"Excellent," Nick said. "In the interim, Oliver can stand up with Miss Brandon."

Julie started, on principle, to decline, but the Captain gave her a hard, quelling stare, and she recalled the nature of her distasteful assignment. "I should be delighted to dance with Sir Oliver," she cooed.

Nick and Miss Vernon led the way to the floor, and Julie reluctantly allowed the baronet to take her in his arms. To her relief and surprise, he was a highly accomplished dancer—far more accomplished than Julie herself—and she was initially compelled to devote her full concentration to the steps of the waltz. When, at last, she was able to follow his lead without effort, she realized that Sir Oliver had yet to utter a single word; obviously she must be the one to initiate a conversation.

"I collect, Sir Oliver," she said brightly, "that you and Miss Crane live in Norfolk as well."

"Yes," he mumbled.

"Near to your uncle?"

"Yes."

"Do you have one estate there or several?"

"Yes," he confirmed.

It was clear that she must pose some question which could not be answered, however incompletely, by a yes or no. "And how long have you been in Bath?" she ventured.

"Upwards of three months."

"Are you enjoying yourself here?"

"I fancy so."

Julie, in desperation, tried another tack. "I myself have not been in Bath before. Nor, for that matter, in Norfolk. I was brought up in Northamptonshire, and prior to this journey I had traveled only to London."

"Umm," Sir Oliver said.

"And that only twice," Julie added.

"Umm."

It was apparent that if she related the entire history of her life, including her mythical career as a Cyprian, she would elicit no more than an "umm."

"What of your education?" she said doggedly, attempting yet another approach. "Did you attend Oxford? Or Cambridge?"

"Yes."

Julie gave up altogether and shifted her attention to the other couples on the floor. At one point she glimpsed Nick and Miss Vernon, towering regally over the rest, whirling and chattering and laughing. Sir Oliver turned her away, and his jaw suddenly clenched, and Julie surmised that he, too, had observed the tall, striking pair now on the opposite side of the room. She wondered which of them—she or the baronet—had been rendered the more miserable.

Julie stood up for the following sets with a variety
of partners, none of them sufficiently memorable that
she could later recollect his name. The final set proved
rather harrowing: she danced a boulanger with a
middle-aged man who looked quite as ill as Lord Arlington claimed to feel. By the end of the rousing set,
her partner betrayed every symptom of an imminent
apoplectic attack, and as he staggered off the floor,
Julie decided to sit out for a time herself. She was
easing her way toward the ladies' withdrawing room
when the orchestra began another waltz, and her elbow was caught in a commanding grip.

"May I?" Nick swept her into motion before she
could respond. "I should have asked earlier, but I
could not penetrate the throng of your admirers. I do
pray I am not risking conflict with someone you've
previously promised. No, I daresay I can't be, for you've
surely danced already with every man here."

"And *I* daresay it is no concern of yours whom I
dance with," Julie snapped.

"It is *every* concern of mine," the Captain corrected.
"In the event you have forgotten, I engaged you to
perform a specific task. I confess that I have not yet
figured the details, but I fail to perceive how we can
maneuver Oliver into a compromising situation if you
continue to flirt with every male in Bath but him."

"I was not flirting!" Julie protested.

"No? It certainly appeared so to me." Nick was
silent for a few bars. "You do look very handsome this
evening," he added at last.

His tone was careless, almost grudging, and it rekindled Julie's wrath. "Do I indeed?" she said frigidly. "I
did not suppose you'd noticed my appearance. Not
tonight or for several days past."

"Are you accusing me of neglect as well? If so,
permit me to remind you that you and I are posing as
the most casual of acquaintances. I have deliberately
kept you at a distance so as to avoid any suspicion of
the relationship between us."

"I was not aware that there *was* any relationship between us."

Julie felt his muscles tighten, and when she gazed up at him, she observed that his eyes had darkened to amber. She sensed that he was remembering London, remembering the interrupted moment in the studio, and her cheeks grew warm. But before she could say anything more, his eyes had lightened again, had turned to shards of yellow ice.

"No, you are quite correct," he agreed politely. "There is no relationship between us, and I apologize if I have needlessly overset you. Let us return, then, to the matter of Oliver. Whatever form our final assault may take, it cannot be carried out until you have weakened his defenses." Evidently the Captain had not entirely overcome his military background. "Which means that you must befriend him. A feat—forgive my repetition—which you cannot accomplish if you scamper about the assembly rooms of Bath with every partner who happens along and leave poor Oliver a wilting wallflower."

Julie guiltily scanned the perimeters of the room. She did not see Sir Oliver, wilting or otherwise, but she admitted that his immediate presence or absence did not much signify. On this head, if on no other, Nick was right.

"I *did* try to befriend Sir Oliver," she said defensively, "but I soon judged it impossible. You must know he is hard put to string three words together."

"I do know that; indeed, it is one reason I took a lease on your charms. Surely you have encountered diffident men before." Julie bit her lip. "If not, you might wish to solicit Emily's advice. Look at her."

Nick tossed his brown-gold head, and Julie glimpsed Mrs. Fitch chattering to Lord Arlington. The latter was smiling, nodding, offering the occasional riposte . . .

"Uncle Edmund has not spoken a civil word to anyone in twenty years," the Captain continued; "yet, in the space of four and twenty hours, Emily has altogether captivated him. I daresay there is a lesson there, and I urge you to seek the benefit of her wisdom."

"Perhaps I shall," Julie lied.

Mercifully the music ended before Nick could pursue their unsettling conversation. He escorted Julie off the floor, exchanged pleasantries with the Earl and Mrs. Fitch, bowed, and wandered away.

"Lord Arlington and I were just discussing the shocking state of modern mores," Aunt Emily chirped.

Julie watched the Captain's retreating figure, belatedly noting that he looked exceedingly well in evening attire. His wasp-waisted coat emphasized his leanness, and his satin knee breeches and silk stockings displayed his long shapely legs to maximum advantage. He melted into the crowd, and Julie looked back at Aunt Emily.

"We agreed that in *our* youth the waltz would have been regarded as a threat to the very fabric of society. But times do change, do they not, milord?"

"They do indeed." His lordship nodded. "I only regret that I have been too unwell to take advantage of the transition. I fancy it would prove most amusing to fondle a woman in full, public view."

To Julie's astonishment, Mrs. Fitch colored a bit. "We were also discussing Lord Arlington's portrait," she said quickly, "and he has consented to begin his sittings tomorrow."

"So let us devise a schedule, Miss Brandon," the Earl suggested. "I normally arise at half past nine and visit the Pump Room in the latter part of the morning. I daresay I can return to the house and be ready to sit by one—"

"Absolutely not," Julie interjected firmly. She distantly counted it odd that she would sacrifice her character, but not her talent, to Nick's shameless scheme. "I must have use of the morning light, so if you are to keep your appointments at the Pump Room, we can begin no later than nine."

"Nine!" His lordship's yelp was but a tame echo of

his customary bellow, but he was clearly annoyed. "I shudder to contemplate what my new physician would say to such a plan."

"Oh, come now," Aunt Emily chided prettily. "If *I* can be ready by nine, you can be ready as well."

"You, Mrs. Fitch?"

"Surely you did not imagine that I would allow dear Juliet to be alone with you? I could not permit her to spend long unsupervised hours in the company of such an attractive man."

"Of course not." Lord Arlington tugged at his immaculately starched shirt-points, fussed with his perfectly tied neckcloth. "Nine it is then, so I fancy my doctor would insist I retire at once. Do you wish to stay on, Mrs. Fitch, or will you accompany me home?"

"I shall accompany you," Aunt Emily said. "We shall send Wyatt back for Julie and Miss Crane."

"Not for me," Julie demurred. "If we are to get an early start in the morning, I should like to retire as well."

Aunt Emily cast her a sharp sidewise glance, for it was not yet eleven, but she evidently elected to offer no comment. She directed Julie to locate the landau while she herself pushed the Earl out, and Julie, without a backward look, hurried to the street.

Bath was very much a pedestrian community, so there were relatively few vehicles drawn up outside the Lower Rooms. Julie glimpsed Nick's carriage perhaps forty yards from the entry and raised her hand. She waited a full minute, she reckoned, but the landau showed no sign of movement, and she strode rather irritably down the footpath. When she reached the carriage, she perceived the reason for Wyatt's failure to heed her signal: he was leaning against one of the rear wheels, conversing with Miss Crane, who was awkwardly perched on the step.

"Miss Brandon!" the latter snapped. "Apparently you have found the rooms quite as insufferably warm as I did. I thought I should perish if I did not seek a breath of air."

"The rooms are a trifle warm," Julie said politely. "However, as it happens, Lord Arlington and Aunt Emily and I have decided to depart. I am sure Wyatt will come back for you later in the evening—"

"Come back for me! I have no intention of returning to that stuffy hole. Indeed, I may well complain to the local authorities that *something* must be done about the ventilation."

Wyatt assisted them both into the landau, and Julie wryly wondered if he would demand some sort of hardship allowance from his master. Surely entertainment of the waspish Miss Crane qualified as service well beyond the realm of Wyatt's normal duties.

They clattered to the entrance, where Wyatt again struggled with his lordship's chair, but at length the Earl and Aunt Emily were safely seated as well, and they drove back to Queen Square in silence. It was possible that they were all tired, Julie conceded, but more likely that Miss Crane's ill-concealed mopes had infected the rest of them. At any rate, when the carriage stopped, Julie did not linger in the drive for the inevitable battle with the chair; she muttered her good-nights and fled to her bedchamber.

Despite her statement to Aunt Emily, Julie was in no rush to retire, and she elected not to ring for Lucy. She undressed herself—hanging her exquisite gown in the wardrobe, placing her toque carefully on the shelf, depositing Mrs. Fitch's jewelry on the dressing table. She was thus reduced to her old, ragged underthings, which she swiftly exchanged for an equally old, equally tattered nightdress and dressing gown. Perhaps it was the shocking contrast between her new garments and her ancient lingerie that set her to worrying about the jewelry: she could not repress the absurd notion that a thief might invade her room in the dead of night and bear Aunt Emily's emeralds away. She decided she would sleep much better if she returned them at once, and she plucked them off the dressing table and knocked timidly at the connecting door.

"Come in, dear," Aunt Emily called.

Mrs. Fitch—clad in a provocative nightdress and peignoir of ecru lace—was reclining on a settee near the windows, but when Julie entered, she sat up and clapped a book facedown on the cushion beside her.

"I am sorry to have disturbed you," Julie said, "but I wished to return your jewelry and thank you once more for permitting me to wear it."

"You're quite welcome, dear, and you need not have returned it, for I'm sure you'll have need of it again. As I told you, I instructed Miss Howard to do you predominantly in green, and I haven't a single thing in that color. I shall keep the jewelry if you wish, but I shall insist you borrow it when the occasion arises."

"We shall see," Julie mumbled noncommittally. She laid the necklace and earrings on Aunt Emily's dressing table, a magnificent lacquered piece with bamboo legs. "I shan't trouble you any further; I shall let you get back to your book."

"In point of fact, I was not *reading* my book," Mrs. Fitch sighed. "I was brooding, and I fancy I was not the only one." She gave Julie another sharp glance. "I collect that you did not entirely enjoy yourself at the ball."

"Not entirely, no," Julie agreed dryly.

"Perhaps we share similar thoughts," Aunt Emily said. "I had not met Miss Vernon prior to this evening, and I assure you that I was prepared to give her *every* benefit of doubt. Indeed, I hoped—*fervently* hoped—she would prove altogether different from the rest of her dreadful family. She *looks* different; I shall grant her that. But insofar as character is concerned, I must unfortunately say that I judged her considerably *worse* than I had anticipated. *If* I had anticipated, which—in view of my objectivity—I naturally had not."

Julie did not want to discuss Miss Georgina Vernon

with Aunt Emily or anyone else. However, Mrs. Fitch's bright blue eyes were probing hers, and she realized that some sort of response was required.

"I was somewhat dismayed myself," she said carefully. "I cannot imagine that Nick will be happy with her—"

"Happy?" Aunt Emily shook her head. "No, I daresay Nick has never imagined that marriage would render him '*happy*.' His own parents were quite miserable, you know."

Julie had *not* known, of course, but Aunt Emily no longer seemed to demand an answer; her piercing eyes had drifted to the dark windows.

"I was not personally acquainted with Mrs. Stafford, but I am given to understand that she was an exceedingly—exceedingly *cold* person. For all practical purposes, she and Henry lived apart the last ten years of their marriage—the years during which I knew him. Nick, to his credit, did not align himself with either party, but I do believe he *sympathized* with Henry. I cannot explain his kindness to me in any other way."

The conversation was horribly uncomfortable, but curiosity perversely seized Julie's tongue. "And then he died?" she ventured. "Admiral Stafford, that is?"

"Actually *she* died first, in a freakish carriage accident. Henry expired in his sleep three months later." Aunt Emily drew her eyes away from the window, looked at Julie again. "I have often wondered what would have transpired if he had survived a year of proper mourning. Would he have wed me? Maybe it's best that I shall never know."

Julie felt the swelling of a lump in her throat, and she gazed down at her bare feet; her house slippers had long since fallen totally apart.

"But I digress again, don't I?" Mrs. Fitch said briskly. "A sure symptom of old age. We were discussing Nick and Miss Vernon, and—much as I regret to say it—perhaps we shall simply have to submit to fate. In the interim, if you are to paint Lord Arlington bright and early in the morning, I fancy we should *both* retire. Good night, dear."

"Good night, Aunt Emily."

Julie trudged back through the connecting door and found herself suddenly, blessedly exhausted after all. She burrowed into the canopied bed and fell at once to sleep.

Chapter 8

The next morning, while Julie nibbled at a wretched breakfast of boiled eggs, charred bacon, and dry toast, she sent Lucy to learn where in Lord Arlington's vast house her equipment had been stored. The efficient little maid speedily returned with the news that Miss Brandon's supplies had been placed in a small parlor just off the morning room. She started to issue directions, but Julie, having consumed as much of his lordship's horrid health food as she could, shook her head and followed Lucy to the designated chamber.

To Julie's relief, the room was generously bathed in morning light, and she moved her easel to one bright corner, set a canvas upon it, and began mixing a palette of colors. She thought she had very nearly approximated the gray-white of the Earl's hair, the pale blue of his eyes, and the ruddy tone of his complexion when the morning room clock struck nine, and Aunt Emily sailed into the parlor. To Julie's further relief, Baxter wheeled Lord Arlington himself through the door just a few seconds later, and Mrs. Fitch at once took charge of the proceedings.

"I daresay you will want his lordship immediately next to the window," she suggested, "so that his *wonderful* hair will be quite illuminated."

She could indeed learn a great deal from Aunt Emily, Julie thought wryly. The spot she had proposed was the only sensible one in the entire room, but the Earl, carefully patting his hair, nodded in sage agreement.

"An excellent notion, Mrs. Fitch."

Baxter had been dismissed, so Aunt Emily pushed Lord Arlington's chair to the chosen location, then stood away for a moment of study.

"I hope you will not take it amiss if I recommend a slightly sidewise view," she said at last. "I personally *adore* a strong nose, milord, but there are those who do not, and I believe if we turned your face just a *little* to the right, it would be minimized. Such a pose would also serve to disguise that very *small* patch on the left where your hair has receded just the *tiniest* bit."

The Earl wholeheartedly concurred with this suggestion as well, and Aunt Emily painstakingly tilted his head at the proper angle, stood back again to review her effort, nodded briskly, and retreated to a chair across the parlor. Julie was compelled to own that Mrs. Fitch had, in fact, posed his lordship in the most flattering manner, and she roughly brushed his features on the canvas and started to correct her colors.

Though Julie had overcome her abject terror of painting Lord Arlington, she had remained rather daunted by the prospect of conversing with him through many hours of sittings. As it happened, however, Aunt Emily shortly allayed her apprehensions: Julie was still struggling with the precise hue of the Earl's eyes when Mrs. Fitch launched into a tale of her youth. She soon had his lordship laughing uproariously, and when she had finished her story, he embarked on one of his own. Julie listened to their interchange at first desultorily, then with genuine interest, but she could not decide whether life had changed a great deal in the past quarter century or had changed not at all. At any rate, their repartee was undeniably amusing, and Julie was astonished when the morning room clock struck twice and Lord Arlington announced that it was half past ten.

"Half past *ten*?" she echoed disbelievingly.

"I trust I made it clear, Miss Brandon, that I cannot cancel any of my visits to the Pump Room. My new doctor insists on regular consumption of the waters and daily baths."

"I am sure Julie has made an excellent beginning," Aunt Emily said. "And that she quite understands that you must follow your physician's instructions." She stood and smoothed the skirt of her blue jaconet walking dress, managing to display her girlish figure to maximum advantage. "If it would not prove inconvenient, milord, perhaps I might escort you to the Pump Room."

"Inconvenient? To the contrary, I should be delighted, Mrs. Fitch. Indeed, if I may venture a suggestion of my own, you might find it beneficial to take a dose of the waters yourself."

They chattered their farewells, Aunt Emily propelled the Bath chair out the door, and Julie returned her attention to the canvas. She *had* made an excellent start, and, her memory fresh, she decided to continue as long as she could. She believed she had almost captured the Earl's "wonderful" hair before the parlor grew so shadowed that she was forced to stop. The morning room clock had just chimed two, and Julie suddenly discovered that she was ravenous. She hurried to the dining room and was initially relieved to find a buffet laid on the sideboard. However, her joy soon evaporated, for the repast proved to consist of cold, overdone meat, stale bread, and an assortment of raw vegetables. She choked down as much of this wretched fare as she could, thinking—after she had finished—to take a brief walk about the neighborhood. But upon consideration, she realized she might well encounter the Captain and Miss Vernon, and instead she borrowed two books from his lordship's splendid library and retreated to her bedchamber.

If Julie had entertained any notion of permanently avoiding Miss Vernon, her hope was rudely and repeatedly dashed during the following hours and days.

Lord Arlington's party was invited to dine that evening with the Countess of Bristowe, another of his lordship's Norfolk neighbors, and Viscount Carlon and his daughter were present as well. Lord Arlington dominated the conversation with a description of the marvelous regimen his new doctor had prescribed. In view of the fact that the Earl wolfed down every one of Lady Bristowe's rich courses—from the thick mulligatawny to the flaky lemon tart—Julie felt his dedication a trifle suspect, but no one else seemed to notice.

As his lordship rattled on, Julie's eyes wandered to Miss Vernon's generous bosom, which was barely covered by the daring corsage of her gown. Despite this provocative display, Miss Vernon apparently feared that Nick and/or Sir Oliver—seated on either side—might miss the magnificence of the exposed bounty. At any rate, she managed to lean well over the table every thirty seconds or so, and Julie soon began to wager with herself as to whether Miss Vernon would eventually plunge her rose satin bodice into her plate. Unfortunately she did not.

As they left Lady Bristowe's, Lord Arlington announced that they were all to attend church the next morning, and at half past ten the group obediently set out in the landau and the barouche, traveling in tandem. After the service had concluded, the Earl insisted that Viscount Carlon and Georgina return to Queen Square for a midday dinner, following which Miss Vernon was persuaded (without great difficulty) to conduct an impromptu piano recital. Though Julie had no great ear for music, she gleefully calculated that Miss Vernon missed approximately three notes in ten, but, again, she was evidently the only one to notice. When the Vernons at last prepared to depart, Lord Arlington cheerfully reminded them of the weekly Monday-night assembly at the *Upper* Rooms.

Much as Julie loathed her constant exposure to Miss Vernon, she was forced to own that the hectic weekend had had one advantage. She had been unable to spend a single private moment with Sir Oliver, and she did not think even Nick could criticize her continuing failure to "befriend" his cousin. She recognized, however, that she must pay the baronet keen attention during the upcoming ball, and after Lord Arlington's morning sitting, after he and Aunt Emily had left for the Pump Room, Julie abandoned his lordship's portrait and concentrated on the evening's task.

In light of Sir Oliver's painful shyness, Julie judged it best to arm herself with a prepared list of conversational topics. She would begin, she decided, by extracting the specifics of his educational background; this would naturally lead to a discussion of the geographical charms of Oxford or Cambridge. After they had talked about every stream, every edifice, every *tree*, Julie would inquire as to the baronet's field of study. If he had read ancient Greek literature, the ensuing conversation might prove a bit strained, but, with luck, he would have chosen something considerably less esoteric.

Julie was beginning to tire of green, so she selected an ensemble in the Captain's colors: a slip of almond satin surmounted by a draped robe of dark brown lace. She did not demur when Aunt Emily offered the use of her pearl necklace and matching teardrop earrings, and she was feeling quite confident when she descended the stairs to the foyer. She had failed to allow for but one minor complication: the absence of her intended victim.

"Oliver is not going?" Lord Arlington roared as Julie and Aunt Emily reached the entry hall. "Why not?"

"You know he has never been one to fancy shallow amusements, Uncle Edmund."

Miss Crane punctuated this explanation with a pointed glance at Nick, but his lordship's glare apparently reminded her that the Earl himself had displayed a recent fondness for "shallow amusements." She hastily took another tack.

"And I do fear that Oliver may be a trifle indisposed. He did not say so, of course, for he has never been one to complain of illness."

Lord Arlington's glare turned distinctly stony, and Julie reflected that Miss Crane was in exceedingly poor form; her waspish tongue seemed to be racing well ahead of her devious mind.

"I daresay that Oliver has inherited your delicate constitution, Uncle Edmund," she sighed. "He is so like you in so many *other* ways."

Evidently it did not occur to the Earl that, as Sir Oliver was not blood-related, there was little likelihood he had inherited *any* of his lordship's traits. He nodded—albeit a bit stiffly—and they adjourned to the drive and clambered into the carriages.

Though the new assembly hall was physically quite different from the Lower Rooms, the crowd looked to be virtually identical, and Julie braced herself for a long, dull evening. She stood up for the first two sets with partners she vaguely recalled from the Friday-night ball and danced the third with a gentleman who introduced himself as Sir Alfred Clay.

Sir Alfred was a reasonably attractive man of perhaps five and thirty, and he immediately let it be known that he was the scion of a very old, very prominent Derbyshire family. Julie disclosed, in turn, that she was residing with Lord Arlington, and by the time the music ended, they were chatting most amiably. Julie recollected Nick's suggestion that she might find a permanent protector in Bath, mentally translated "protector" to "husband," and judged Sir Alfred a definite, if remote, possibility. It was not until he led her off the floor that she observed the numerous ill-darned holes in his stockings and surmised that Sir Alfred had come to England's premier resort with the hope of winning a wealthy bride, which certainly eliminated her from the picture.

"Perhaps you might present me to Lord Arlington," he cooed, his eyes fairly sparkling with interest.

"I'm afraid that isn't possible," Julie said regretfully. "I am only his housekeeper, you see, and while he does allow me out in the evenings, he has made it very clear that we are not to mingle socially. But I'm sure he would not object if you wished to call."

Sir Alfred bowed hurriedly away, and Julie permitted herself an evil chuckle. She heard a low echo behind her and whirled around.

"Excellently done." The Captain bobbed his brown-gold head.

"Are you on the listen for all my private conversations?" Julie said coldly.

"Not all or any; I merely chanced to overhear. And, I repeat, you did well to nip Sir Alfred's attentions in the bud. He hasn't a feather to fly with."

"I somehow collected that without your expert advice," Julie snapped.

"I wonder if you have been too much with Hester," Nick said. "I fancy so, for you are beginning to sound quite like her. If you have not fallen under Hester's influence, I can only conclude that my slightest comment is sufficient to send you flying into the boughs, and I am at a loss to conceive why that should be the case."

The Captain's tone was mild, but there was a dangerous glint in his eyes, and Julie turned her gaze to her brown satin slippers. His every word *did* seem to annoy her, and she was no more able than he to account for her irrational reaction.

"I am sorry," she muttered. "If you will excuse me now—"

"Not just yet, for there's an imperative matter we need to discuss."

The orchestra had begun the first waltz of the evening, and Nick propelled Julie rather forcefully onto the floor. She had paid scant attention to his ballroom skills on Friday, but she now rated him an even more accomplished dancer than Sir Oliver. She recalled Lord Arlington's rather coarse remark and became suddenly, intensely aware of the Captain's strong arm around her, his long, lean fingers holding hers. She closed her eyes, foolishly speculating as to what might have transpired had they met under different circumstances. Met at Almack's perhaps, during the course of a very proper assembly . . .

"The matter we must discuss is Oliver." Nick abruptly shattered the spell, and Julie's eyes flew open. "Obviously some factor—one I've yet to puzzle out—has changed his relationship with Hester."

"Hester?" she echoed. "I should have guessed that Sir Oliver has wearied of Miss Vernon's game."

She had not intended to say it, and, too late, she bit her lip. The Captain's jaws briefly hardened, then relaxed; apparently he had elected not to challenge her.

"Whatever Oliver's reasons for refusing to attend the ball, he did, in fact, decline to come. I should stake my last groat that he is not 'indisposed'; Oliver's impeccable habits have rendered him supremely healthy." Nick flashed a rather weak grin. "Barring illness, then, Hester—in times past—would have *commanded* him to accompany Uncle Edmund, to the gates of hell, if necessary. And as I'm sure you've observed by now, Oliver invariably obeys his sister's orders."

"Yes, indeed," Julie agreed dryly. If memory served her correctly, Sir Oliver's normal discourse consisted of three words, two phrases: "Yes, Hester" and "No, Hester."

"So, to reiterate, I assume that Oliver has somehow wriggled out from under Hester's thumb. I should add that she was quite candid on one head: Oliver has never fancied the customary entertainments."

Julie was reminded of their conversation at the Captain's house in London—the unfortunate conversation which had drawn her into this morass. "What is your point?" she asked, somewhat testily.

"My point is that Oliver may well refuse to join us

at any future gatherings. Consequently, you will have to befriend him in some other way."

"What would you advise?" Julie was starting to snap again. "Am I to creep into his bedchamber and seduce him after all?"

"Indeed not!" Nick said sharply. "That is to say, I believe any such approach would be decidedly premature. No, I suggest you seek Oliver out in the afternoons, after Uncle Edmund leaves for the Pump Room."

"I do not know where Sir Oliver *is* in the afternoons," Julie protested. Actually she had not pondered the baronet's activities until that very minute, but, in truth, she had never glimpsed him about the house or the garden.

"Umm." The Captain frowned. "Now you mention it, neither do I."

Which meant, Julie thought, that when Nick paid his daily visit to Miss Vernon, Sir Oliver was not present. She glanced over the Captain's shoulder and chanced to spy the lady in question just at the edge of the floor, watching their progress with dark, narrowed eyes.

"Do you not realize that our charade is entirely gratuitous?" Julie said. These words had slipped out as well, and she could only assume that her long-dormant conscience was demanding to be heard. "It is quite clear that Miss Vernon much prefers you to Sir Oliver."

"That may be true." Nick's voice, his angular face, were equally blank. "However, as I informed you at the outset, Lord Carlon will make the ultimate decision, and his choice will follow Uncle Edmund's."

He had not told her that "at the outset," of course, and perhaps it was this small fabrication which rekindled Julie's wrath. "I do not perceive that Lord Carlon has a thing to do with it," she hissed. "You and Miss Vernon are both of age; you can marry with no one's permission. I daresay you could procure a special license and be wed tomorrow if you wished."

She had gone too far; Nick's jaws clenched again, and his eyes turned to fearful yellow slits. "And *I* do not perceive that it is any part of your responsibility to examine my motivations. Your responsibility is—or should I say *was?*—to compromise Oliver. Evidently you find the task no longer to your liking. If such is indeed the case, I should hate you to exhaust your fertile imagination on lame excuses. You need but request release from our agreement; I shall pack you back to London at the earliest opportunity."

Julie would have loved to accept his offer; would have adored to stalk off the floor, rush back to Queen Square, bundle her new wardrobe into her new trunk, and depart on the first coach out of Bath. But she reminded herself that Lord Arlington's home was presently the only one she had, and she swallowed a furious retort.

"I have no wish to terminate our arrangement," she said stiffly. "I shall try to think of something."

"Pray do."

The Captain's voice was strained as well, but fortunately the music stopped before he could continue. He took Julie's elbow to escort her from the floor, and she found some small satisfaction in jerking it from his grasp and stalking a bit after all.

"Good evening, Miss Brandon."

Julie had forgotten Miss Vernon, and she hurriedly assumed what she hoped was an innocuous smile. "Good evening, Miss Vernon."

"I am somewhat surprised to see you here." Miss Vernon negotiated a chilly smile of her own. "I should have supposed you might be busily at work on Lord Arlington's portrait. You *were* hired to paint him, were you not?"

Julie wondered if Nick had told his beloved Georgina the truth about their enterprise and judged it most unlikely. "I was not *hired,* Miss Vernon," she corrected. "I am painting his lordship as a favor to Captain Stafford. And, even had I been employed, I should be unable to work at night."

"I see." Miss Vernon's pale face turned distinctly pink, and she snapped open her ivory fan and started to wave it about.

"Perhaps after Miss Brandon has finished Uncle Edmund's portrait, she might do yours," the Captain proposed.

"Mine?" Miss Vernon laughed. "When I have my portrait done, it will be by Gainsborough or Constable."

"Oh, I fear not." Julie was beginning to enjoy the interchange. "Mr. Constable paints only landscapes, and Mr. Gainsborough has been dead for nearly thirty years. You might, however, *hire* Sir Thomas Lawrence."

Miss Vernon's flush deepened, and Julie thought she detected a slight twitch at one corner of Nick's mouth. The orchestra struck up a new tune, and Miss Vernon smashed her fan shut.

"It's a quadrille, Nick," she said rather shrilly. "My very *favorite* dance, and I really must insist you stand up with me."

The Captain nodded and led her out, and Julie— unable to repress a smirk of triumph—sped to the ladies' withdrawing room.

Her assurance to Nick notwithstanding, Julie was most reluctant to seek out Sir Oliver. Her odd new perception of morality had somehow permitted her to justify compromising the baronet so long as he was openly vying for the favors of Miss Vernon, Lord Carlon, and Lord Arlington. She viewed it as quite another matter to track him down—as she might a helpless animal—with the express objective of destroying him. She therefore dallied for several days, hoping he had, after all, been indisposed and would soon deliver himself into her hands.

But Sir Oliver did not attend Lady Dartmouth's dinner on Tuesday, the theater on Wednesday, Mrs.

Powell's card party on Thursday, and by Friday Julie recognized that, indeed, she must "try to think of something." Consequently, after the Earl and Aunt Emily had left for the Pump Room, she fairly combed the public rooms of the house and prowled every inch of the garden. Her fruitless effort rendered her hot, tired, and irritable, and when she slipped back into his lordship's library, she peevishly slammed the door.

"Were you looking for something, Miss Brandon?"

Baxter's inquiry caught her entirely unawares, and Julie whirled around. "In—in point of fact, I was," she stammered. "An—an earring. A pearl teardrop. I daresay I lost it Monday evening."

"You were not in the garden Monday evening," the butler pointed out.

"No? No, I fancy you're right, Baxter. Thank you."

"Perhaps you dropped it in the house," he suggested. "I shall direct the staff to initiate a search at once."

"No!" Julie yelped. "That is to say, I've searched the house already, and I now surmise I must have lost it at the assembly rooms."

"Then I shall dispatch a footman to the rooms. I believe Archer has the sharpest eyes—"

"No!" Julie said again. "I probably dropped it in my bedchamber; let me have another look."

She fled the library and dashed up the stairs, reflecting that her talent for subterfuge was excessively limited. If she could not manufacture a facile lie for Baxter, she certainly could not successfully deceive Sir Oliver; and this reasoning, though admittedly rather weak, seemed to provide the perfect excuse to dally another six and thirty hours. On Sunday, she briefly thought her patience had been rewarded, for Sir Oliver joined the rest of the party for church. However, the baronet excused himself immediately after dinner, before Miss Vernon's musicale, and he failed to appear at the Monday-night ball or the Tuesday-evening concert.

On Wednesday Julie decided she must make at least

one further effort to flush out her quarry, and, following the Earl's sitting, she donned her bonnet, snatched up her reticule, and left the house. She soon found herself in Milsom Street, reputed to be one of the finest shopping locales in England, and under the pretext of inspecting the merchandise arrayed in the windows, she peered into every library, every confectionery, every tailoring establishment. But there was no sign of Sir Oliver, and as she approached George Street, she glimpsed Nick and Miss Vernon emerging from a milliner's shop. The Captain was burdened with several enormous boxes—in addition to the weight of Miss Vernon clinging to his arm—and Julie hastily crossed the street to avoid them. She had proceeded but a few dozen yards when she spotted Miss Crane and Wyatt just in front of her, the latter laden with boxes as well. Julie crossed the street again and strode briskly back to Queen Square; Sir Oliver, she thought grimly, would have to wait yet awhile.

After Lord Arlington's Thursday sitting, Julie recognized that she could not continue to procrastinate indefinitely. His lordship's portrait was almost finished; indeed, she confessed, she *could* have completed it several days since had she wished. As it was, only his neckcloth and a few details of his waistcoat remained undone, and Julie reluctantly settled on a Sunday attack. If all else failed, she vowed, she would trail Sir Oliver out of the dining room and literally corner him in the entry hall.

The next morning Julie painstakingly painted and repainted the Earl's neckcloth throughout his sitting, and when the morning room clock chimed half past ten, he cleared his throat.

"Forgive me, Miss Brandon." His words to the contrary, Lord Arlington's tone was not in the least apologetic. "I quite understand that you are not a professional artist, and I have attempted to make every allowance for that circumstance. Nevertheless, I must point out that I have been posing for nearly two weeks, and frankly my backside is beginning to pain me." Aunt Emily emitted an appreciative titter. "In short, I should like to know just when my portrait will be finished."

"Tomorrow," Julie said.

"Excellent." His lordship beamed. "Then I shall schedule the unveiling for tomorrow evening. I intend to invite Lady Bristowe, Lady Dartmouth, and various others to whom I owe an entertainment—"

"No!" Julie protested. "Begging your pardon, Lord Arlington, but I should prefer to wait till Sunday."

"I am sure Julie fears the paint might not yet be dry," Aunt Emily said smoothly. "However, if we instruct the guests not to touch the portrait, I fancy there will be no difficulty. Will there, Julie?"

Aunt Emily's piercing blue eyes discouraged, nay, *forbade*, further argument, and Julie shook her head.

"No difficulty," she muttered.

"Excellent," the Earl repeated. "If you, Mrs. Fitch, will write the cards, I shall arrange for their delivery this afternoon."

"I shall write the cards at once." Aunt Emily rose, rearranged her skirt most fetchingly about her narrow hips, frowned. "If I might proffer the *smallest* suggestion, milord, I do believe you might want to brighten up the house a bit. I have observed that the foyer, most particularly, is rather—rather depressing."

"A splendid idea, Mrs. Fitch."

Lord Arlington nodded, and Aunt Emily went to the Bath chair, stopped, and frowned once more.

"Perhaps you'll entertain another of my foolish notions," she said. "Since your health has improved so dramatically, you might wish to spice up the food just a trifle. *I* have the greatest respect for your new physician, but I daresay Lady Bristowe can be somewhat—somewhat critical."

"*Very* critical," the Earl agreed darkly. "I shall issue the instructions immediately, Mrs. Fitch."

Aunt Emily wheeled his lordship's chair out the

door, and Julie gazed despairingly back at the portrait. She had delayed too long: the ostensible reason for her presence in Bath was shortly to evaporate, and for all her progress, Sir Oliver might be residing on the moon. She painted in the final fold of Lord Arlington's neckcloth, shuddering as she contemplated what Nick would say when he learned of her abysmal failure.

Chapter 9

"Tonight?" Nick hissed. "Could you not have extended his sittings a trifle longer?"

He gave Julie an exasperated glare, and she elected not to remind him that he had once counseled a speedy completion of his uncle's portrait. She looked away and gazed studiedly about the foyer, noting that it had, indeed, been "brightened up." Several pieces of furniture had been removed, including the hideous pedestal and urn in front of the window, and a soft twilight glow spilled across the marble floor. There was an arrangement of fresh flowers on the Chippendale side table at one side of the entry hall, and atop the dwarf cupboard on the opposite side, two lighted lamps dispelled the evening shadows.

"He was growing impatient, Nick," Aunt Emily said soothingly. "I encouraged Julie to finish before he set his back up altogether."

"I hope, then, that Julie is prepared to report substantial progress with Oliver."

Julie transferred her inspection to the greenery on the plant stand, which had obviously been pruned. "No," she murmured. "I was never able to locate him."

"You conducted an intensive search, of course," the Captain snapped.

"I am sure Julie has done the best she can—"

"Well, I am not sure of that at all." Nick had reverted to his hiss. "And I must say that neither of you

126

seems to grasp the gravity of our situation. You have been here in excess of two weeks, and with his portrait done, Uncle Edmund may well begin to hint that you should think of returning to London."

"I doubt that," Aunt Emily said mildly. "However, if it would ease your mind, I shall try to conceive a suitable approach to Sir Oliver."

"It would ease my mind enormously. I daresay it would ease Julie's mind as well, for she appears quite unable to devise *any* approach to Oliver."

Julie, who was now examining the mirror above the side table, sensed rather than saw the Captain's latest glare and groped for some sort of dignified response. Fortunately, she was rescued by the peal of the doorbell, and as Baxter rushed into the foyer, Nick stalked out. Aunt Emily floated after him, and Julie trudged woodenly in their wake, wondering—for perhaps the thousandth time—how she had got herself into this wretched coil.

None of the dining room furniture had been changed, but the heavy drapes were open, and additional fresh bouquets bloomed on the sideboard, the pier table, and the mantel. Julie's eyes flew to the spot in front of the center window, where, some hours since, she had supervised the placement of her easel. She had finished Lord Arlington's portrait the day before so as to give the paint time to dry, and the canvas was now swathed in heavy, black velvet. She remembered every detail of the picture, of course, and she believed it was far and away the finest work she'd ever done. She was hardly in a position to challenge Sir Thomas Lawrence, but on the whole—

"Well, I collect that we are to see your masterpiece this evening, Miss Brandon."

Julie whirled around and found, as a result of the difference in their heights, that she was staring at Miss Vernon's scantily clad bosom. She raised her eyes and was rewarded with a chilly smile.

"I daresay everyone is anticipating the unveiling with my own degree of eagerness."

Miss Vernon's smile did not waver, but her black eyes were hard and cold as jet, and Julie's confidence dissolved.

"I do hope so," she murmured politely. "Now, if you will excuse me, I should like to greet the other guests."

Even as she spoke, Baxter escorted Lady Bristowe through the door, and Julie hurried forward to exchange a few words with the elderly, rather flighty Countess. She observed, from the corner of her eye, that perhaps a dozen guests had preceded Lady Bristowe and were milling about the dining room. Sir Oliver was present as well, she noted; evidently Miss Crane had decreed the occasion a command performance. In fact, it appeared that their host was the only person missing, and as Lady Bristowe related an interminable description of her dispute with the mantua-maker in Bond Street, Julie glanced toward the head of the table. To her horror, she saw a chair situated in Lord Arlington's normally empty place, and she trembled to imagine the Earl's reaction to this embarrassing error. She decided to move the chair herself and was desperately attempting to interrupt Lady Bristowe's endless narrative when his lordship stepped into the dining room.

Lady Bristowe abruptly stopped talking—indeed, the entire company fell silent—and Julie's preoccupation was such that she seized the opportunity to creep toward the offending chair. She was halfway to her goal before Mrs. Powell found her tongue.

"Lord Arlington!" she gasped. "You are *walking!*"

The Earl peered down at his legs, as if to verify Mrs. Powell's astonishing pronouncement. "Yes, I am," he agreed at last. "I fancy I have mentioned my new physician, and I can only conclude that his advice was sound. Naturally, I do not yet know whether my improvement will be permanent." Everyone sighed in unison. "However, I do feel sufficiently optimistic that

I have instructed Baxter to remove my Bath chair to the attic." Everyone flashed a happy smile. "In any event, let us all enjoy the moment. Let us eat."

His lordship walked, nay, *strode,* to the head of the table, and Julie noticed that he was considerably taller than the average and that his legs appeared quite as strong as his thick, muscular arms. She recalled Nick's comment that his uncle's illness had always been largely imaginary and sought the Captain's eyes across the table. But Nick was seating Miss Vernon, who promptly leaned over her plate so as to expose her bosom still further, and Julie reluctantly took the place next to Lady Bristowe.

Apparently Lord Arlington judged himself enough "improved" to have abandoned his diet as well as his chair, for the food was both bountiful and excellent: a rich turtle soup, oyster patties, a heavily sauced saddle of mutton, pigeon and beefsteak pies, an assortment of vegetables and wines. Lady Bristowe remarked favorably on each and every course (which Julie thought would have pleased the Earl) and, between compliments, chattered of her various homes, her servants, and the late Lord Bristowe, in no particular order. The Countess's discourse required, *permitted,* no response, and Julie initially attempted to eavesdrop on the surrounding conversations. But her ladyship was a trifle hard of hearing, as a result of which she fairly shrieked her ceaseless commentary, and Julie soon gave up, wishing she had somehow been able to avoid the whole wretched evening.

After the party had consumed dessert—cheesecake and several varieties of tart—and generous glasses of Tokay and brandy, Lord Arlington cleared his throat.

"I planned this little gathering not only to celebrate my return to health, but to display the portrait for which I've been sitting in recent weeks." There was a courteous ripple of enthusiasm. "I daresay, as the artist is with us, she should be granted the honor of unveiling the canvas. If you would, Miss Brandon?"

Julie had half expected this duty, and she rose with what she hoped was considerable aplomb. But as she paused to shove her chair beneath the table, she caught Miss Vernon's obsidian eyes upon her and felt her confidence once more begin to shred. She crossed the dining room, which now seemed at least a hundred feet in length, on unsteady legs and paused again in front of the easel. At length she realized that it was far too late to escape, and she took a deep, ragged breath and snatched the velvet covering off the portrait.

There was another chorus—one of "oohs" and "ahs" —but Julie did not attach any importance to the compulsory admiration of his lordship's friends. She glanced at Nick, but, as was so often the case, his craggy face was blank. She looked on up the table, looked at the Earl, and, to her inexpressible relief, he nodded, slowly at first, then more vigorously, until at last he gave her a definite beam of approval.

"Excellent, Miss Brandon," he said. "Really excellent. I am exceedingly pleased."

"Thank—thank you," Julie croaked.

"Are you not pleased, Mrs. Fitch?" the Earl demanded. He turned to Aunt Emily, who was seated at his right hand.

"Very much so though I fear it immodest of me to commend my own niece. Unfortunately, however, the portrait does not begin to do you justice."

"I was just thinking the same thing." Miss Vernon sounded a bit shrill. "I was just thinking that the portrait does not resemble Lord Arlington at all."

"You misunderstood me, Miss Vernon." Aunt Emily assumed a cool, devastating smile. "I meant to suggest that a portrait—while it may be excellent—is, after all, nothing more than paint and canvas. A portrait can never capture the spirit of the subject, especially not a spirit as lively as Lord Arlington's."

Miss Vernon's rosy cheeks flushed to deep brick-red, but the Earl did not appear to notice; he was busily straightening his already immaculate neckcloth.

"A point well taken, Mrs. Fitch." He nodded again, "However, I daresay we can all agree that *this* portrait is as good as any, better than most, and I shall be proud to hang it in my home. In fact, I have a specific place in mind; there is a great, empty wall in my library at Arlington Court. I believe Miss Brandon's work will look excessively well there; indeed, I can hardly wait to install it."

"A *great* wall, you say?" Aunt Emily frowned. "Then it occurs to me, milord, that you may require a family grouping to fill the space."

"A family grouping?" The Earl knitted his own white brows.

"Yes—portraits of you and your beloved nephews. I may have failed to mention that before we left London, Julie painted Captain Stafford." Miss Vernon crashed her wineglass on the table, where it rocked alarmingly for a moment, but Aunt Emily seemed oblivious to the interruption. "If Julie could paint Sir Oliver as well, I fancy you would have a most impressive collection."

"A splendid idea, Mrs. Fitch!" His lordship, like a small boy, clapped his hands together. "Do you not agree, Oliver?"

"No." Insofar as Julie knew, this was the first word the baronet had spoken since his arrival in the dining room. "That is to say, it may be a splendid idea, but I should much prefer not to sit for a portrait—"

"Nonsense," Aunt Emily interjected firmly. "Do *you* not agree, Miss Crane?"

"I beg your pardon?"

Though Julie had been quite occupied with Lady Bristowe, she had absently observed that Sir Oliver's sister did not seem herself at all. Miss Crane now focused on Aunt Emily with obvious difficulty, as if she had torn her eyes from some distant, entrancing scene.

"I was saying," Aunt Emily reiterated, "that I believe Sir Oliver should pose for Julie so as to allow a family grouping. Captain Stafford has posed already," she added pointedly. "Do you not concur, Miss Crane?"

"Oh, certainly; certainly I do. Yes, Oliver must sit for Miss Brandon."

"Well, it is settled then," Lord Arlington said cheerfully. "Since I do not approve of Sunday labor, Oliver will begin his sittings on Monday."

The Earl rose, and there was a considerable scramble as the rest of the guests leaped to their feet. Amidst the confusion, Julie looked up the table once more, and Aunt Emily gave her a tiny but triumphant wink. It was, as Lord Arlington had stated, all settled; the ruination of Sir Oliver Crane was to start in six and thirty hours.

At half past eight on Monday morning, Julie trudged to the parlor off the morning room, set a new canvas on her easel, and began to mix a palette of colors. She had never had any enthusiasm for this loathsome project, and adding to the great leaden ball in her stomach was the suspicion that Sir Oliver would prove a very poor subject. She examined her palette and, as she had feared, beheld an assortment of bland colors, so similar that they seemed to run all together. Perhaps the baronet would at least wear vivid clothes . . .

"Miss Brandon? I trust I am not too late? Nor too early?"

"No, you are precisely on time, Sir Oliver," Julie said brightly. In fact, the morning room clock was just chiming the hour. "If you will take the chair next to the window, we shall start at once."

The baronet plodded to the designated place, and Julie collected that his level of enthusiasm was, if possible, even lower than her own. She observed, to her dismay, that his attire was hopelessly neutral: a dove-gray frock coat, an ivory waistcoat, a white neckcloth.

"How do you wish me to sit?" Sir Oliver asked.

Julie glanced up and decided it hardly signified *how*

he sat: he looked quite as blank as the empty canvas on the easel. "Just assume a natural position," she muttered.

The baronet's notion of a "natural position" was one in which his shoulders were thrown stiffly back, his hands rigidly grasped the arms of the chair, and he stared—wide-eyed—at some imaginary vista well over Julie's head. She was at the point of suggesting some small degree of relaxation when it occurred to her that this was, indeed, Sir Oliver's normal posture. She sighed and brushed his outline on the canvas.

"Ah, you have begun then," Mrs. Fitch said cheerfully, peering through the door.

"Yes, we have." Julie narrowly quelled a deep breath of relief. "And I daresay you could be of considerable assistance, Aunt Emily—"

"I fear I haven't the time, my dear." Mrs. Fitch regretfully shook her gold-and-silver head. "Lord Arlington *insists* we take our tour of Bath today." She frowned, very prettily and very artificially, but her expression was wasted on the baronet, whose eyes remained riveted to the far wall. "I fancy I could be criticized for leaving the two of you alone, but I shall simply have to trust Sir Oliver not to take advantage of your privacy."

The baronet did not flush, did not bat the first pale eyelash, and Julie surmised that misconduct was so foreign to his nature that he had altogether failed to perceive Aunt Emily's meaning.

"Well, I shall go along then." Even the redoubtable Mrs. Fitch sounded somewhat dubious. "I shall speak with you later in the day, Julie."

She floated away, and Julie grimly realized that she had been left entirely to her own devices. She studied her initial effort—a few strands of Sir Oliver's hair—and attempted to persuade herself that the color was wrong. But it was not: the baronet's hair and her own rendering were the same dull blond. She recalled the list of conversational topics she had prepared some weeks since, but upon consideration, she doubted they would elicit more than monosyllabic responses. And it was certain that Sir Oliver would initiate no discussion; he would sit for hours, days, weeks if necessary, in perfect silence.

She was, Julie mentally reiterated, on her own, and this was positively her last chance. She groped about for an opening and cleared her throat.

"I have been most disappointed to have enjoyed so little of your company, Sir Oliver," she said.

"Umm."

The baronet moved his lips not at all, and Julie was reminded of Nick's sitting. There was no real comparison, of course: the Captain's eyes paled and darkened according to his mood, and the sharp bones of his face twitched and danced, hardened and softened . . .

"Yes," she continued doggedly. "You have missed most of the assemblies and parties and performances."

"I have never particularly fancied such amusements, Miss Brandon."

"Neither have I." It was not altogether untrue; Julie had had no opportunity to participate in the customary entertainments. "And that circumstance enormously exacerbates my regret, Sir Oliver, for I daresay you and I could have provided one another excellent company."

This *was* a lie; Julie was barely able to choke the words out and hated herself when she succeeded. There was a long silence, and she sensed another cul-de-sac. She glanced up again, and the baronet's gray eyes abruptly met her own.

"I have found the recent amusements—those few I did attend—especially painful," he blurted out. "I can scarcely bear the sight of Nick and Georgina making sheep's eyes at one another."

She must be very cautious, Julie thought. Her mind churned for a second or two; what should she know? What *shouldn't* she know? "Yes," she said at last, "I

believe someone did mention that you and Captain
Stafford are both courting Miss Vernon."

"There is no competition, Miss Brandon." Sir Oliver
did not sound bitter; he sounded tired, resigned. "I
must own that I entertained certain—certain *delusions*
during Nick's most recent absence, for Georgina paid
me a great deal of attention. I now recognize that she
regarded me as a substitute, a toy. She clearly prefers
Nick—always has and always will."

The baronet stopped, and Julie cast about for the
proper, comforting response. But nothing came, and
Sir Oliver went on.

"I want you to understand that I harbor no animos-
ity toward Nick or Georgina either one. It's only to be
expected that she should favor him: he cuts a dashing
figure, and he had a splendid military career, and I
daresay he's traveled halfway round the world. I have
spent my life in Norfolk and London and Bath, and
I've yet to drive a curricle."

Sir Oliver's lips twisted into a wry, totally unchar-
acteristic smile, and Julie quite forgot the Captain's
shameless scheme.

"You love Miss Vernon very much, don't you?" she
said gently.

"I don't love her at all!"

Julie started, painting an inadvertent blond line
down the baronet's nose, across his mouth, and over
his chin. She hastily swabbed the canvas and looked
back at Sir Oliver.

"I am courting Georgina—or *was*, as the case may
be—because Hester favored the match. Hester favored
it because she believed it might influence Uncle
Edmund. And I have—all my life, it seems—tried to
please Hester." The baronet flashed another mirthless
smile. "So if I lose the battle—and I fancy I shall—I
shan't regret the loss of Georgina or even of Uncle
Edmund's estate. I shall simply regret that I lost."

Sir Oliver's armor was fairly riddled with holes, and
Julie recollected her distasteful assignment. Though

she had had scant experience of flirtation, she reckoned that a few well-chosen words of sympathy would
likely ensnare the baronet, for as long, at least, as it
would take to destroy him. But she could not dispel
the image of Sir Oliver as a helpless animal, now a
wounded one, and she lacked the heart to chase him
down. Whatever the consequences, she would not turn
his own sorrow, his own failures against him and
render him still less a man.

"Yes," she murmured, "I can readily comprehend
why you have elected to avoid Captain Stafford and
Miss Vernon. But what is it you do in the daytime
hours? I have searched for you on many occasions"
—she despised herself for saying even this—"and I've
yet to find you."

"I ride." For the first time that Julie could recall,
the baronet's pale face grew animated, and his gray
eyes glowed. "It has always been my favorite pastime
and one it's easy to pursue in Bath. As you're no doubt
aware, the city is quite small, and the countryside but
a few miles distant."

Another, and most significant, chink. Julie had not
ridden since Mama's death, but as a girl she'd been a
reasonably accomplished horsewoman. And in view of
the sudden rapprochement between herself and Sir
Oliver, she felt certain she need only ask to accompany him—

"I daresay I took to riding because it was a means of
escape," the baronet continued. "It was—is—a way for
me to be alone. But then I don't suppose you could
possibly understand that, Miss Brandon."

Julie understood perfectly, further understood that,
all unknowing, he had once more eluded her. Her
sense of morality had not been sufficiently twisted
after all, it seemed; she could not steal his only moments of happiness with the express intent of slipping
a figurative knife between his ribs. She would have to
think of something else.

"I suppose you began to ride as a boy, Sir Oliver?" she said. "On one of your estates in Norfolk?"

They chatted quite amiably until half past ten, at which juncture the baronet announced that he had instructed his horse be saddled as usual. If it would pose no difficulty, he would like to embark upon his daily ride; he would, of course, return for a second sitting tomorrow. At Julie's assenting nod, he bowed out of the parlor, and she watched his departure with mixed emotions.

On the negative side, the portrait, as she had anticipated, was thus far wretched: a great blob of straw-colored hair and a pair of lifeless gray eyes. Moreover, she had utterly, *deliberately,* failed to fulfill her task, and some ancient regard for duty delivered a sharp, almost physical, stab of guilt. On the other hand, she had, at last, "befriended" Sir Oliver, and she was confident that over the ensuing days she could devise an approach she would somehow find acceptable.

But she did not, for on Tuesday morning it became immediately clear that the baronet had retreated into his shell. When Julie inquired about his ride, he tersely replied that it had been "pleasant," and, in desperation, she reverted to her original list of questions. She eventually elicited the information that he had attended Oxford, where he had read sixteenth-century history, but she was unable to extract more than a few words of opinion on Henry VIII, any of his six wives, or either of the queens he had sired. On Wednesday and Thursday the conversation deteriorated still further: after three hours of grueling effort, Julie managed to establish that Sir Oliver was six and twenty, that he had been orphaned by the age of ten (he never did explain how), and that "Hester" had assumed responsibility for his subsequent upbringing.

By the time the baronet departed the parlor Thursday morning, Julie could only fancy that she had been punished, by whatever God or gods there were, for failing to answer the fickle knock of opportunity. Aunt Emily would surely have guessed that Sir Oliver's warmth was a temporary aberration; Julie had not. To make matters worse, the supernatural retribution extended to the portrait: following four full days of sittings, the canvas consisted of hair, eyes, a highly unsatisfactory nose, and a great expanse of dead, fair skin. Julie suppressed a rising wave of panic and assured herself she had ample time in which to rekindle the baronet's well-banked fires.

On Thursday evening Lord Arlington's retinue—with the exception of Sir Oliver, of course—attended another of Mrs. Powell's card parties. Julie normally enjoyed cards and played quite well (Papa, alas, had been a gamester), but on this night she lost successively at piquet, Pope Joan, and whist. She was initially inclined to attribute her lack of concentration to the impasse with Sir Oliver, but she was soon compelled to own that she was growing bored with Bath. When the games were over, Mrs. Powell served mince pie, coffee, and brandy, and as Julie nibbled and sipped, she peered furtively about the drawing room. She was unsurprised to discover that she had encountered the other guests at least a dozen times before, and she reflected that if she stayed in Bath forever, she would undoubtedly forever see the same faces. No, that wasn't quite true. Mrs. Powell would ultimately die, and her daughter, an insipid matron named Mrs. Brewer, would conduct the weekly card parties in her stead.

"Well, what of next week?" Lady Bristowe shouted. She might have been reading Julie's thoughts. "I believe there is a concert on Tuesday." Everyone nodded. "Then I shall have a dinner on Wednesday. I should send proper cards, but my butler recently ran off with my abigail. I am sure I needn't tell you that my entire household has been quite upended . . ."

The Countess rattled on, but Julie had heard the story before. She closed her eyes, wondering how much longer—however poorly—she could play her part.

". . . but, at any rate, you are all invited," Lady Bristowe shrieked in conclusion. "I only pray the cook will not elope with the coachman, for I've had suspicions in that direction as well."

"Your invitation is very kind," Lord Arlington said, amidst a general murmur of acceptance. "However, I fear I must decline, for I do not expect to be in Bath next Wednesday."

Julie's eyes flew open, and she bolted up in her chair.

"Indeed," the Earl went on, "Wednesday is the very day I have selected for my departure. As you know, my health is vastly improved, and I feel it time to return to Arlington Court. Mrs. Fitch and Miss Brandon are to travel with me to Norfolk, so I must regretfully ask you to omit the three of us, Lady Bristowe."

"Eh?"

The Countess cupped one hand to her ear, and Lord Dartmouth, seated beside her, roared out a summary of Lord Arlington's message. After that, there was nothing more to say, and the group struggled to their collective feet. Julie thanked Mrs. Powell for a wonderful evening and trailed the Earl and Aunt Emily and Miss Crane to the landau in the street.

Chapter 10

It was late when they returned to Queen Square, and Julie was too tired to ponder Lord Arlington's sudden change of plans. She tumbled into the canopied bed and slept astonishingly well, but when she woke, she collected that her mind had been busy during the night. At any rate, no pondering remained to be done: she had firmly, irrevocably decided not to go to Norfolk.

The prospect was a tempting one, of course. She sat up and gazed around her bedchamber, fairly inhaling the luxury to which she'd never quite grown accustomed. She couldn't conceive why the Earl had invited her and Aunt Emily to accompany him to Arlington Court, but since he had, she doubted he would soon withdraw his hospitality. No, they might well be able to linger in Norfolk for weeks, months, enjoying all the benefits of country life amongst the *ton*.

And that, perversely, was the very factor which rendered his lordship's proposal unacceptable. At some juncture, Julie had to escape the Captain's charade, had to find herself, had to construct a real existence. So it was better, far better, to make her escape now, before she *had* become accustomed to the trappings of wealth and position.

She considered Nick's scheme for a moment and felt an odd blend of shame and relief. She had failed in her mission, had betrayed the Captain, and the guilt was stabbing at her innards again. On the other hand, she had spared Sir Oliver—a kind, decent man who desired nothing more than to ride alone in the country-side. It occurred to her that her emotions must be much like the baronet's own: he would be sorry to lose his battle but not in the least regretful to escape Miss Vernon's deadly clutches.

In any event, right or wrong, Julie would not go to Norfolk, and she believed Nick should be the first to learn of her refusal. The corridor clock was just strik-ing seven, and she leaped out of bed and tugged the bell rope. If she dressed quickly, there would be plenty of time to speak with the Captain and meet Sir Oliver in the parlor at nine. Though that was another failure, she reflected—the baronet's portrait. It was, at best, a third finished, and the extant canvas looked like the work of a precocious toddler. Julie saw no way to complete it—even retaining its horrid beginning—in five days. Four, she amended; his lordship would not permit a Sunday sitting. There was a light tap on the hall door, and she shook her head. If the Earl wanted Sir Oliver's picture in his library at Arlington Court, he could well afford to engage Sir Thomas Lawrence after all.

Lucy, with her customary efficiency, completed her ministrations in under an hour, and Julie dismissed her. She had permitted Lucy to select an ensemble from the wardrobe, and now, examining her reflection in the mirror, she judged the maid's choice singularly appropriate: it was the black, rather funereal bomba-zine she had worn upon her arrival in Bath. She sighed and stood up, wondering where the Captain might be at this hour of the day. She stepped rather tentatively into the corridor and beheld the object of her search not five yards distant, stationed outside Aunt Emily's door.

"Nick!" she screeched.

"Shh!"

He peered furtively about, but the hall, except for

themselves, was empty. Julie crept forward and stopped beside him.

"I was just going to look for you," she whispered. "I must talk to you, Nick—"

"Ah, it is you, children." Mrs. Fitch, who had barely cracked the door, was whispering as well. "Come in."

Nick cast a final glance over his shoulder, then shoved Julie into Aunt Emily's bedchamber and slipped in behind her, nearly treading on the heels of her black chamois shoes.

"I was expecting you." Mrs. Fitch, assuming a normal tone of voice, gestured them toward the settee while she herself took the satinwood armchair. "I should naturally have consulted you before agreeing to accompany Lord Arlington to Norfolk, but I was unable to do so. You may recall that Mrs. Powell and Mrs. Brewer left our table to see to the refreshments, and it was not until then that he issued the invitation. I judged it best to accept at once, calculating that I could always claim a later change of heart."

"An excellent decision, Emily." The Captain nodded.

Mrs. Fitch drew a small breath of relief and settled back in her chair, and Julie clenched her hands. She had hoped to prepare a speech of sorts to explain her own decision, which she feared Nick would deem far from "excellent," but there was no time. Her mouth had gone quite dry, and she discreetly licked her lips.

"Yours was, indeed, the wisest course of action, Aunt Emily," she said. "However—"

"In fact," the Captain interjected, "you have set the stage very nicely, Emily. By the time of your departure, you *will* have a change of heart, for Julie can't possibly go to Norfolk."

His final words were so entirely unexpected, so wonderfully welcome, that Julie scarcely registered his introductory comments. She, too, heaved a sigh of relief and relaxed her hands.

"That is *exactly* what I intended to say," she babbled.

"I intended to say that I can't possibly go to Arlington Court—"

"No." Nick continued as though he had not heard her, and Julie suspected he had not. "No, it is quite clear to me that we must strike before we leave Bath. So you, Emily—having observed Oliver's shocking attempt to seduce Julie—will be compelled to send your innocent niece far from Norfolk, to protect her against another shameless assault." He flashed a devilish grin. "It will work out splendidly. Splendidly."

"No!" Julie protested. She couldn't guess precisely what the Captain was at, but she well understood that he was moving to block her escape. "There is not enough time—"

"There is ample time," he corrected coldly. "Five full days. Unless, of course, you elect not to cooperate." His eyes turned to yellow slits. "Let us consider that point once and forever, Julie. Do you wish to fulfill our agreement or do you choose to terminate it?"

There was a long silence, and as Julie frantically groped for a response, she glimpsed Aunt Emily's keen blue eyes upon her. She should take another lesson from the clever Mrs. Fitch, she thought: she should keep every option open as long as she could. In the end, as Aunt Emily had pointed out, she could always change her mind.

"I shall fulfill our agreement," Julie said stiffly.

"Very well." It was Nick's turn to draw a rather ragged breath. "As you've no doubt inferred, I have given the matter some thought already. I have concluded that ideally Emily should *observe* Oliver's horrifying—let us for the moment term it an 'attack' —upon her dear niece. It would be even more ideal if Uncle Edmund could witness the odious proceedings as well. It is unlikely that any such attack could occur inside the house; Julie would shriek for assistance, and half a dozen servants would pound to her rescue. Consequently, the incident must take place elsewhere, and I now solicit your ideas."

The Captain's eyes—golden again—darted between Julie and Mrs. Fitch, and eventually the latter tapped her teeth with one long fingernail.

"Lord Arlington did chance to mention that Sir Oliver fancies riding," she said.

"Yes, he does," Julie confirmed. Her mind seemed split in half; one half was plotting Sir Oliver's ruin while the other desperately sought a means to avoid it.

"You knew that?" Nick snapped at Julie. "Knew it and failed to capitalize on your knowledge?"

"I—I am afraid of horses," Julie lied.

"I have never observed that you are in the least afraid of horses," the Captain said frigidly. "I *have*, however, observed that you display a continuing reluctance to compromise Oliver—"

"Children, children, let us not bicker," Aunt Emily chided. "Let us assume that Sir Oliver's love of riding is his fundamental weakness. Let us further remember that Nick wishes Lord Arlington and myself to be present at the—the performance. His lordship and I do not ride. We must therefore devise a plan that will put Sir Oliver on horseback and allow for an accompanying party *not* on horseback." It was perhaps the clearest example of basic logic Julie had ever heard.

"A picnic!" Nick snapped his lean brown fingers.

"A picnic!" Aunt Emily repeated. "A picnic in the country."

"A picnic," Julie echoed miserably.

"A picnic it is then," the Captain said. "How are we to persuade Oliver and Uncle Edmund to join us?"

There was another silence, and at length Mrs. Fitch tapped her teeth again. "We shall say it has something to do with Sir Oliver's portrait. Lord Arlington is most enthusiastic about the family grouping."

"We shall say"—Nick took up the theme—"that Julie must paint Oliver outside, in the full light of day, so as to capture him to maximum advantage."

"I cannot take my canvas and my easel and all my

paints to the countryside," Julie objected. "So I fancy we shall have to abandon the notion after all—"

"You can take your sketch pad and simply draw him," the Captain interrupted. "You can claim to be working on his 'lines,' or whatever it is artists work on."

"I shouldn't require full daylight to get his lines," Julie said indignantly.

"But neither Oliver nor Uncle Edmund knows that."

Another defeat. Julie picked at an imaginary thread on the black crepe flounce around her hem.

"To the details then," Nick said. "Oliver and I shall go on horseback, and the rest of you will occupy one of the carriages—you, Julie, and you, Emily, and Uncle Edmund and Georgina."

"Georgina!" Julie very nearly tore the flounce from the fabric of her skirt.

"If you will listen a moment, I shall explain why Georgina is necessary to the plot." Julie was still inspecting her flounce, but she would have wagered her last farthing that the Captain's eyes had turned yellow again. "We shall proceed to an appropriate site and have our lunch. When the meal is over, you will state that you need some privacy in which to sketch Oliver."

"Lord Arlington will perceive that fabrication at once." Julie looked triumphantly up. "Aunt Emily was there during every minute of his sittings—"

"Will you listen?" Nick's eyes *were* yellow. "I shall offer to take Georgina for a drive, and Emily will insist on chaperoning our excursion. She'll persuade Uncle Edmund to go as well. We'll drive about for precisely half an hour, and when we return, we shall find you and Oliver in a most embarrassing situation. Do you have a watch?" he demanded abruptly.

"No," Julie replied. "So I daresay we shall have to think of something else—"

"Lend her your watch, Emily," the Captain ordered.

"Now?" Julie croaked. "As you yourself pointed out, we have five full days."

"That is true, but there is no reason to delay. To the contrary, delay invites poor weather or some other complication. No, we shall have the picnic tomorrow. Emily will engage Uncle Edmund, he'll engage Oliver, and I myself shall invite Georgina. I shall also speak with you, Julie, about the specific nature of the embarrassing situation I have in mind. Are we agreed then?"

Mrs. Fitch nodded, and Julie—though far from agreed—bobbed her head as well. Nick suggested they disperse at once, lest someone discover their clandestine meeting, and Aunt Emily ushered him toward the corridor. They were still reviewing the Plot when Julie stole through the connecting door and closed it firmly behind her.

"What do you wish to wear, Miss Brandon?"

Julie was inclined to ask Lucy's opinion as to which of her costumes was most suitable for a seduction, but she bit her lip. "The yellow, I suppose," she mumbled.

"I must say you don't appear very enthusiastic about the picnic." Lucy went to the wardrobe and withdrew an open robe of yellow jaconet and a slightly darker spencer trimmed in bronze satin. "I think it sounds most amusing, and I daresay the food will be *wonderful*. Mrs. Vester has been cooking and packing the hampers since dawn."

"Umm," Julie muttered.

She had desperately hoped that the Captain's latest scheme would come to naught, but by the end of last evening's assembly, both he and Aunt Emily had been able to report complete success. Lord Arlington had agreed to the excursion at once; he lived in constant fear of a relapse, he said, and he felt that a dose of fresh air might help to maintain his delicate health. Upon learning that an outdoor sitting was essential to the completion of Sir Oliver's portrait, his lordship insisted that the baronet join the party; and Miss Vernon, of course, required no persuasion whatever.

"So all is in readiness," Nick concluded, during a

hurried conference following their return from the Lower Rooms. "We are to depart the house at eleven, and I shall meet with Julie at a quarter before the hour to establish the final details."

The hall clock struck half past ten, and Julie started.

"Is something wrong, miss?" Lucy inquired anxiously. "Is there some problem with your hair?"

"No; no, my hair is fine." Julie was mumbling again.

"If you will excuse me then, I shall see to Mrs. Fitch. And do try to brighten up, for I fancy you'll have a bang-up time."

Lucy scurried toward the connecting door, and Julie gazed at her reflection. Perversely enough, she had selected precisely the right attire: she looked fetchingly fresh and innocent, ripe for "attack" by a hot-blooded suitor driven wild by her girlish charms. Aunt Emily's watch was lying on the dressing table, and Julie picked it up. It seemed hot to the touch, seemed almost to burn her fingers, and she hastily shoved it in a pocket of her skirt. She need never consult it, she reminded herself; she had hours remaining in which to change her mind. When the rest of the group came back from their drive, they could find her calmly sketching Sir Oliver—

There was a soft but urgent tap on the corridor door, and Julie jumped again. In point of fact, her change of mind could occur at this very instant. She could refuse to answer the Captain's summons, could send word that she had been taken suddenly ill. The Earl, at least, would believe her . . . The door opened, and Nick slipped through and pulled it carefully to behind him.

"Good God!" he hissed, striding across the room. "Would you leave me standing in the hall all day, in full view of every passing footboy?"

"I—I am sorry," Julie murmured. She distantly noted that the Captain looked exceedingly well in country clothes; he might have been born in his buckskin breeches, his riding coat, his top boots.

"Never mind," he said rather peevishly. "We've little time so I suggest we rehearse your role without delay."

"Rehearse?" Julie echoed.

"I have put myself to a great deal of trouble to engineer the upcoming scenario," Nick snapped. It was clear that he was in very poor humor, and Julie entertained a guilty notion that he had somehow read her recent thoughts. "Consequently, I do not intend to leave matters to chance, and, yes, we shall rehearse. Get your sketchbook please."

Julie had placed her pad and pencil on the dressing table as well, and she obediently plucked them up.

"Very good. Now sit down."

"I *am* sitting," Julie pointed out.

"I wish you to sit on the floor."

It occurred to Julie that the Captain's "rehearsal" might be designed, in part, to weaken her own resistance. It would be so much easier to reenact a familiar performance . . .

"On the floor!" he repeated sharply.

Julie reluctantly stood, then lowered herself to the rug, and Nick moved to a point perhaps ten feet away.

"You must imagine that you are sitting on a blanket in the grass," he counseled.

Julie found it extremely difficult to visualize the rose-and-pink Brussels carpet as grass, but she nodded.

"You must further imagine that I am sitting as well, and you are drawing me. Drawing Oliver, that is."

It was even harder to see the dark, towering Captain as a pale baronet reclining on a blanket, but Julie nodded once more and poised her pencil over her sketch pad.

"Very good," Nick said again. "Now, precisely five minutes prior to our return, you are to drop your pencil in the grass."

Julie could not but wonder how she was to sketch Sir Oliver while consulting Aunt Emily's watch every thirty seconds or so. Nevertheless she dropped her pencil on the rug.

"Your pencil is now buried in the grass," the Captain said, "and you begin to search for it."

In fact, Julie's pencil was in plain view approximately three inches from her right hand, and she could not repress a giggle.

"Search for your pencil!" Julie patted all around her "lost" implement, and Nick bobbed his head approvingly. "Grope about for a time and then request Oliver's assistance."

"Oh, Sir Oliver," Julie chirped, "I seem to have dropped my pencil. Could you possibly help me locate it in this terrible deep grass?"

The Captain—obviously unamused—stalked across the room, squatted beside her, and began fumbling about the carpet as well. "Observe that at this juncture Oliver will be off-balance," he said sternly. "Just as we are about to come within view, I shall give you a signal. I shall"—he frowned—"I shall shout, 'Is that a fox?' If you then tug at Oliver's arm, he will tumble down, and surely I can leave the rest to your own invention."

"Like this?"

Julie could not have explained her motivation: perhaps she acted from sheer mischief; perhaps she was sick to death of his interminable plotting. In any event, she jerked Nick's sleeve, and he lost his balance and began to teeter toward her. She started to laugh again, but when he tried and failed to break his fall, she belatedly realized that either or both of them stood to sustain serious injury. She instinctively extended her arms, but she could not begin to support his superior weight, and he drove her relentlessly backward. Her shoulders thudded to the carpet, then her head, and, lest her arms be broken, she threw them desperately round his back. She closed her eyes just as he collapsed atop her, and she lay still a moment, gasping for breath.

When Julie was persuaded that she was not dead, that *he* was not dead, she tentatively opened her eyes, bracing herself for the furious scold which—she conceded—she richly deserved. But Nick, who had raised his head a bit, was staring down at her, his own eyes darker than amber.

"Yes, like that," he said hoarsely. "And since you apparently wish to rehearse the entire performance, I shall oblige you."

His lips smashed down on hers, and for a moment Julie struggled to free herself. She wanted to tell him that she had *not* invited this brutal assault, but she was suddenly unsure of that; she couldn't seem to sort anything out. And then his mouth turned soft, gentle, but, at the same time, hungry; and she ceased to resist, ceased to think. Her lips—with a will of their own, it seemed—eagerly parted, and her fingers crept into his hair. His mouth moved to her ear, her neck, and she moaned deep in her throat and arched up against him.

"Julie," he whispered. "I fear I've made a dreadful error—"

But she didn't want to talk. She could not name the thing she *did* want, could not define her shameless yearning to feel his hands on her body, to touch his dark, bare skin. So, lacking words, she pulled his head down again, bringing his lips back to hers, and this time it was he who struggled away.

"Please listen to me, Julie. I must explain—"

"Are you ready, dear?"

Aunt Emily's voice, emanating from just beyond the connecting door, might have been a great splash of icy water. The Captain scrambled to his feet and yanked Julie up so abruptly that she feared her arm had been wrenched from its socket.

"Nick!" Mrs. Fitch had opened the door and was peering across the threshold. "Ah, yes, you did have some final details to discuss, didn't you? Well, I hope you have done so because it is time to leave."

As if in confirmation, the hall clock began to chime

the hour, and Aunt Emily's shrewd blue eyes darted to Julie.

"Get a headdress, dear," she instructed. "Though I personally *adore* freckles, I fancy you have enough without adding to your collection."

Julie's knees were so weak that she was hard put to stand, but she somehow walked to the wardrobe, pulled her yellow French bonnet from the shelf, and tied the bronze ribbons under her chin.

"And don't forget your props."

Mrs. Fitch airily waved toward the sketchbook and pencil, as if she had quite expected to find them strewn about the carpet. Julie—cheeks flaming—stumbled across the room once more, snatched them up; and they were ready to depart.

Chapter 11

Julie never knew precisely where they picnicked or how long it took them to reach the site, for during the better part of the drive she was wrapped in a fog. Not a literal one, of course; she did recall that it was a bright, warm day. They used Lord Arlington's barouche, and Julie occupied the rear-facing open seat. She recollected this detail because Nick and Sir Oliver, on horseback, trotted along on either side of the carriage, and the first time Julie glanced up, she caught the Captain's eyes—amber, unfathomable eyes—fixed upon her. She felt the onslaught of another furious blush and gazed swiftly back at the hamper in her lap.

What had happened? she wondered wildly. Had she, indeed, invited Nick's advances? Or had he, after weeks of discretion, elected at last to take advantage of his intimate acquaintance with a Cyprian? She thought he had murmured something about an error; if so, what error?

More to the point, where was she, were they, to proceed from here? Julie had never been kissed before, not once in all her two and twenty years. Mr. Howe, after consuming a slight excess of champagne at Mrs. Wainwright's Christmas assembly, had *tried* to kiss her, but Julie had deftly turned her cheek at the last instant. She had found even that experience distinctly repugnant, and she was utterly at a loss to explain her shameless response to Nick.

Yes, *shameless* was the only fitting word to describe her behavior. Worse yet, she was compelled to own that given the same circumstances, she would react again in exactly the same way: Nick had only to touch her, and she would fairly fall into his arms. The notion was so exquisite, yet so appalling, that she closed her eyes and shivered.

"Are you all right, dear?" Aunt Emily asked anxiously.

"All right?" Julie's eyes flew open. "Yes; yes, I am fine."

"It appeared for a moment you were suffering a chill. Perhaps you should pull your bonnet down a bit."

Julie obediently adjusted her hat, and they rattled on through the countryside.

Whatever its location, the picnic site was perfect: a small grassy clearing entirely surrounded by thick stands of trees. Nick and Sir Oliver tied their horses to a convenient beech as Wyatt unloaded both passengers and equipment from the barouche. When the carriage was empty, the Captain's man drove it to the edge of the clearing, secured the team, and trudged back toward the rest of the group. Though Julie was still in something of a daze, she did observe that Wyatt seemed rather morose. Maybe, she decided absently, he resented driving Lord Arlington's equipage while the Earl's own coachman dallied with the maids in Queen Square.

At any rate, everyone else appeared to be in high spirits. His lordship cheerfully helped Nick and Sir Oliver spread the blankets, and Miss Vernon sacrificed her dignity to the astonishing extent of unpacking one of the baskets. After the food and dishes and utensils had been laid out, after the Captain had uncorked and poured the wine, there was a brief debate as to where the various members of the party were to sit. Aunt Emily soon resolved the issue by declaring that she and Lord Arlington and Wyatt would take one blanket and the "young people" would share the other. Wyatt glowered a bit—evidently he did not care for the implication that he was an "old" person—but he heaped his plate nevertheless and joined Mrs. Fitch and the Earl.

Lucy had been right on one head: the food was wonderful. Her preoccupation notwithstanding, Julie wolfed down two servings of lobster salad, fully half a cold roast chicken, several generous portions of fruit and cheese, and an enormous slice of blueberry pie. As she ate, she was distantly aware of the merry conversation flowing between the blankets: Lord Arlington and Miss Vernon reported a recent scandal in Norfolk; Aunt Emily described a recent scandal in London; and even Sir Oliver ventured a few remarks about the recent weather in Bath. Julie and Wyatt remained silent, and Nick—though he tossed out the occasional comment—seemed largely immersed in an inspection of his wineglass.

"Well." At length Aunt Emily patted her lips and laid the linen napkin aside. "The meal was quite good, was it not?"

"Very good indeed." The Earl massaged his stomach and emitted a little belch of appreciation. "And very *healthy,* Mrs. Fitch; I daresay my doctor would heartily approve."

"*Very* healthy," Aunt Emily agreed. "And now we're finished, I fancy Julie would like to begin sketching Sir Oliver."

This was Julie's cue, of course, the moment at which she was to announce that her artistic effort would require uninterrupted privacy. She was staring at her ravaged plate, but she sensed Aunt Emily's keen blue eyes upon her, and she toyed with the possibility of claiming illness after all. No one would question her statement; the entire party had heard Mrs. Fitch's reference to a chill. She tried to open her mouth, but her lips seemed paralyzed, and the opportunity passed.

"Julie is a trifle hesitant," Aunt Emily said smoothly,

"because it quite oversets her to work in view of an audience. As you know, Lord Arlington, she is not a professional artist."

"I do know that, and *I* shall not disturb her in the least. I shall take my blanket into the trees and enjoy a brief snooze. My physician says that afternoon rest is most beneficial."

"As I am sure it is," Mrs. Fitch said. "However, I fear Julie will be distracted by the others."

There was a long silence, and eventually Julie dared to raise her eyes. Aunt Emily was gazing pointedly at Nick, but the Captain—his glass now drained and put aside—was studying one of the empty wine bottles.

"I was saying, Captain Stafford"—Aunt Emily cleared her throat—"that Julie should start to sketch Sir Oliver while there is ample daylight. And, as I believe you are aware, she finds it difficult to work in public."

Nick looked up as well, and for the first time in the course of their acquaintance, Julie detected an air of uncertainty about him. His yellow eyes darted from Mrs. Fitch to Sir Oliver to Julie herself, darted so quickly that Julie doubted anyone else had noticed. She could not surmise what he was searching for, what he found, but at last he tossed the wine bottle on the grass.

"Far be it from me to impede Miss Brandon's effort then," he drawled. "Perhaps I can persuade Georgina to drive around a bit."

Miss Vernon leaped eagerly to her feet, and Aunt Emily essayed one of her pretty frowns.

"I am afraid Lord Carlon would be *exceedingly* distressed if I were to permit you and Miss Vernon to depart unchaperoned," she said. "No, I shall have to accompany you." She rose and plucked an imaginary piece of grass from one of the lilac rosettes at the bottom of her skirt; then her frown deepened. "Of course, if I accompany *you,* I shall be compelled to leave Julie and Sir Oliver alone." She feigned an agonizing inner debate. "But, as Sir Oliver has shown himself altogether trustworthy in the past, I daresay I can afford the risk." Aunt Emily was setting the stage very nicely indeed, Julie thought wryly.

"There is no risk whatever, Mrs. Fitch," the Earl said. "As I indicated, I shall take my blanket just into the trees. Miss Brandon will therefore be quite unaware of my presence, but I shall be nearby."

Julie was hard put to quell a hysterical giggle. Evidently Lord Arlington—their sole and entire audience—was determined to squelch the performance.

"As you will." Aunt Emily sighed. "I had hoped—since you are so very knowledgeable about the local flora and fauna—that you might serve as my guide. However, if you feel you need to rest ..." Her voice trailed despondently off, and her lower lip quivered a bit with disappointment.

"I do not *need* to rest, Mrs. Fitch," his lordship said indignantly. He bounded up, popped one of the buttons off his waistcoat, and hastily clasped his hands over the gap. "If you wish me to show you about, I shall certainly do so. Wyatt!" he roared.

The Captain's man, seated virtually at the Earl's feet, started, then jumped up as well.

"Untie the horses, Wyatt," Lord Arlington commanded grandly. "We are going to take a splendid drive round the countryside."

Within three minutes the barouche was loaded—Aunt Emily and the Earl in the forward-facing seat, Nick and Miss Vernon in the other—and thirty seconds after that, it had clattered into the woods and disappeared from sight. Julie discreetly consulted her borrowed watch. It was exactly two, which meant that at exactly two twenty-five, she was to drop her pencil. *If* she elected to carry out the sordid charade ...

"Where do you want me to sit, Miss Brandon?"

"On the other blanket," Julie muttered.

She had placed her sketchbook and pencil in the picnic hamper she had carried, which she could readily identify because Mrs. Vester had adorned it with a pink bow. But Julie rooted amongst all the baskets a full five minutes before "finding" her implements and resuming her place on the blanket. At that juncture, she grimly noted that the Captain's rehearsal had been remarkably accurate: give or take an inch or two, Sir Oliver was positioned the predicted ten feet away.

"I must own, Miss Brandon"—the baronet emitted an apologetic cough—"that I was a trifle puzzled about the necessity for an outdoor sitting. I was under the impression that light was critical for color alone, but I observe that you are drawing in pencil."

"Pencil." Julie nodded and desperately borrowed from the Captain. "The fact is, Sir Oliver, that I wish to capture your lines. So if you could move your head just a bit to the right . . . Yes, that is it precisely. I must now ask you to be very still, not to talk at all."

The baronet held his pose as if he'd been turned to stone, and Julie dashed a few preliminary strokes on her pad. She calculated that she still had approximately fifteen minutes in which to reach a decision, but if she chose *not* to entrap Sir Oliver, she must have a reasonably competent sketch to display to Lord Arlington. She concentrated on the baronet's bone structure and grudgingly conceded that the light was of some help: the nose which took shape in her sketchbook was far superior to that on the canvas at Queen Square. Not that it signified; no matter what her immediate course, she did not expect to finish Sir Oliver's portrait. But, by force of habit, she proceeded from the baronet's nose to his chin and suddenly realized that her pad had grown shadowed.

"Ahem." Sir Oliver coughed again. "Forgive me, Miss Brandon, but I must point out that it has quite clouded over."

Julie glanced up and perceived at once that "clouded over" was a monumental understatement: the sky had become a low, black, seething sea. Even as she contemplated the astonishing change in the weather, a chill wind rose, and there was a fork of lightning just overhead, followed by an ominous rumble of thunder.

"In fact," the baronet continued nervously, "I fancy it is about to rain."

Julie snatched Aunt Emily's watch from her pocket and read a time of twenty past two. "I daresay it *is* going to rain," she concurred rather shrilly, "but perhaps it will hold off another ten minutes, till the others return from their drive."

"How do you know they will return in ten minutes?" Sir Oliver's question was nearly lost in another great crash of thunder.

"Well, I do not *know,* of course." Julie was forced to raise her voice over the ever-strengthening wind. "I meant to suggest that in view of the weather, they will no doubt come back as quickly as possible."

"I must disagree with you, Miss Brandon." The baronet's words were punctuated by a jagged bolt of lightning and a further roar of thunder. "To the contrary, I should think they might well continue to town. They departed in the direction of Bath, you know."

Julie had *not* known, and she gazed apprehensively at the sky, pondering this new and absurd dilemma. Consequently, the first drops of rain fell directly into her face, and almost before she could lower her head, the clouds seemed to burst apart. There was no accurate way to describe the downpour; "torrent" was entirely inadequate. It was as though some malign force of nature had combined all the world's great waterfalls and moved them to a small corner of Somerset, and within a scant ten seconds Julie was totally soaked. She struggled to her feet, distantly wondering what good *that* might do, and found Sir Oliver standing beside her.

"I propose we head for town ourselves, Miss Brandon."

Julie thought he was shouting, but she could barely hear him over the cacophony of wind and rain. She nodded, and the baronet seized her elbow and began to drag her across the clearing. For the first time in her life, Julie wished she were a man, unrestricted by the leaden weight of skirt and petticoats twining soggily about her ankles. By the time they reached the horses, she was panting for breath, and she sagged against Sir Oliver, idly observing that her yellow slippers, not to mention her beautiful saffron flounces, were black with mud.

"Do you ride, Miss Brandon?" the baronet yelled.

On a clement day, properly attired, Julie thought she could. But not in the driving rain, the shrieking wind, not in a sodden walking dress, and she shook her head.

"I shall put you up behind me then."

Sir Oliver untied his horse and swung into the saddle, then reached down his hand to her. Julie wished for the second time that she were of the opposite gender, but the situation quite precluded false modesty. She hitched her skirt and petticoats above her knees, and, with Sir Oliver's help, managed to scramble astride the broad, bare, wet rump of his black stallion.

"You must hang on very firmly," the baronet shouted over his shoulder. "Very firmly indeed."

"Yes, I shall." Julie's teeth were chattering—whether with cold or fright she wasn't sure—and she wrapped her arms round the baronet's waist and laced her fingers together.

"Are you ready then?"

"Yes," Julie whimpered.

Sir Oliver slammed his heels into the stallion's belly, and the horse launched into a headlong gallop. Julie suspected that ten years since she would have regarded the frantic ride as a thrilling experience, but she was now compelled to attribute her chattering teeth to abject terror. She closed her eyes, pressed one cheek against the baronet's back, and tried not to notice that the stallion was slipping and sliding about in the mud. She vaguely recollected Sir Oliver's statement that the countryside was but a few miles from

Bath, and after an eternity (perhaps five minutes), she hopefully cracked one eyelid. But she glimpsed only trees and rain, and she hastily shut her eye again and attempted to wriggle a bit closer to the saddle.

After a further eon, Julie detected a new sound, a new rhythm to their movement, and she tentatively ventured another peep. To her unutterable relief, she discovered that they had reached the fringes of Bath; though the blinding rain virtually obscured the buildings, the horse was unmistakably racing on paving stones rather than mud. She did not believe she had drawn a single breath since they left the clearing, and she now heaved an enormous sigh and gave Sir Oliver a small squeeze of gratitude. She well realized that a less accomplished horseman could never have guided the skittish stallion through deluge and thunder, lightning and mud; as it was, they were safe.

Julie's arms relaxed, and she became aware that her bonnet had slipped almost to her nose and was showering great drops of icy water on her bare knees. She cautiously raised her left hand and attempted to tug it back into place, but the ribbons were plastered to her chest. She lifted her right hand, and just as she found the straggling streamers of bronze satin, the horse splashed through a veritable lake in the road and began to shy.

Julie distantly awarded the baronet further points: in the hands of an inferior rider, the stallion would surely have fallen. In the event, however, the horse merely danced, and had Julie been "hanging on" as she should, there would have been no difficulty. But she was foolishly fussing with her hat, and she felt herself tilting sidewise.

"Sir Oliver!" she shrieked. "I am—I am—"

Before she could finish, she perceived that nothing could prevent her fall, and she desperately strove to land on her feet. By some miracle, she managed to slide off the stallion's back and plant her ruined slippers on the cobblestones. She was at the point of counting herself most fortunate when her right ankle buckled and she tumbled into a gigantic puddle on the pavement.

"Are you all right, Miss Brandon?"

Julie collected that she had been rendered momentarily insensible because she could not recall the baronet dismounting, coming to her side, or kneeling in the street, which was fast becoming a river. "I—I am fine," she stammered. "Please do not give it another thought; I am fine."

Sir Oliver rose and tugged her up as well, and Julie vainly tried to stifle a moan of pain.

"It is my ankle," she gasped. "Nothing serious, I am sure, but if you could help me just a bit . . ."

He half led, half carried her back to the horse and somehow maneuvered her onto the stallion's rump again. They were not far from Queen Square, he assured her, and—soaked as they were—they might as well proceed at a walk. Julie managed a nod, and the baronet clucked the horse to a start, then held him at the promised leisurely pace. Julie buried her face in his back once more and gritted her teeth, but she was fairly dizzy with pain. Her injury *was* nothing serious—insofar as she was unlikely to die—but she suspected her ankle was broken or badly sprained at least. Broken, sprained; broken, sprained—the words became a terrible litany as they plodded along in the rain.

"We are home, Miss Brandon."

Sir Oliver was standing beside the horse, his arms outstretched, and Julie surmised that she had drifted off again. Maybe it was for the best, she thought groggily, for her ankle no longer pained her at all. She peered optimistically down and was horrified to observe that it had already started to swell, had already turned a pale unhealthy blue. She once more slid off the stallion's back, but this time the baronet caught her up.

"Place your weight on your *left* leg, Miss Brandon," he counseled, "and I shall assist you into the house. I shall then send for Dr. MacCallum—"

He was interrupted by the clatter of a carriage, and—through an almost impenetrable curtain of rain— Julie saw the barouche turn into the drive. When the carriage stopped at the front door, it was somewhat protected by the house, and Julie was able to discern a most wretched party of picnickers. Lord Arlington had gallantly surrendered the covered seat to Aunt Emily and Miss Vernon, and they, as a result, were merely wet. The Earl himself, in the open seat, was positively drenched—his coat, waistcoat, shirt-points, and neck-cloth appearing to have dissolved into a single shape-less mass of fabric.

"Julie?" Aunt Emily clambered out of the barouche unassisted and rushed toward the front steps. "Are you all right, dear?"

"She has injured her ankle a bit," Sir Oliver responded, "but I daresay it is nothing serious. Once she is settled in her bedchamber, I shall send for Dr. MacCallum."

"Dr. MacCallum," Julie echoed weakly.

Lord Arlington was handing Miss Vernon out of the carriage, and though they both looked considerably the worse for wear, they seemed largely undamaged. Nevertheless Julie sensed something amiss, and at last it came to her.

"Nick," she croaked. "Where is Nick?"

"Captain Stafford?" Aunt Emily corrected. "We were very near the clearing when the rain set in, and Captain Stafford walked back to see to you and Sir Oliver and the horses. Had you taken both horses, Wyatt was to return for the Captain; obviously that will not be necessary. But come, Julie, dear, you need your rest."

Mrs. Fitch and Sir Oliver jointly propelled Julie up the stairs—the Earl and Miss Vernon trailing just behind—and at the moment they reached the porch, Baxter threw the door open.

"Miss Brandon!" the butler exclaimed.

Julie could hardly believe that her injury was visible to the casual eye, but she peered downward. No, her ankle was properly covered, so perhaps Baxter was reacting to her mud-spattered clothing.

"You might have informed me you were expecting a guest, Miss Brandon," the butler hissed accusingly. "As it was, she caught me entirely unawares."

"A guest?" Julie repeated feebly.

She glanced over Baxter's shoulder, and a familiar form emerged from his lordship's library.

"Julie?" Louisa said. "Thank God you have arrived at last; I was at the point of being cast out."

Louisa gazed curiously at Sir Oliver and Mrs. Fitch, at Lord Arlington and Miss Vernon, and Julie's knees began to sag.

"Louisa?" she whispered. "Surely you remember our dear Aunt Emily."

Her legs gave way altogether, and everything went black.

Chapter 12

Julie woke in the canopied bed and lay still a moment, marveling at her exceedingly peculiar dream. She was dry and rather too warm, for the bedclothes were pulled up to her neck. She started to kick them away and was rewarded by a vicious stab of pain in her right ankle. Not a dream then? She fearfully opened her eyes and beheld Louisa sitting in a chair beside the bed.

"Louisa," she said resignedly.

"Yes, it is I. Aunt Emily instructed me to watch after you; she has gone to change her clothes." Louisa frowned. "Who, pray, *is* Aunt Emily?" she asked.

"Her real name is Mrs. Emily Fitch." Louisa betrayed no sign of recognition, and Julie drew a small breath of relief. "She is posing as my aunt because she and I and Captain Stafford are engaged in a—a project."

"A project?" Louisa echoed suspiciously. "What sort of project?"

"It is far too complicated to explain," Julie replied truthfully. "And it no longer signifies, at any rate; the project has altogether failed."

She struggled upright, wincing as her ankle issued a sharp protest, and tugged the covers down to her waist. She discovered, in the process, that she was clad in one of Aunt Emily's ensembles; apparently Mrs. Fitch and Louisa had been unable to locate Julie's own tattered nightclothes. The ensemble was relatively modest—a peignoir of pale blue lace over a matching satin nightdress—but nevertheless far more revealing than Julie's ancient flannel attire. She felt the threat of a blush and repressed an inclination to burrow beneath the bedclothes again.

"I see," Louisa said. It was clear that she did not see at all. "And just where *is* Captain Stafford?"

"I believe he is riding back to town; he may have arrived already. Or he might be waiting for the rain to abate." Louisa had assumed another, impatient frown, and Julie described the picnic—omitting, of course, the matter of Sir Oliver's aborted "attack."

"I see," Louisa repeated. "I collect, then, that Sir Oliver Crane is the very *attractive* man who was standing with you at the door."

Julie was hard put to judge the baronet "very attractive," but she nodded.

"And the older gentleman is Lord Arlington? He is quite handsome as well."

Julie nodded once more.

"I must give you credit," Louisa said grudgingly. "You are far bolder than I: I should never *dare* to become embroiled with three men at the same time. And most particularly not if they were residing under a single roof."

Louisa shook her head with reluctant admiration, and Julie's cheeks blazed.

"You have gravely misconstrued the situation," she snapped. "I am not *'embroiled'* with any of them; I was, as I have stated, engaged as part of a project . . ."

But her denial sounded dreadfully lame, even in her own ears, and her voice trailed off. Louisa looked—not surprisingly—unconvinced, and Julie elected to yield some ground in hopes of attaining a larger victory.

"Very well," she said stiffly. "I do have a—a relationship with Captain Stafford, but Sir Oliver and Lord Arlington believe me to be entirely respectable. And you must do nothing, say nothing, to bring my character into question. Indeed, you yourself must behave with the utmost propriety so long as you are here." Julie was frantically eager to change the subject, and her final words seemed to provide the perfect opportunity. "Which leads me to inquire, Louisa, how long you intended to stay, and what it was that brought you to Bath in the first place."

"The factor that brought me to Bath is the late, unlamented Lord Romney." Louisa pursed her lips and primly patted her hair, which was glowing a rich, warm red in the lamplight.

"Late?" Julie gasped. "He is dead then?"

"He is dead to *me*," Louisa responded regally. "Do you recollect that he had leased a house for us?"

Julie recollected this circumstance all too well, and she bobbed her head again.

"I had seen it only from the outside until the very day we moved in, at which point I found it to be little more than a cottage. There was insufficient room for my furniture; I was compelled to place fully half my things in the coach house. This presented no great problem because Godfrey shortly informed me that there was to be no carriage. No horses. He next declined to pay my bills—the very few, very modest bills I had accumulated—and I had to transfer my custom to a most inferior mantua-maker. You can observe the result for yourself."

Louisa gestured disdainfully down at her gray bombazine carriage dress, which, insofar as Julie could determine, easily rivaled even Miss Howard's elegant work.

"However," Louisa continued, "I should not like you to conclude that I am entirely mercenary. No, I soon discovered Godfrey to be frightfully dull. You may find that difficult to credit, Julie, for you observed him at his best. Consequently, you will simply have to believe me when I report that he is a man of very limited intellect."

As Julie recalled, Lord Romney's "best" was utter silence, and she sternly bit back a smile.

"In any event," Louisa went on, "five weeks of Godfrey's unadulterated company proved *quite* enough. I was confident you would take me in until I could locate another"—she seemed to remember Julie's admonition of propriety—"another place to live."

The way Louisa had so generously taken *her* in, Julie thought bitterly. But, at this juncture, she felt recimination would be useless and degrading.

"How did you locate me?" she said aloud.

"It was not easy," Louisa replied accusingly. "I found Captain Stafford's house readily enough, but it was deserted. I then went about the neighborhood, posing inquiries, and eventually a butler at the end of the street, a friend of Captain Stafford's man, directed me to Lord Arlington's house in Bath. When I arrived— after two full days on the road—you were cavorting about in the woods, and Baxter was extremely reluctant to admit me. But it ended well after all, and I bear you no ill will, Julie."

How very noble! Julie silently fumed. She wondered how best to advise Louisa that her journey to Bath had been in vain, that in four short days they would *both* be homeless again. She was pondering several alternative approaches when there was a rather timid knock at the door. Louisa glanced about the bedchamber and—when no servant magically materialized from the woodwork—went to answer.

"Ahem. Good afternoon." The open door obstructed Julie's view into the corridor, but she recognized Sir Oliver's apologetic cough. "I am Sir Oliver Crane."

"Sir Oliver!" Louisa trilled. "Julie has told me a great deal about you. I am her cousin, Louisa Linley."

"Miss Linley." There was a brief pause, and Julie suspected the baronet was negotiating one of his stiff bows. "May I take the opportunity to welcome you to Bath?"

"You may indeed. Though I should regard your welcome with a *most* jaundiced eye if I suspected for a moment that you had arranged the weather."

"It *is* wretched, isn't it?" Sir Oliver rejoined. "Perhaps Miss Brandon has mentioned our harrowing ride to town."

"She did mention it," Louisa confirmed, "and she indicated that you are an *exceedingly* accomplished horseman, Sir Oliver."

Another silence; Julie assumed that the baronet was now blushing. "It was really nothing," he mumbled at last.

"Hardly *nothing*," Louisa said. "To the contrary, it appears that without your expertise Julie might well have been *killed*."

"Oh, scarcely *killed*," Sir Oliver protested. "Severely *injured* perhaps."

Julie was beginning to speculate as to just how long this insipid conversation could continue when she heard another, unidentifiable cough.

"Speaking of injuries," the baronet said, "this is Dr. MacCallum. I summoned him to examine Miss Brandon's ankle. This, Dr. MacCallum, is Miss Linley."

"Miss Linley." A deep but gentle voice. "I, too, welcome you to Bath, and I assure you that *I* am not responsible for the appalling weather either."

Laughter all round; more chatter. She might well *die*, Julie fretted, while Louisa and Sir Oliver and the physician exchanged banalities in the corridor. But at length a bearish man of middle years backed into the bedchamber.

"Please wait outside," he said. Since Louisa had already vanished into the hall, his instruction seemed a trifle gratuitous. "I shall give you a full report after I have examined Miss Braden."

"My name is Miss Brandon," Julie corrected, as he closed the door and strode across the room.

"Miss Brandon," he agreed, "and we shall have just a *look* at your ankle . . ."

Dr. MacCallum's notion of "a look" was a seemingly endless interval of agonizing probing and prodding, but he eventually pronounced his diagnosis: the ankle was not broken, only badly turned. Though it was nothing to be trifled with, he added sternly, winding a bandage halfway to Julie's knee. She must stay off her feet a week at the least, possibly ten days; he would check back. He repacked his case and marched across the Brussels carpet while Julie was still writhing in pain.

The physician left the door ajar, and after an indecipherable murmur of conversation in the corridor, it eased open again. Julie gritted her teeth, fearing that Dr. MacCallum had decided to inflict further torture after all, but it was Sir Oliver who peered across the threshold, then hurried to the bed.

"I took the liberty of apologizing to Miss Linley for Baxter's neglect," he said. "I also directed that she be shown to the bedchamber next to Hester's, where I daresay she will be quite comfortable."

"Umm," Julie muttered. The baronet obviously attached more importance to Louisa's needs than to her own recent travail, and she could not quell a twinge of annoyance.

"She is a charming young woman," Sir Oliver added. "Miss Linley, that is."

He looked expectantly down at Julie, apparently hoping to elicit additional information about her "charming" London cousin. But Julie was too tired to manufacture a suitably respectable background on such limited notice, and she emitted a loud (and largely genuine) moan.

"Miss Brandon!" The baronet perched on the edge of the bed and contritely seized her hand. "Pray forgive my thoughtlessness. Dr. MacCallum has assured me that your injury is not serious, but you must be suffering a good deal of pain."

"A *great* deal of pain," Julie confirmed. This was, again, substantially the truth.

"I am deeply sorry to have been the cause of your distress." Sir Oliver did, indeed, shake his blond head in a most sorrowful manner. "Pluto was bred for a jumper, but his fear of water has precluded any such activity. I should have been more alert—"

"Please do not blame yourself," Julie interposed. "Had you not handled Pluto as skillfully as you did, I fancy my injury would have proved considerably worse."

"Well, as Miss Linley pointed out, I *am* a rather accomplished horseman."

To Julie's astonishment, the baronet preened a bit, but she was in no frame of mind to contemplate his odd new behavior. Her ankle had begun positively to throb, and she wanted only to be alone, to drift again to sleep. She was casting about for the proper courteous words of dismissal when the hall door—which Sir Oliver had left ajar as well—squeaked and came fully open.

"Well," Nick drawled, "it seems I have come at an inopportune moment. Pray excuse me; I shall return at a more convenient time."

"No, it is quite all right, Nick." Sir Oliver guiltily dropped Julie's hand and sprang to his feet. "I wished merely to ascertain Miss Brandon's condition; I was at the point of taking my leave. So I shall ask *you* to excuse *me*."

The baronet's bow was so abbreviated as to be little more than a nod, and he fled across the bedchamber and into the hall. The Captain closed, nay, *slammed,* the door in his wake and stalked to Julie's bedside.

"Another opportunity lost," he snapped, glaring down at her.

She had expected him to display some slight degree of concern, at least a flicker of sympathy, and his actual remark struck her with the force of a physical blow. Dr. MacCallum's unpleasant ministrations had left her literally prostrate, but her exhaustion abruptly evaporated, and she wriggled furiously back to a sitting position.

"An opportunity lost?" she hissed. "Am I now to be held responsible for the weather?"

"I was not referring to our ill-fated picnic." His

voice was utterly frigid, and his eyes were slivers of yellow ice. "I was alluding to the cozy scene I so recently, so rudely interrupted. I daresay Uncle Edmund would have found it *enormously* interesting: Oliver ensconced in your bed, you undressed—"

"I am not undressed!" Julie was so enraged that she altogether neglected to blush. She *did* steal a discreet downward glance and assured herself that Aunt Emily's ensemble—though considerably more provocative than her own—was in no way indecent.

"Oliver pawing you," Nick unheedingly continued.

"Sir Oliver was not *'pawing'* me!" Julie screeched. "He had taken my hand to impart some comfort, which is certainly more than *you* have chosen to do."

"I chose to ride like hell through the rain, and I got here as fast as I could."

Julie belatedly observed that the Captain's buckskin breeches were plastered most revealingly round his legs and that his riding coat had degenerated to a limp travesty of its former splendor. Her fury moderated a bit, and she plucked at the bedclothes, carefully rearranging them round her stomach.

"Not that I need have bothered," Nick went on. "Oliver was caring for you most conscientiously. It was a highly indelicate situation, but was there anyone to observe it?" Julie opened her mouth, but the Captain answered his own rhetorical question. "No, there was not."

Julie wondered what it was he fancied she should have done: had she attempted to summon Lord Arlington or Mrs. Fitch, Sir Oliver would have bolted, like a terrified rabbit, out of the room. But Nick *had* been concerned, it seemed, and she was prepared to be tolerant. She essayed a forgiving smile.

"I can only speculate," he concluded darkly, "as to what might have transpired had I not arrived when I did."

Julie's tolerance, her budding forgiveness, were quite submerged in a veritable flood of renewed rage. She considered a dozen scathing retorts, but before she could select the perfect, devastating response, she realized that he would disbelieve anything she said. He had always thought her a Cyprian, always would, and she had resolved long since not to challenge his opinion.

"You may speculate to your heart's content," she said coldly, "for I do not intend to discuss the matter any further."

"No? Then speculate I shall. I observed, virtually from the beginning, that you were peculiarly reluctant to compromise Oliver, and I am embarrassed to own that it took me so long to puzzle the situation fully out. Be that as it may, it is now clear that you regard Oliver as the perfect target: innocent, vulnerable, infinitely susceptible to your charms."

"Sir Oliver?" Julie gasped in disbelief. "You believe I have settled on him as my—my new protector?"

"I should not do you such injustice, Julie; I believe you are far more clever than that. No, I think you view Oliver as a potential *husband*. If he inherits Uncle Edmund's estate—which you seem well in the way of ensuring—he will be a very wealthy man, will he not?"

He had rendered her quite dumb; her throat worked, but no words emerged.

"Added to which, I suspect you have developed something of a *tendre* for Oliver. I have always found female thinking entirely incomprehensible, but I daresay Oliver is sufficiently handsome, sufficiently intelligent, to garner some favor—"

"Get out," Julie hissed.

"I am sorry if I have overset you," the Captain said politely. "I wish to assure you that I shall not murmur a word to Oliver—"

"Get out!" she shrieked.

"As you will." He negotiated an elaborate bow, backed away from the bed, stopped. "How *is* your ankle, by the by?" he growled.

"My injury is unlikely to prove fatal. So, as you

needn't wait about for my demise, I shall once more request—"

"Julie?" Aunt Emily bounded through the connecting door but ground to a halt just inside. "Oh, do pardon me; I shall come back—"

"Never mind," Nick snapped. "Julie has ordered me out, and I was at the point of acceding to her wishes." He strode across the room, threw open the corridor door, and whirled back round. "I neglected to mention that your sketchbook was quite ruined by the rain; I perceived no reason even to carry it back. But I daresay you can soon reconstruct your work, eh? And I am sure you will find it no sacrifice to spend a few additional hours with Oliver."

He proceeded into the hall and flung the door to with a resounding crash. Aunt Emily gazed after him a moment, then walked to Julie's bed.

"Well, my dear," Mrs. Fitch sighed, "I collect that you and Nick have had a bit of a disagreement."

It was an understatement of such magnitude that Julie started to giggle, but the laugh died in her throat, and she found herself dangerously near to tears. Her anger had drained away, leaving her with no emotion except a great, inexplicable sense of desolation.

"It was nothing," she murmured. Her voice was wretchedly unsteady, and she clamped her teeth upon her quivering lower lip.

"Oh, my poor, dear child." Aunt Emily lowered herself to the bed and took one of Julie's hands in both her own. "I can scarcely bear the notion that I might have been able to prevent this lamentable development. I repeatedly thought to warn you, but I fancied that any advice, coming from me, would be decidedly hypocritical."

Julie surmised that her injury had rendered her a trifle delirious because Aunt Emily's words made no sense whatever. "Warn me?" she echoed weakly. "Hypocritical?"

"Hypocritical in the extreme," Mrs. Fitch said. "You

are aware of the feelings I entertained for Henry; how could I have counseled you to behave as I myself did not? I was, as I have stated, frequently tempted to warn you of the consequences, but why should you have listened? Who was I to point out the awful bumblebath that surely would ensue?"

"*What* consequences?" Julie's head was fairly spinning. "*What* bumblebath?"

Aunt Emily frowned and touched Julie's brow as though she, too, suspected the existence of a debilitating fever. But eventually she shook her head and reclasped Julie's hand.

"I am referring, dear, to the gravest error a woman such as ourselves can make—that of falling in love with a client. Or a *prospective* client, as the case may be."

It all came clear at last: Mrs. Fitch had obviously taken the Captain's parting remark to heart and believed, as he did, that Julie had conceived a great *tendre* for Sir Oliver. Another giggle welled up in her chest and tickled the corners of her mouth, but Aunt Emily looked so very sincere that Julie carefully straightened her face.

"Pray do not tease yourself about it any longer," she said solemnly. "I assure you—"

"I have not yet told you the worst," Mrs. Fitch interposed grimly. "The worst is that I was rather inclined to *encourage* the relationship. There was never any doubt in my mind that it would be the best thing for you, and I rapidly came to believe it would be the best thing for him as well. So I ignored every untoward incident, pretending to myself that they were quite meaningless. I knew better, of course, for I saw it coming early on, saw it coming even in London." Aunt Emily bit her own lip and once more shook her gold-and-silver head.

"London?" Julie repeated. "I did not even *know* Sir Oliver when I was in London."

"Well, of course you didn't, dear," Mrs. Fitch agreed kindly.

She was speaking in riddles again, and Julie was assailed by another wave of dizziness. She thought she might be able to concentrate if her ankle weren't aching so dreadfully, but when she attempted to reposition it, a great bolt of pain shot from her foot to the roots of her hair. She tried and failed to stifle a groan and collapsed against the headboard.

"But I daresay you should rest now."

Aunt Emily's voice seemed to come from far away, and Julie was but vaguely aware of gentle hands maneuvering her down amongst the pillows, tugging the bedclothes back to her neck.

"Yes, you must rest, dear, and if you wish, we shall discuss it later."

Discuss *what* later? Julie groggily wondered. But her eyes were already closed, and she did not even hear the opening and closing of the connecting door.

Chapter 13

Julie had slept, by her reckoning, for approximately thirty seconds when a hand on her shoulder shook her rudely awake. She reluctantly opened her eyes and found Lucy peering down at her.

"Forgive me, miss." Lucy swiftly withdrew her hand. "However, if you wish to join the others for dinner, it is time for you to dress."

Julie did not wish to join the others for *any* activity, tonight or ever, and she shook her head. "No, thank you, Lucy," she murmured.

"Shall I bring up a tray then?"

"No, thank you," Julie said again. "I am not in the least hungry." This, in fact, was true: the food she had consumed at the picnic had apparently been jarred about during the course of her wild ride, and she detected a distinct queasiness in the vicinity of her rib cage.

"Very well," Lucy said. "I daresay it's for the best because it is extremely late indeed. I should have come sooner, but Eliza, the other lady's maid, is ill, and I had to attend Miss Linley as well."

"Louisa!" Julie bolted upright, shuddering to contemplate the damage her cousin might do during a long unsupervised dinner conversation. "I fancy I *am* hungry after all, Lucy; indeed, I am quite ravenous. You must help me dress at once."

The task was more easily stated than done, for Julie

immediately discovered that her injured ankle would not support the slightest bit of weight. She perched precariously on her left leg while Lucy fairly jammed her into the pale-green evening gown. Julie then managed to hobble to the dressing table, where she beheld a most distressing sight: her hair—dampened and subsequently slept upon—was tumbling about her face in wild, uncontrollable curls. She suspected she looked much as she had on the dismal night she'd met Captain Stafford, but she certainly didn't intend to give *him* another thought, and she grimly pursed her lips.

"I am doing the best I can, miss," Lucy snapped, misreading Julie's expression in the mirror.

"I am sure you are." Julie nodded, and the brush snagged painfully in an especially obstinate tangle. "But you must *hurry*, Lucy."

Lucy's "best" was astonishingly good: the finished coiffure scarcely rivaled Mr. Paul's effort, but Julie no longer resembled a dairymaid recently tumbled in the barn. She wondered why that particular image had occurred to her, but there was no time to dwell on it; the corridor clock was already striking seven. Julie struggled to her feet and—half-hopping, half-limping, leaning on Lucy all the while—made her painful way to the stairs, at which point it became clear that they could proceed no further.

"I can't get you down, miss." Lucy merely confirmed Julie's own opinion. "Not without killing both of us. Wait here, and I shall summon Mr. Baxter."

Lucy rushed down the steps, and Julie sagged against the wall, listening to the mocking tick of the clock. Louisa had no doubt reached the dining room long since, but did it really signify? At worst, Louisa would blurt out the whole history of their lives—hers and the life she fancied to be Julie's—and Lord Arlington, with righteous horror, would order them out of his home. But did it matter if they left tonight rather than on Wednesday? To the contrary, a premature departure would be a distinct relief: Julie would be spared further exposure to the odious Captain.

Julie's stomach began to churn again, and she peered down the hall, speculating as to whether she could hobble back to her bedchamber unassisted. She had just determined to make the attempt when Lucy galloped into view, dragging Baxter in her wake.

"Lord Arlington has arranged a wonderful surprise, miss," Lucy panted, reaching Julie's side. "It is waiting in the entry hall, so you must bear with us while we carry you down."

As it happened, a good deal of bearing with was required. Lucy and Baxter, joining hands to elbows, formed a perilous seat, scooped Julie indelicately up, and began to stagger down the stairs. Unfortunately, they could not find a mutual pace: Lucy scampered ahead and waited for Baxter to catch up, whereupon *he* labored down a step or two and paused for Lucy. By the time they reached the foyer, Julie could well imagine the torments inflicted by the medieval rack and wheel.

"And here is Lord Arlington's surprise!" Lucy gasped triumphantly. She and Baxter deposited Julie most unceremoniously in the Earl's abandoned Bath chair. "He had it brought down from the attic just a few minutes since."

Julie quite believed this, for traces of cobweb remained on the seat. "I appreciate his lordship's concern," she said politely. "However, I fancy I can walk from here—"

But Baxter was already pushing the chair industriously forward, and Julie gritted her teeth, dreading the spectacle she would present as she was wheeled dramatically into the dining room. However, her fears proved groundless, for when Baxter halted the chair in the doorway, there was no lull in the conversation. Conversations, Julie amended, peering about. Aunt Emily and Lord Arlington were chatting at one end of the table while Sir Oliver and Louisa, at the other, conducted a separate, equally spirited discussion. Miss Crane, as seemed to have become her habit, was gazing sightlessly into space, and the Captain was drawing aimless designs on the tablecloth with the tines of his silver fork. Julie waited fully half a minute for someone to note her entry and eventually, rather irritably, cleared her throat.

"Miss Brandon!" The Earl leaped to his feet, rushed to the door, and seized Julie's hand. "Permit me to express my deep dismay that you should have suffered such distress while a guest in my home. I directed that dinner be held for you because—as a former invalid myself—I quite recognize the difficulty, the *agony,* with which you dragged yourself from bed. Nevertheless it is imperative that you eat; you must husband your limited strength. If you will position Miss Brandon just there, Baxter, we shall begin."

"Just there" was, unfortunately, the place immediately next to Nick's. One of the footmen scurried forward to remove the chair, Baxter propelled Julie to the table, and the Captain acknowledged her with a nod so cool, so slight, that Julie fancied she might well have imagined it. His lordship resumed his own place and signaled the footmen for the soup.

The soup was mulligatawny, one of Mrs. Vester's perennial failures, and Julie's stomach fairly wrenched as an overpowering odor of curry wafted up to her nostrils. She was inclined to shove the bowl as far as possible across the table, but the Earl was regarding her with a worried frown. She essayed a weak smile and began swirling her spoon about the bowl with great enthusiasm.

"I have already told Mrs. Fitch"—his lordship spoke through a mouthful of soup—"how delighted I am that her *other* niece could visit us as well." He beamed down the table at Louisa. "I am given to understand that Mrs. Fitch was sister to your father, Miss Linley, and to Miss Brandon's mother."

Julie nodded; Louisa shook her vivid red head; Sir Oliver frowned.

"*I* was given to understand that Mrs. Fitch is Miss Brandon's *father's* sister," the baronet said. His tone, not surprisingly, was one of puzzlement.

"I am 'sure you *mis*understood, Sir Oliver," Aunt Emily said kindly. "I am sure that what dear Louisa explained is that I am Julie's father's *cousin.* Her mother's sister and her father's cousin."

"Would that not make Miss Brandon's father and mother cousins as well?" Lord Arlington inquired.

"*Step*cousin, I should have said," Aunt Emily responded smoothly.

Julie heard a small, strangled sound at her right and watched, from the corner of her eye, as Nick hastily buried his mouth in his linen napkin.

"But . . ." Sir Oliver started to protest, then took refuge in his soup; apparently the relationship was so complex that it quite defied his comprehension.

"In any case," the Earl said, "I wish to assure you that you are most welcome, Miss Linley. Both here in Bath and later in Norfolk."

"Norfolk?" Louisa echoed sharply.

"Evidently Miss Brandon neglected to inform you that I intend to return to Arlington Court on Wednesday."

His lordship had finished his soup, and he waved imperiously for the entrée. There was a long pause as the footmen bounded forward, whisked the bowls away, and presented plates of ham and duck, cauliflower and peas. Another pause followed as the footmen retreated, and Julie fervently hoped that Lord Arlington would forget the subject of his discourse.

"That is to say that I *planned* to return on Wednesday." The Earl continued as though there had been no interruption whatever. "I fear Miss Brandon's accident will necessitate a change of schedule." He turned his pale blue eyes directly on Julie. "I spoke with Dr.

MacCallum prior to his departure, and he advised me that you are to remain off your feet at least a week."

"Yes," Julie choked; "yes, that is what he told me as well."

Lord Arlington sighed. "I cannot but wish that Oliver had summoned my *new* physician, for I daresay he would have had you up and about in a matter of hours. But I hesitate to impose upon him at this late juncture, so we shall simply wait.

"Yes"—his lordship's eyes now flew round the table—"we shall wait until Miss Brandon can comfortably travel, and *then* we shall leave for Norfolk. And, as I have stated, Miss Linley, you will be *most* welcome to join us."

Dear God, Julie thought. She cast Louisa a great quelling glance across the table, but her cousin was smiling at the Earl.

"That is very kind of you, Lord Arlington," the Red Fawn murmured throatily. "Very kind indeed, and I shall certainly consider your invitation."

"Excellent." Lord Arlington had somehow managed to devour every morsel on his plate, and he sat back, lacing his fingers contentedly across his waistcoat. "I have always subscribed to the philosophy that whatever may happen is for the best. Your injury is a case in point, Miss Brandon."

Julie's ankle had begun to throb again, and she could not conceive that her pain was of any advantage to anyone. But she bit her lip and dutifully nodded.

"Our journey to Norfolk would surely have delayed your completion of Oliver's portrait," his lordship continued. "In fact, the portrait might not have been finished at all. I know how such matters go." He sighed once more. "One becomes distracted; one develops new interests in a new place. As it is, however"—the Earl brightened—"you can complete Oliver's portrait before we go. Can you not, Miss Brandon? I shan't allow a sitting tomorrow, of course, but if you resume work on Monday, you will have a minimum of six days left."

Julie judged it time—long since time—to extricate herself from this absurd predicament. She had only to stand, to issue a firm refusal, to march out of the dining room. But she could not stand, much less march; and was she to embark boldly upon a new life while imprisoned in a Bath chair? She sensed the Captain's cold yellow eyes upon her and drew herself up.

"I fancy I *can* finish Sir Oliver's portrait," she said.

"Excellent," Lord Arlington repeated.

He signaled for dessert, and Julie—suddenly hungry after all—wolfed down two slices of cheesecake, an enormous bunch of grapes, and three full glasses of dark, sweet sherry.

Julie studied her sketchbook, marveling at the realization that she had somehow produced a superb full-color drawing of the Captain. Yes, there was no mistake about it: her simple pencil had created amber eyes, sun-bronzed skin, brown hair generously streaked with gold. She glanced up, glanced at the other blanket, and Nick gave her an approving smile.

"You must not drop your pencil, Julie," he cautioned. "We should never find it in the grass."

"No, I shan't," she promised.

There was a rumble of thunder, and a few great drops of rain splashed down upon the clearing. Fortunately, the water was warm, pleasant, and evaporated before it reached the ground. Nevertheless the Captain rose languidly to his feet, walked very slowly to Julie's blanket, and drew her up beside him.

"I daresay we should take one of the blankets into the trees," he suggested. "My physician says that afternoon rest is most beneficial."

"Dr. MacCallum?" Julie asked.

"No, my *new* physician."

Julie nodded, and they strolled into the woods, where Nick spread the blanket just a few inches from Pluto's hooves. Julie inquired if they weren't a trifle too close to the horse, but the Captain shook his head.

"Pluto has no fear of water," he assured her. "And I have never observed that you were in the least afraid of horses."

They stretched out on the blanket, and though the rain was now pounding all about them, they remained miraculously warm and dry. Nick soon pulled Julie into his arms and began to kiss her, to kiss her mouth and her ears and her throat. Julie tried to move closer, but the rain had reached her feet, and her skirt and petticoats were firmly plastered round her ankles. She attempted to kick them away—vigorously, then frantically—but the more she struggled, the heavier her clothes became.

"I suspect it's Emily's doing," the Captain sighed, "for she fears you've made a grave error. Falling in love with a client, that is. She saw it coming early on, you know; even in London."

"But it wasn't raining in London," Julie protested. "And now my flounces are growing quite ruined, and I *have* lost my pencil."

She kicked at her sodden garments one final time, but her right ankle got entangled, and she felt a vicious stab of pain. Added to which, the drenching rain had crept to her waist, her neck . . .

Julie's eyes flew open, and she raised her head to find the bedclothes piled in hopeless disarray about her feet. She sat up, gingerly freed her injured ankle from the twisted sheets and blankets, and lay back down. Shafts of morning sunlight were poking round the draperies, but Julie's nightgown was soaked with perspiration, and she was quite as damp and chilly as if she *had* awakened in the clearing. She fancied Aunt Emily would counsel her to pull the bedclothes up again.

Aunt Emily. Julie was drifting somewhere between sleep and wakefulness, night and day, awareness and oblivion; and she wasn't sure whether she smiled or merely *thought* a smile. In any case, she groggily conceded, Aunt Emily was always right. Aunt Emily had advised her to purchase modest attire and to cut her hair and not to fall in love with Nick. Though the latter admonition had been issued a bit tardily, so perhaps Aunt Emily wasn't infallible after all . . .

Julie came instantly alert, totally awake, and—as often happened with dreams—the absurdities fell away, exposing a terrible, bright core of truth. It was *Nick* Aunt Emily had belatedly sought to warn her of. Not Sir Oliver, never Sir Oliver; it was Nick. Aunt Emily had divined the truth when she stepped through the door of the London studio, and Julie herself had missed it.

Julie briefly wondered how she could have been so blind, but—her mind open at last—she perceived the answer in a flash. She had not loved before, and she had always fancied that her great *tendre,* if ever it came, would be a joyful time of shared laughter and mutual tenderness and confidences exchanged. In contrast, her alliance with Nick had been founded on deceit and clouded almost from the start by his affection for another woman. It was scarcely surprising that Julie had failed to recognize her intense attraction to the Captain, her jealousy of Miss Vernon as symptoms of love. Perfectly reasonable that she had misunderstood even her passionate response to Nick's physical advances, had judged her inexplicable behavior "shameless."

But now that the truth was clear, it was equally clear that she must escape at once. She could not linger about, falling increasingly under the spell of a man she could never have. Like wealth, like position, love was a luxury to which she could not afford to grow accustomed.

Julie sat up and lowered her feet to the floor, at which point a nasty jolt of pain reminded her of her predicament. As she had realized the previous evening, she was in no condition to venture boldly toward a new life. Furthermore—a factor that had *not* occurred to her last night—her financial circumstances were little short of dismal. She belatedly recollected that the Captain had agreed to pay her only if he was designated his uncle's heir. And, though Lord Arlington might eventually rule in Nick's favor, it was most unlikely that the Earl would render his decision by the time Julie's ankle healed. She would therefore be compelled to set out with a rather splendid wardrobe and funds of under five pounds—a circumstance, she thought grimly, quite befitting her role as a supposed Cyprian.

But it didn't signify, for she would *not* go to Norfolk. Indeed, she might well return to Northampton and marry Mr. Howe after all. She did not love him, of course, but she didn't expect to love anyone again; and Mr. Howe would no doubt prove an excellent husband. Though that did not presently matter either, for she had some days during which to select a final destination. In the interim, she would avoid the dashing Captain—the irrepressible, impossible Captain—insofar as she could.

Julie limped to the dressing table, where she had placed her extra sketch pad and pencil, and scrawled a note to Lucy, advising the maid that she was entirely too ill to join the rest of the party for church. She hobbled to the corridor door and propped the note against the outside knob, limped back to the bed, and stretched out atop the rumpled covers. Her nightgown had dried by now, but her cheeks were oddly wet, and she told herself that it must be an unusually warm day.

Chapter 14

At five minutes before nine on Monday morning, Baxter and Lucy once more wrestled Julie down the stairs and deposited her in Lord Arlington's Bath chair. The butler then pushed Julie to the parlor off the morning room, where she found the Earl himself, closely supervised by Mrs. Fitch, fumbling with her easel.

"I have observed, Miss Brandon," his lordship said, "that you normally stand while you paint, and, in view of your disability, I was attempting to adjust your easel. However, the damned thing is improperly designed, so we shall have to saw the legs down. See to it, Baxter!" he barked.

The butler rushed out of the parlor, and Lord Arlington turned back to Julie. "Naturally," he added, in a somewhat more temperate tone, "when you have recovered, I shall buy you a new easel."

Julie did not suppose she would ever paint again either, but she nodded and allowed the Earl to wheel her to a spot just behind the recalcitrant easel. Baxter returned with two footmen and two saws in tow; Sir Oliver arrived immediately thereafter; and everyone proffered generous measures of advice as the footmen whittled away.

"A bit lower on the back right," his lordship roared.

"Lower on the back *left*," Aunt Emily corrected.

"I fancy the back legs are at proper height," Sir Oliver put in. "It's the *front* legs that require reduction."

Eventually Lord Arlington pronounced the work complete and placed Sir Oliver's unfinished portrait back on the easel. Julie could not but notice that the top of the canvas was still situated well above her head and that there was a definite left-to-right tilt. However, she feared that any further "adjustment" might well put the portrait in the vicinity of her knees, and she managed a polite, appreciative smile.

"We shall leave you to it then, Miss Brandon," the Earl said heartily. He glanced at the canvas and frowned. "You *can* complete Oliver's portrait before we depart for Norfolk, can you not?"

"Oh, yes," Aunt Emily cooed. "Yes, Julie always begins slowly and finishes in a rush. Though not if we continue to pester her, milord."

Mrs. Fitch propelled Lord Arlington out of the room, Baxter and the footmen trailed after them, and Julie studied the canvas. It was quite as awful as she recalled, but she was determined to complete it to the Earl's satisfaction. If his lordship furnished her a reference, she might be able to paint professionally after all, might be able to avoid marrying Mr. Howe . . .

"We missed you yesterday, Miss Brandon."

Julie had nearly forgotten the baronet's presence, and she started and glanced up. She perceived at once that Sir Oliver's appearance had undergone a subtle change, and she was initially inclined to attribute the transformation to a slight, becoming flush high on his cheekbones. However, as her practiced eye flew from the baronet to the canvas and back, she realized that Sir Oliver seemed more relaxed as well; indeed, he was fairly sprawled in his chair.

"Missed me?" she rejoined absently.

"Yes, at church and at dinner thereafter. Though I trust you will not take it amiss when I report that Miss Linley took your place on both occasions."

"Umm," Julie muttered.

She was attending the baronet only vaguely, but he chattered on while she attempted to reconstruct the drawing she had lost in the deluge. Yes, the nose on the canvas lacked that tiny flare about the nostrils, and the chin was far too weak. Julie painted in the revisions and leaned back to evaluate her effort.

"And then," Sir Oliver was saying, "after dinner, Miss Linley played the piano for us. This was after Georgina had played, and I judged your cousin's performance far superior. I daresay Georgina shared my opinion, for she left in a bit of a miff."

Julie briefly wished she *had* been present, if only to witness Miss Vernon's humiliation. But she would have been compelled to face the Captain, and he no doubt fancied his love remarkably accomplished ... Julie's hands started to tremble, and she bit her lip.

"Yes, Louisa does play quite well," she said. She thought her voice was commendably light, wonderfully casual.

"Evidently talent is a family trait," Sir Oliver said gallantly. "Though Miss Linley tells me her father was a naval officer."

"Yes, he was." Julie began adding a splash of rose to Sir Oliver's pale, painted cheeks. "And my mother was not particularly artistic. Odd, is it not?"

"Miss Linley also indicated that her father died some years since. He must have left her quite well-fixed."

The conversation had suddenly grown treacherous, and Julie lowered her brush. "I was not aware of Uncle John's circumstances at the time he died," she responded carefully, truthfully.

"But Miss Linley did not marry or take a position," the baronet pointed out. "I therefore assume that her father's estate has provided an adequate income."

"I assumed so as well," Julie said.

"Then I collect she remained in London to enjoy the excitement of the city. Does she hold a salon or some such thing?"

"Some such thing," Julie choked.

"I wonder why she elected to come to Bath?" Sir Oliver mused. "She seems in good health."

"Louisa is in excellent health indeed." Julie was still coughing a bit.

"It is all very puzzling." The baronet shook his blond head. "But, whatever the case, your cousin is a lovely woman, Miss Brandon."

"Perhaps you might introduce her to Pluto," Julie suggested desperately. "Just how *is* Pluto, by the by? Has he recovered from our mad ride?"

The black stallion had recovered very nicely, Sir Oliver replied, and through the remainder of the sitting, Julie insisted they relive—detail by excruciating detail—their ill-starred picnic. Nevertheless, when the morning room clock struck half past ten and the baronet excused himself, Julie mopped her brow with one sleeve of her emerald-green spencer. Despite her weeks of practice, she was a sorely unaccomplished deceiver, and she reckoned it inevitable that she would eventually make a fatal error. All the more reason to finish Sir Oliver's portrait as quickly as possible, she thought, and she set grimly to work on the baronet's largish ears.

By one o'clock Julie's unaccustomed posture had rendered her back and neck exceedingly stiff, and, judging that she had made sufficient progress, she decided to stop for the day. She soon realized that if there was any way one could propel a Bath chair unassisted, she did not know it, and she was preparing to hobble to the bell rope when Aunt Emily and Lord Arlington sailed into the parlor. The Earl immediately crossed to the easel, inspected the painting, and, to Julie's relief, pronounced himself pleased with her progress as well.

"We were just setting out for a walk, dear," Aunt Emily said, "and his lordship was kind enough to propose that you accompany us."

The prospect was a tempting one until Julie recalled that they might well meet up with the Captain and Miss Vernon. "Lord Arlington's invitation *is* very kind," she murmured. "However, I fear I am too tired for an outing."

"Nonsense!" the Earl boomed. "You must keep in mind, Miss Brandon, that fresh air is essential to your recovery."

Julie did not believe that fresh air would have any effect whatever on her throbbing, swollen ankle, but his lordship's expression brooked no further objection, and she sighed and nodded. Mrs. Fitch scurried up-stairs to fetch Julie's leghorn hat, and within a few minutes they were under way.

It seemed that everyone in Bath was taking advantage of the fine weather, for Milsom Street was fairly jammed with pedestrians, sedan chairs, and dozens of Bath chairs similar to Julie's. They had scarcely passed the Octagon when they encountered Lady Bristowe, who demanded to know—in her customary shriek—what dread disease had attacked Miss Brandon. Lord Arlington was compelled to bellow out the details of Julie's accident, an explanation which attracted the attention of several passersby. Julie, her face flaming with embarrassment, looked studiedly away and glimpsed Miss Crane and Wyatt on the opposite side of the street, gazing into one of the shop windows. It was the second time she had seen them thus, Julie recalled; evidently Miss Crane had permanently ap-propriated Nick's man as her own personal servant. They turned away from the window, and Miss Crane caught Julie's glance and hastily averted her eyes. At least, Julie thought, she had the grace to be discomfited by her shameless exploitation of the Captain's gener-osity.

Julie reluctantly returned her attention to Lady Bristowe, but, to her unutterable joy, the Countess suddenly remembered an imminent luncheon engage-ment. Her ladyship shouted a few final words of commiseration, then sped away, and the Earl began pushing the Bath chair along the street again. They reached the intersection of George Street, crossed over, and as Aunt Emily and Lord Arlington pondered aloud whether to treat themselves to a box of chocolates, Julie saw Louisa and Sir Oliver perhaps half a block ahead. She had naturally assumed the baronet to be riding, especially on such a splendid day, and she initially fancied her eyes had tricked her. But, at second look, there was no mistaking the vivid red curls spilling from the back of Louisa's French bonnet, no mistaking the tall, rather ungainly figure attempting to juggle the several large parcels with which he'd been burdened. Julie was still figuratively shaking her head with astonishment when she was interrupted by a most unwelcome voice.

"Mrs. Fitch!"

Julie gratuitously turned her head and beheld Miss Vernon literally dragging Nick across the footpath.

"Mrs. Fitch," she repeated. "Lord Arlington. And I am pleased to observe that your condition has improved, Miss Brandon."

She did not sound pleased at all; indeed, she did not sound remotely interested.

"I am in hopes you can settle our disagreement, Mrs. Fitch," Miss Vernon continued. "I have found the *loveliest* bonnet." She tossed her head toward the milliner's shop behind them. "It would perfectly complement my primrose walking dress, which I have not yet been able to wear precisely because I have no suitable hat to match. This one, as I say, is *perfect*, but Nick does not care for it at all." She threw the Captain a flirtatious glare. "But I daresay that if *you* were to approve, Mrs. Fitch, Nick would be forced to own himself wrong. You will have a look, will you not?"

"Of course I shall," Aunt Emily said. "Perhaps we can solicit Lord Arlington's opinion as well."

The three of them retreated into the shop, and Julie waited for Nick to follow. But the Captain continued to stand beside the Bath chair, his yellow eyes flickering up and down and across the street. Julie's heart began to crash against her ribs, and—inexperienced as she was in matters of love—she wondered how he could possibly fail to perceive her feelings.

"I trust your condition *is* improved?" he said politely, looking down at her for the first time.

"Some—somewhat," Julie stammered.

"Excellent." He directed his scrutiny back to the street.

What might transpire if he knew the truth about her? Julie speculated wildly. If, as she'd imagined once before, they had met under proper circumstances? It was too late to undo that, of course—their meeting—but what if she now explained all the absurd particulars? Would he believe her? And, if he did not, what had she to lose?

"Nick." Her voice emerged a very squeak, and she cleared her throat. "There is a matter I should like to discuss—"

"Is that *Oliver*?" The Captain squinted into the midday sun as though, in command of a ship again, he had spotted land where his charts showed only empty sea. "Oliver and Miss Linley?"

"I believe it is," Julie said. "And, coincidentally, Louisa bears upon the topic at hand—"

"What an exceedingly interesting development," Nick drawled. "Did you neglect to inform Miss Linley of your designs on Oliver? I collect so, for apparently *she* judges him a juicy plum as well."

"Nick, please—"

"A most fascinating development indeed. Perhaps I can salvage my project after all; perhaps I can strike a bargain with Miss Linley."

"Nick—"

"But I shan't because I have already burned my fingers once, have I not? I daresay I should retire gracefully from the fray and lick my wounds in peace."

It was no use, no use whatever, and Julie felt a familiar stir of anger. "It does not signify a whit to me what you choose to do," she said coldly.

"No? Then at this juncture I choose to extend a bit of advice. If I were you, I should keep a very sharp eye on Miss Linley, lest she steal Oliver quite away."

"I am not in the least concerned that Louisa might steal Sir Oliver away."

"No?" the Captain said again. "Evidently you are confident of his affection then."

"I am confident that Sir Oliver entertains as much affection for me as ever he has."

"I do hope you are correct." Nick looked down at her once more, and his eyes darkened briefly to amber. "I should find it most ironic if—after all our machinations—we both failed to attain our goals."

"Most ironic indeed." A terrible threat of tears was clogging Julie's throat, prickling her eyelids, and she desperately prayed for deliverance. If only she could operate the damned chair—

"Mrs. Fitch *adored* the hat!"

For the first time (and surely the last), Julie welcomed Miss Vernon's intervention. She blinked her eyes dry, peered gratefully up, and narrowly repressed a hysterical peal of laughter. The bonnet was quite the most hideous thing she had ever beheld: a French walking hat several sizes too large, adorned by an enormous plume of ostrich feathers which spilled almost to Miss Vernon's nose.

"I did not intend to wear it with *this* dress, of course," Miss Vernon said rather defensively, "so you must overlook the yellow trim."

Julie glanced suspiciously at Aunt Emily, but Mrs. Fitch returned a bright, bland, innocent smile.

Sir Oliver and Louisa made for such an implausible pair that Julie did not attach undue importance to the Captain's remarks; she assumed the baronet had escorted her cousin to Milsom Street as an act of mere courtesy. She did count it somewhat more significant when Lucy delivered her dinner and chanced to mention that Sir Oliver was escorting Miss Linley to the

Monday-night assembly as well. But it was not until Tuesday morning, not until Louisa accompanied the baronet to his sitting, that Julie began to sense that something was indeed afoot.

"I trust you do not object, Julie?" Louisa said, firmly ensconcing herself in the window seat. "Oliver finds his sittings so *tedious.*"

Tact had never been among Louisa's transcendent virtues, and Julie bit back an irritated response and turned her attention to the baronet. She observed at once that his cheeks were even more highly colored than they had been the day before and that his gray eyes were fastened on Louisa with an expression which could only be described as adoration.

Good God! Julie thought, what could Louisa possibly be at? The Red Fawn was no doubt sufficiently clever to have recognized Sir Oliver's vulnerability, but she must be aware that his financial circumstances quite precluded an elaborate London establishment. So what, for that matter, was *Sir Oliver* at? Had his longing for adventure impelled him to make promises he could never fulfill?

Julie glanced discreetly at the two of them—who were glancing not at all discreetly at each other—and conceived a far more probable explanation. She had asked Louisa not to disclose her background, and it was extremely unlikely that the ingenuous baronet had independently divined the truth. No, he surely presumed himself to be courting the respectable cousin of the highly respectable Miss Brandon.

Good God! Julie thought again. She wondered if she should intervene—not now, of course, but later, privately. However, she soon realized that she did not know precisely whom to warn, nor of what, and she further recollected that Louisa and Sir Oliver were both well above the age of consent. Their situation was, in short, not her affair (a rather provocative choice of words), and she hastily began to paint the outline of the baronet's jaw.

Whatever Louisa's motives, her continuing presence at Sir Oliver's sittings spared Julie the necessity of engaging in idle conversation with her subject. She could not determine whether it was this factor that speeded her work, her own passionate desire to be done with the portrait, or some combination of the two, but following the Friday-morning sitting she was pleasantly surprised to discover that the painting was virtually finished. She spent several additional hours correcting the folds of Sir Oliver's neckcloth, adjusting the collar of his coat, and as the morning-room clock chimed half past one, she leaned back in the Bath chair and studied the completed portrait. To her greater astonishment, she beheld a most attractive man with a decidedly firm jaw and an unmistakable liveliness about the eyes. Her rendering was so dissimilar to the pale, timid baronet she had first encountered that she feared that—succumbing to the great temptation of the society artist—she had produced a flattering canvas bearing scant resemblance to the subject.

It was, therefore, with considerable trepidation that she displayed the portrait to Sir Oliver and Louisa the following morning, and their long mutual silence was in no way designed to bolster her confidence.

"It is quite good, Julie," Louisa conceded at last. "I do feel that Oliver's hair is somewhat too dull, and I believe you might have made his mouth a trifle larger. But on the whole it is quite good."

"It is *very* good," the baronet corrected, "and I am exceedingly pleased."

He turned to Julie and smiled, and she recognized, with a flood of pride, that she had captured him exactly.

"I understand that you do not accept monetary recompense," Sir Oliver continued, "but if there is any way I can reward you, I hope you will advise me."

Naturally, Julie would have been *delighted* to accept monetary recompense, but she did not judge it the proper time to discuss her perilous future.

"You may reward me by summoning Dr. Mac-

Callum," she said. "A full week has passed since my accident, and I should like him to reexamine my ankle."

Julie had believed for some days that her injury was healing: she had been able to limp about with decreasing difficulty and for extended periods of time. Nevertheless she fairly shuddered when, late that afternoon, Dr. MacCallum unwound the bandage and began jabbing enthusiastically at her ankle bones. To her inexpressible relief, his poking and prodding generated only the tiniest twinge of pain, and he eventually gave up.

"You are much improved," he said. "I shouldn't wish you to go hiking about the woods, but if you exercise care, I daresay I can discharge you."

"I shall not go hiking about the woods," Julie promised dryly.

"Very well."

Dr. MacCallum shoved the bandage into his case and left the bedchamber, and Julie laid her head against the back of the Sheraton armchair. This was the moment she'd awaited: Sir Oliver's portrait was finished; her health was restored; and she could at last escape the Captain's horrid plot. She fervently wished that—as often happened in the childhood tales Mama and Papa had related—she could simply disappear. But real life did not permit such feats of magic; she would now be compelled to report her situation to Lord Arlington and, in the next breath, to announce her defection.

Julie sighed, rose, and walked gingerly across the Brussels carpet. She paused for a moment with her hand on the bell rope, but there was no other way, and she tugged the rope with as much confidence as she could muster.

Chapter 15

As it happened, Julie was not required to deliver a progress report; the turtle soup had scarcely been distributed round the dinner table when Lord Arlington addressed the matter of Sir Oliver's portrait.

"I took the liberty of inspecting the painting this afternoon," the Earl said.

Julie suspected he had taken that liberty *every* afternoon, but she merely nodded.

"I found it eminently satisfactory," his lordship continued, "and I most heartily congratulate you, Miss Brandon. Mrs. Fitch advises me that Nicholas's portrait was left at her home in London, and I am most anxious to retrieve it. I believe the three canvases together will make for a very handsome grouping indeed."

"I do pray so," Julie murmured politely.

"My eagerness to hang the paintings greatly enhances my desire to return to Arlington Court. I was consequently delighted when Dr. MacCallum informed me that there is no further obstacle to your departure from Bath."

"N—no," Julie stammered. She had hoped to broach the matter very carefully, very gradually, but the Earl had fairly snatched the words from her mouth. "That is to say, yes; there is no further obstacle."

"Excellent." His lordship beamed impartially about the table. "Since I do not, of course, subscribe to Sunday travel, we shall leave for Norfolk day after tomorrow. On Monday."

Lord Arlington returned full attention to his soup, and there was a silence, punctuated only by the staccato clang of silver spoons against china bowls. Now, Julie realized frantically—she must speak now.

"Insofar ..." A bit of turtle meat seemed to have lodged in her throat, and she coughed. "Insofar as our departure is concerned—"

"I daresay Carlon and Georgina will wish to leave Monday as well," the Earl interposed.

Julie agreed, for she fancied the Viscount and Miss Vernon would pursue their quarry to Antarctica if such a journey proved necessary. "I daresay so," she said. "However—"

"We must therefore give considerable thought to the precise logistics." Lord Arlington had finished his soup, and he signaled the footmen for the entrée. "Carlon brought his landau to Bath, but if I may be perfectly frank, I judge his equipage totally unfit for human habitation. I consequently propose to use Carlon's conveyance exclusively for luggage. That procedure will enable the nine of us to fit most comfortably in my barouche, my curricle, and Nicholas's landau."

Between swallows of mutton and boiled potatoes, great bites of veal and green beans, his lordship chattered on, arranging and rearranging the members of the party amongst the various carriages. Julie perceived, as she had on so many previous occasions, that her opportunity was slipping away, and she eventually managed a deep breath and clattered her fork on her plate.

"Excuse me, Lord Arlington," she said firmly, "but I do not plan to travel to Norfolk."

There was another lengthy silence, following which the Earl was first to find his tongue. "Not go to Norfolk?" His own fork was poised in midair, dribbling drops of gravy on the tablecloth. "Then just where *do* you intend to go, Miss Brandon?"

"I . . ."

She had been at the point of blurting out that she had not yet selected a destination, but she caught herself up at the last instant. It would not do at all for a respectable young woman to venture forth entirely alone; she must play her part to the very end.

"I plan to visit my other aunt," she responded. "My grandaunt, I should have said—Aunt Sophia, who lives in Northampton."

Mrs. Fitch raised one blond eyebrow, and the Captain shot Julie a penetrating sidewise look.

"Aunt Sophia?" Louisa repeated. "But Aunt Sophia—"

Julie sent *her* a penetrating look, and Louisa assumed a hasty smile.

"Aunt Sophia will be *overjoyed* to see you," she cooed. "Please do extend her my regards, Julie."

"Oh, I shall," Julie promised solemnly.

"Well, I must own myself most disappointed," Lord Arlington said. "I've a great number of relatives in Norfolk, and I had hoped to fill the walls of Arlington Court with family portraits. But I well understand that you cannot shirk your own familial duties, Miss Brandon."

"No, I cannot." Julie sighed.

"I do trust that after you have paid your respects to—er—Aunt Sophia, you will feel yourself welcome to come to Norfolk."

Julie thought she would present herself at the gates of hell before she crawled to Arlington Court, but she nodded again. "I shall always feel myself welcome," she dissembled. "In the interim, it occurs to me that I might wish to paint the occasional portrait. I should like to believe that if such a situation arose, you would furnish me a reference, Lord Arlington."

"Of course; of course."

Evidently the Earl did not count it odd that an amateur artist anticipated a need for references; he expansively waved one of his large, rather stubby hands. The first footman misinterpreted this gesture as a demand for dessert—a fortunate mistake, Julie decided, because the mutton and veal had grown cold, and the gravy was quite congealed. She had long since lost her appetite, but the chocolate blancmange at least *looked* more appealing than the aging entrée. She toyed with her pudding and eventually managed to choke down a spoonful or two.

"So Miss Brandon is not to go to Norfolk," his lordship reiterated. "I hope, Miss Linley, that you will not permit your cousin's decision to influence your plans. As I have previously stated, you are entirely welcome to accompany us."

"I shall follow my own course without regard to Julie's," Louisa said demurely.

Julie received a distinct impression that her cousin was dissembling as well, and she cast another sharp glance across the table. But Louisa, ever endowed with a healthy appetite, was wolfing down her blancmange and did not look up from her bowl.

"Back to the logistics then," Lord Arlington said. "I believe it would be best if Miss Linley were to travel with Mrs. Fitch and myself in the barouche. Oliver and Hester will join the Vernons in the landau, and you, Nicholas, will drive my curricle. On your way out of the city, you can drop Miss Brandon at the coach."

Her weakened ankle notwithstanding, Julie would vastly have preferred to *walk* to the coach, but one did not argue with Lord Arlington. Everyone else assented to his final plan as well, and at last the interminable meal was over.

Julie fled up the stairs and down the hall to her bedchamber and sank onto the canopied bed. The escape she had so passionately desired was now within view, but her relief was generously tempered with a growing sense of panic. She had *not* chosen a destination, and the alternatives tumbled about in her mind, rendering her literally dizzy.

If, in fact, she wished to become a professional artist, she should obviously go to London. Mr. Compton had no doubt forgotten the young woman he'd encountered on the stage, but his memory would surely be jogged if Julie appeared on his doorstep. And she believed she had learned enough, over the past difficult weeks, to elude any impropriety his offer of assistance might have included.

On the other hand, even if Mr. Compton's offer proved perfectly proper and sincere, Julie could not remain with him forever. No, she would shortly be compelled to locate lodgings of her own, and the cost of London living was frightfully high: she would have to become very successful, and very quickly, if she was to support herself in any state beyond abject poverty.

So perhaps she should return to Northampton after all. She need not marry Mr. Howe at once; she could stay temporarily with him and his widowed mother. By the time Mr. Howe began to press her for a decision, she might well have arranged several handsome commissions. And then what? she speculated grimly. There could not be above a year's work in all Northamptonshire.

Julie sighed and heard the soft click of Aunt Emily's corridor door. That was it, of course; she would seek Mrs. Fitch's advice. Of all the people Julie presently knew, she suspected that Aunt Emily was the only one who truly cared for her; and Aunt Emily, she reminded herself wryly, was always right. She leaped off the bed, walked across the room, and knocked on the connecting door.

"Julie, dear."

Mrs. Fitch's smile was a bit too wide, her voice a trifle bright, and Julie glanced over her shoulder. She could not see the settee from where she stood, but she did glimpse a pair of long legs stretched out upon the Axminster rug. Long, slender legs clad in the sable-colored pantaloons the Captain had worn at dinner.

"I should adore to chat, dear," Aunt Emily said, "but you've arrived at a rather inconvenient time. Might you come back in an hour or so?"

"No," Julie muttered; "no, I only wanted to say good night."

"Good night, dear, and do sleep well. I suggest you pack tomorrow, for I am sure Lord Arlington will wish to get an early start on Monday."

Mrs. Fitch closed the door, and Julie trudged back to her bed. She should have recollected that Aunt Emily's first loyalty was to Nick, but she had not, and she felt utterly betrayed. Mrs. Fitch had not even inquired about her plans . . .

Julie lay down on the counterpane and closed her eyes, but the tears seeped out nevertheless and trickled down her cheeks. She would become even more successful than Sir Thomas Lawrence, she vowed furiously. She would become the most famous artist in English history, and they would all regret most bitterly that they had paid her such scant attention when they had the chance.

Toward the end of Sunday dinner, Lord Arlington announced that they were to depart Bath at eight o'clock the following morning.

"Consequently"—the Earl addressed Lord Carlon—"I should like you and Georgina to come at seven. We can breakfast while the servants tend the baggage."

"Very well." The Viscount had appeared somewhat miffed by Lord Arlington's earlier pronouncement that the Vernon carriage was to bear only the party's luggage, but he now seemed to have overcome his indignation. "We shall be here at seven precisely."

Miss Vernon stated that her packing would require the rest of the day; she could not play even one song on the piano. Everyone looked suitably disappointed, and Lord Carlon and his daughter sped back to their rented lodgings.

Julie devoted much of the day to packing as well,

but there were numerous items that could not go into her trunk till the last minute: her threadbare night-clothes, her comb and hairbrush, her limited supply of cosmetics. She therefore decided to retire early and asked Lucy to awaken her at five. The maid agreed and scurried out, and Julie burrowed beneath the covers, but she could not sleep.

She had yet to determine where she would go and less than half a day left in which to reach a decision. She reviewed every advantage, every fault of London and Northampton and eventually glimpsed a means of further procrastination. She would follow Aunt Emily's example, would leave both options open as long as possible. If she went to London, she could readily change to a Northampton coach, and during the journey she might well perceive the *sensible* solution to her dilemma. She drew a ragged breath and began to count the stylized roses on the canopy above her head.

Julie slept only lightly—tossing and turning and dreaming peculiar dreams—and when she felt Lucy's hand on her shoulder, she remained wretchedly un-refreshed.

"Please let me rest awhile longer, Lucy," she mumbled. "Come back in fifteen minutes; I can still be ready by seven—"

"It is not Lucy!" a voice hissed in her ear. "Come, Julie, wake up."

Julie reluctantly opened her eyes, and Louisa tugged her to a sitting position. The room was still dark, but Louisa had lighted the bedside candle, and in its flick-ering glow Julie saw that her cousin was fully dressed.

"Did Lucy fail to wake me?" she asked groggily. "Assure Lord Arlington that I shall hurry—"

"No, you've plenty of time," Louisa interposed. "I came because"—she hesitated a moment—"because I wished to bid you a private farewell."

Louisa had never exhibited any measurable degree of cousinly feeling, and Julie studied her with consid-erable suspicion. She thought Louisa looked somehow

different—that her face was softer, her eyes warmer—
but perhaps that was a trick of the dancing flame.

"Farewell, Louisa," she said. "I hope you will have a
pleasant journey and a pleasant stay in Norfolk. I
further hope you will permit me to go back to sleep."

She started to wriggle beneath the bedclothes again,
but Louisa seized her arm and gave her a vigorous
shake.

"*Please,* Julie," she pleaded. "I must talk to you, and
there is not much time."

Julie was quite sure that not half a minute since
her cousin had said there was *plenty* of time. But she
was far too tired to argue over trivialities, and she
jerked her arm from Louisa's grasp.

"Very well," she snapped. "What is it you want to
discuss? And pray be quick about it."

"Quick about it." Louisa nodded and perched on the
edge of the bed. "I shall begin, then, by advising you
that I have told Oliver the entire truth about my
past."

"Louisa!" Julie became, in the same instant, fully
awake and thoroughly annoyed. "I specifically requested
you—"

"Allow me to finish, Julie. I was at the point of
adding that I have not told Oliver, nor anyone else,
the truth about *you.*"

Julie was sorely inclined to correct, once and forever,
her cousin's sordid notion of the "truth." But she realized that any such correction would require endless
explanations, and at this juncture the benefits did not
appear to justify the effort.

"Thank you," she said dryly.

"However," Louisa continued, "I should like to take
this final opportunity to attempt to—to redirect your
life."

"To redirect my life," Julie echoed. She briefly fancied she was caught up in another ludicrous, but highly
realistic, dream.

"Yes," Louisa said. "You may recall that when we

were in London, I stated my opinion that the lot of a Cyprian is not altogether a bad one."

"I do recall that," Julie agreed.

"I have not entirely *changed* my view," Louisa said, "but I have modified it." Julie wasn't certain whether this was a contradiction or not. "I have come to believe that the best course is to seek the affection of an honest man. To marry, to have children—in short, to be *respectable*."

She *must* be dreaming, Julie thought, and she shook her head to jar herself awake.

"I was afraid you would not concur," Louisa said sorrowfully, "and it pains me to own that I encouraged your wanton ways. And I understand your financial situation all too well: you and Captain Stafford have fallen out, and you've been left with nothing but the clothes on your back."

Though the former Red Fawn was quite mistaken about the nature of the "falling-out," she had deduced the result with frightful accuracy, Julie reflected grimly. But she did not choose to discuss her monetary hobble either.

"Do not tease yourself about it, Louisa," she said. "I fancy I shall muddle through—"

"But you *won't*," Louisa protested. "If you leave Bath without a farthing, you'll stumble into another liaison, then another, and you *will* follow in my footsteps. I speak from experience, Julie, and that is why I want you to have this."

Louisa fumbled in the pocket of her gray carriage dress, withdrew her hand, and laid Viscount Romney's diamond-and-emerald ring on Julie's palm. "It is worth a great deal of money, and I daresay it will support you for many months."

Many *years*, Julie amended, recollecting her cousin's extravagant tastes. But . . .

"I deeply appreciate your concern, Louisa." A great lump had formed in Julie's throat, and she tried to cough it away. "However, I can't possibly accept—"

"Of course you can." Louisa sounded a bit tremulous as well. "Regard it as a contribution from Godfrey; his first charitable act in his whole miserable life."

The corridor clock started to chime, and Julie distantly noted that it was only four. There *was* plenty of time, but Louisa sprang off the bed and straightened her leghorn hat.

"I must go now." She leaned down and kissed a spot in the general vicinity of Julie's right cheekbone. "I wish you the very best of luck; I shall be most disappointed if you do not become the premier artist in all the Empire."

Louisa hurried across the Brussels carpet, slipped out of the room, and closed the door behind her. Julie had wanted to wish her cousin luck as well, to wish Louisa success in her pursuit of an "honest man"; but it was too late. She brushed the tears from her eyes and fastened her fingers round Lord Romney's ring.

Chapter 16

Exhausted though she had fancied she was, Julie could not fall back to sleep, and when the hall clock struck half past four, she sighed and gave up. By the time Lucy arrived, Julie was half dressed, and within an hour the efficient little maid had repaired her coiffure and packed the last of her things. Lucy fastened the trunk and turned away from the canopied bed.

"In the event I don't see you again, I have enjoyed serving you, Miss Brandon."

Julie felt the swelling of another lump in her throat and sternly gulped it back; this was not the moment for regrets. "Thank you, Lucy; you have been most helpful. I daresay Aunt Emily needs you as well, so I shall summon a footboy to carry my trunk downstairs."

"I shall see to the trunk while I'm tending Mrs. Fitch, miss. Then, if I can, I'll help you with your art supplies."

"My art supplies!"

Julie had quite forgotten them, and, with a hasty nod at Lucy, she rushed to the parlor. Following her completion of Sir Oliver's portrait, she had left the room in dreadful disarray, and she gazed unhappily about. She saw no way to lug her sawed-down easel, her palette, and her extra canvases the length and breadth of England, but she could at least salvage the paint. She frantically tugged the bell rope and began gathering up and cleaning off the various containers. The footboy who eventually answered her summons was not overly clever; it took him nearly half an hour to locate a suitable box and another ten minutes to arrange the paints inside. When Julie was reasonably sure that he had finished, she instructed him to bear the box to Lord Arlington's curricle, and she herself dashed across the morning room and into the breakfast parlor.

Lord Carlon and Miss Vernon had obviously come early; they were already seated at the table, enthusiastically devouring great portions of eggs and bacon, kidneys and muffins. Aunt Emily, Lord Arlington, and Nick were serving themselves from the mahogany sideboard, and Julie—though she had no appetite at all—slipped into the line behind them. She placed a single muffin and two rashers of bacon on her plate, and just as she assumed her customary chair, the morning room clock started to chime the hour.

"Seven!" the Earl announced peevishly. "I thought I had made it clear that we were to breakfast at seven and depart at eight. Where is the rest of the party? Where is Hester? Where is Miss Linley? Where is Oliver?"

Baxter, who had been pouring coffee into Aunt Emily's cup, straightened and wiped the spout of the silver pot on a napkin draped over his forearm. "Miss Linley?" he repeated. "Sir Oliver? Begging your pardon, sir, but I assumed you knew; they left the house some three hours since."

"Left?" his lordship bellowed. "Left for where, Baxter?"

"I'm afraid I couldn't say, sir. That is to say, I *can* say that Sir Oliver ordered out a carriage to bear them to the White Hart, from whence, I collect, they were to embark upon a coach. But where the *coach* was going, I simply couldn't say. As I say, milord, I thought you knew."

The butler's numerous *say*'s had rendered Julie most

confused, and it appeared she was not alone: the table had fallen into puzzled silence. The interlude was interrupted by the arrival of a young man Julie vaguely recognized as Robinson, the baronet's valet.

"Pardon me, Lord Arlington." Robinson panted to a halt at the threshold of the breakfast parlor. "Pardon me, but it is seven o'clock, is it not?"

"It is long *past* seven," the Earl growled.

"I am sorry for that, but Sir Oliver instructed me to deliver a message exactly at seven, and I fancy the clock in our corridor is a trifle slow—"

"Get on with it, Robinson!" his lordship roared.

"Yes, sir," the valet gulped. "Sir Oliver desired me to tell you that he and Miss Linley have gone to Scotland to be married. They will shortly return to Norfolk, where they will pay their respects to you. Sir. Milord. Your lordship."

"Is that all, Robinson?"

"Yes, sir. Milord. Your—"

"Never mind, Robinson! You are excused!"

The valet bowed and fled into the morning room, and there was another long, astonished silence.

"Oliver and Miss Linley have eloped," the Earl said at last. His words, his tone suggested that he alone possessed the wit to have reached this startling conclusion.

"So it would seem," the Captain agreed politely.

"But why?" Lord Arlington crashed his fork on his plate, and a morsel of scrambled egg slithered to the tablecloth. "Miss Linley is a *lovely* girl; surely Oliver cannot have supposed that I should offer an objection."

Julie choked on a bit of muffin and hurriedly washed it down with a swallow of coffee.

"It is difficult to surmise just what may have been in Sir Oliver's mind," Aunt Emily said soothingly.

"Most difficult indeed," Lord Carlon snapped. "And I must own myself both shocked and disappointed by your nephew's conduct, Arlington. He has courted Georgina for many months, and it is now apparent, *painfully* apparent, that he was merely toying with the poor child's affections. How fortunate that he revealed his true character before you designated him your heir. And how fortunate you have *another* nephew worthy to follow in your honorable footsteps." The Viscount beamed at Nick.

"Yes, yes," the Earl said impatiently. "Of more immediate import, however, is the question of how best to break the matter to Hester."

"Break *what* matter to Hester?"

Miss Crane was standing in the doorway, and, despite her preoccupation, Julie noted that her appearance had changed over the weeks as well. Her pale eyes—though now narrowed with suspicion—had acquired a definite sparkle, and her pasty complexion had turned an unmistakable pink. Indeed, Julie thought, Miss Crane might almost be termed pretty.

"What matter?" she repeated.

Lord Arlington gazed pointedly around the table, and everyone else pointedly avoided his gaze.

"My dear Hester," the Earl said heavily. He rose and crossed the room, took Miss Crane's arm, guided her to the nearest empty chair, seated her. "Try to be brave, my dear, for we have news I fear you will find quite distressing." He patted her hand and drew a deep breath. "Do we not, Mrs. Fitch?"

Aunt Emily shot him a glare but quickly assumed one of her wide, bright smiles. "Let us not call our news 'distressing,'" she said. "The fact is, Miss Crane, that Sir Oliver and my dear niece Louisa have gone to Scotland to be wed. I can well imagine that you may initially find this turn of events somewhat disturbing, but I daresay, once you have grown accustomed to the notion—"

"But that is wonderful!" Miss Crane snatched her hand from his lordship's protective grasp and clapped both hands together. "I fancy Oliver will be extremely happy with Miss Linley."

Miss Crane's reaction was so entirely unexpected

that Julie felt her mouth drop open. Nor, again, was she alone: every eye at the table had visibly widened, and Lord Arlington was clutching Miss Crane's chair as if for support.

"Furthermore," Miss Crane continued, "Oliver's course eliminates any final doubts I might have entertained about my own." *She* drew a deep breath and straightened her rather bony shoulders. "I shall not travel to Norfolk either, Uncle Edmund, for I have decided to marry Mr. Wyatt."

In contrast to Miss Crane's announcement, the news of Sir Oliver's elopement was relegated to the status of a commentary on the weather. Wide eyes grew to saucers, and the ensuing pause could only be described as stunned. She had missed the obvious again, Julie reflected distantly; she had attached no significance to Miss Crane's excursions with Wyatt. Though, in that respect, the Captain had been equally remiss: he had failed to puzzle out Miss Crane's sudden lack of interest in her brother's future.

"Wyatt?" Miss Vernon was first to recover. "You intend to wed a *servant?*"

"Charles is far from being a '*servant*,'" Miss Crane retorted testily. "As Nicholas could tell you if he saw fit to do so—"

"Yes, Wyatt does act in a number of capacities," the Captain hastily interjected. "Be that as it may, I am delighted by the match, Hester, and I shall certainly assist you insofar as possible. Which leads me to inquire just where it is you and—er—Charles plan to go."

"Charles felt you would not object if we were to occupy your house in London while we searched for lodgings of our own. He further suggested that if we rearrange the carriages a bit, you could drop us at the White Hart along with Miss Brandon. She could take the coach to Northampton, we the one to London."

Julie recollected that she had not yet informed Nick of her intention to travel to London as well. She did not plan to sell Lord Romney's ring at once, but if the necessity arose . . . She felt in the pocket of her skirt. Yes, if the necessity arose, the ring was there. She opened her mouth, but it was too late.

"I have a better idea," the Captain said. "I propose that you and Wyatt drive the landau to town. Indeed, if you've no objection, I should very much like to make the carriage and team a wedding gift."

"I have no objection," Miss Crane responded. "However, as I am sure you understand, I must consult Charles."

"Of course." Julie thought a wayward grin tickled the corners of Nick's mouth, but he continued very solemnly. "In the interim, I should regard it as a favor if you and—and Charles would see my equipage safely to London. You will naturally wish to instruct the servants to transfer your luggage from Lord Carlon's vehicle."

Julie wondered if she should ask the newly engaged couple to drive her to the city as well. But as she debated how best to explain her sudden change of plans, her opportunity once more vanished: Miss Crane sprang to her feet and hurried out of the breakfast parlor. Lord Arlington stared after her a moment, then turned back to the group and cleared his throat.

"Well. Ahem." He coughed again. "In view of these very—very remarkable developments, I perceive no reason to withhold my own intelligence. I had thought to wait until we reached Norfolk, but, as I say . . ." He strode to Aunt Emily's chair and placed his hands on her shoulders. "I am exceedingly happy to inform you that Mrs. Fitch—my dear Emily—has consented to be my wife."

Good God! Julie thought, what was to transpire next? Were they to learn that Baxter and Lucy were also betrothed? Eliza and Robinson? Mrs. Vester and the first footman?

"Naturally," the Earl went on, "our marriage will affect the disposition of my estate. Unfortunately, it is a trifle late for Emily and me to be blessed with children." Mrs. Fitch blushed. "However, now my health has been restored—a circumstance I attribute largely to my future wife—I fully anticipate another quarter century of active life. At the—ah—proper time, I shall divide my wordly goods equally amongst Emily, Nicholas, and Oliver."

"An excellent solution," Lord Carlon choked; "yes, eminently fair."

He tugged at his neckcloth and—though Julie found the room pleasantly cool—snatched his napkin off his lap and began to mop his brow.

"May I suggest, Arlington," the Viscount added silkily, "that a *double* wedding might be in order? There can be no advantage in delaying the inevitable, eh?"

He beamed once more at Nick, then at Miss Vernon; evidently, Julie thought wryly, he judged a third of a loaf infinitely better than none.

"We shall have ample time to settle the details en route to Norfolk," Lord Arlington said. "Since Hester and Wyatt are to take Nicholas's landau, you and Georgina will be in the barouche with Emily and myself."

"Oh, I fancy not, Lord Arlington," Miss Vernon said coyly. "I should prefer to go in the curricle with Nick; it appears we have a *great deal* to discuss."

"Very well," the Earl agreed. "Nicholas will drive Miss Brandon to the coach and return for you, Georgina. Are we ready then?"

As long and as eagerly as Julie had awaited this moment, she was *not* ready. She had developed a genuine fondness for the blustery Earl, and when he came around the table, assisted her from her chair, awkwardly patted her shoulder, she was hard put to gulp down a new threat of tears. She looked from him to Aunt Emily, who was standing just beside him, and managed a shaky smile.

"I wish you both every happiness," she said. She feared her dignity was somewhat impaired by the fact that her nose had started to run.

"Oh, my dear."

Mrs. Fitch opened her arms, and Julie was lost. She truly loved Aunt Emily, had long since forgiven her one moment of neglect, and she fairly collapsed into the proffered embrace and buried her face in Mrs. Fitch's bombazine collar.

"Do not cry, dear," Aunt Emily whispered. "Everything will be all right. I promise you—if you permit it—that everything will be all right."

It was the empty comfort a mother might extend a fretful child, but Julie was determined not to humiliate herself. She emitted a single great sniff and drew away, and they all trooped out to the drive. Lord Arlington handed Mrs. Fitch into the barouche, Lord Carlon clambered in behind them, and the carriage—followed by the Viscount's baggage-bearing landau—rattled into the street. The Captain helped Julie into the curricle and took the seat beside her.

"Good-bye," Miss Vernon called, waving gaily from the porch. "I shall see you in half an hour, Nick."

The Captain clucked the team to a start, and they trotted into the street as well. Julie had not been to the White Hart, but she collected from Miss Vernon's parting remark that it lay approximately fifteen minutes from Queen Square. A brief journey, and Julie was in no mood for idle conversation, but the silence very shortly grew oppressive.

"Well," she said brightly, "the morning has certainly provided an abundance of surprises, has it not?"

"Indeed it has. *Pleasant* surprises, in my estimation. Though I shudder to contemplate the consequences if Oliver were ever to learn of Miss Linley's past."

"But Sir Oliver *knows* about Louisa's past," Julie said. "She came to my bedchamber at an appalling hour this morning to tell me so. I didn't realize the significance of her revelation at the time, of course ..." Julie's voice trailed off. "One wonders, for that matter, how Lord Arlington would react if he discovered Mrs. Fitch's background."

"He knows as well." Nick's yellow eyes were fastened on the street, but Julie thought she detected a familiar telltale twitch about his mouth. "Uncle Edmund's engagement to Emily was *not* a surprise. Not to me, at any rate; she informed me of their plans Saturday night. Emily is an exceedingly clever woman: she somehow confessed her own circumstances without blackening the rest of us. Until the day he dies, Uncle Edmund will believe that you and I and Miss Linley are utterly beyond reproach."

"But why would Lord Arlington wed an avowed Cyprian?" Julie demanded. "He seems so very upright."

"Oliver seems very upright, too; do you not agree?" It was another of the Captain's rhetorical questions. "I can only surmise that love works many miracles."

"But you do not believe in love," Julie pointed out.

"No, I never did."

Nick steered the curricle round one corner, then another, and Julie grasped the side of the seat lest she lose her balance.

"In any event," she said at length, "it appears the situation has been resolved to your benefit. You will—it is true—inherit only a third of Lord Arlington's estate, and that not for some years. But I daresay a third is quite enough, and I fancy his lordship will make some interim provision—"

"I don't care a deuce for Uncle Edmund's estate," the Captain interposed. "As you are no doubt aware, I took advantage of my naval career to accumulate objects of interest from throughout the world."

"Yes, I remember your house."

"The items in my home are the very few I elected to keep for myself. No, by the time of my retirement, I had collected a small warehouseful of goods, and

I—well—I set myself up as a merchant. Wyatt is my chief assistant in the enterprise; as Hester so eagerly pointed out, he is far more than a servant. I started to tell you of my endeavor in London, but I feared you might inadvertently mention the matter to Uncle Edmund. And I did not suppose that he, nor Lord Carlon either, would approve of my participation in trade. In any case, while I hardly count myself a wealthy man, I earn enough to be quite comfortable."

"So you were never seeking Lord Arlington's money," Julie said, "and you advised me at the start that you've no desire for a title. You devised the entire plot solely to win Miss Vernon."

"Yes," Nick admitted, "it was all for Georgina. I naturally preferred to lay the blame on Lord Carlon, but the truth is that Georgina had made it abundantly clear she wouldn't wed me unless I could afford to support her in very handsome style indeed. And I realized that marriage to Georgina would force me to terminate my business activities. In the first place, she wouldn't wed me if she learned I was a merchant; in the second, she bitterly resented my travel. All of which serves to explain, I trust, why *I* resented your comments about Georgina. You consistently—if unwittingly—managed to remind me of her attitude."

"How fortunate for you," Julie said stiffly, "that Miss Vernon seems prepared to modify her 'attitude.' Since Sir Oliver is no longer available, both she and Lord Carlon appear *most* anxious to cement your alliance."

Her nose was starting to run again, her eyes to water, and she stared stonily out her side of the curricle. She had attended their route but vaguely, and she now perceived that they had left the city and entered the woods. She had presumed the White Hart to be located in town, and when Nick brought the carriage to a halt, she peered about.

"I think you have lost your way," she said, seeing nothing but forest in every direction.

"No, I think I have *found* my way." The Captain turned to face her, his eyes sweeping from the brim of her French bonnet to the toes of her chamois slippers, and Julie quelled a familiar, maddening inclination to blush. "Though I hardly know where to begin."

Since Julie had no notion what he was at, she could offer scant assistance. "Well, you must begin somewhere," she said briskly. "And quickly, too, for Miss Vernon is waiting."

"Georgina; yes, I believe I shall begin with her. Can you possibly understand that over the years Georgina had grown to be a—a habit?"

Julie distantly recalled that Aunt Emily had once used the very same word, but she elected not to respond.

"I came to *assume* a certain fondness for Georgina," Nick continued, "and as I have indicated, I did not expect to entertain warmer feelings for any other woman. Consequently, I declined to recognize those circumstances which tended to prove me wrong. I couldn't delude myself entirely, of course, so after the incident in London, I judged it best to ignore you. To *try* to ignore you, that is—"

"You succeeded in ignoring me very well," Julie snapped. "Except when you were ripping me up."

"Yes, I fear my behavior was rather odious."

"More than 'rather,' " she corrected coolly.

"Please allow me to finish, Julie. Even when I found myself criticizing Georgina, observing the numerous flaws in her character, I refused to acknowledge the truth. I was persuaded that if only I could secure Uncle Edmund's estate, my life would be put aright again. So I was furious when you avoided Oliver, dallied with your other suitors—"

"I *had* no other suitors!" Julie screeched.

"*Will* you let me finish! As time passed, I wanted Georgina less and less, but despite my waning enthusiasm—no, perhaps *because* of it—I grew increasingly annoyed with you. It appeared that you were deliberately undermining our project . . ."

Nick rattled on, and Julie recollected that he invariably rambled in just such fashion when he had a troublesome message to impart. If he wanted to apologize for his "rather odious" behavior before he drove her to the coach . . .

"Will you please get on with it?" she interjected at last. "What are you attempting to say?"

"I am attempting to say that I love you!" the Captain roared. "And you are making it damned difficult!"

Julie once more fancied she was dreaming, but when she blinked her eyes, he was there; his angular face, his sun-streaked hair, his long, brown hands were there. "Oh, Nick."

He took her in his arms—an exceedingly awkward procedure in the cramped seat of the curricle, but Julie didn't care a whit. His mouth on hers was just as she remembered it, just as she *had* dreamed it: soft and probing, gentle and hungry, all at the same time. Her lips parted, and she pressed closer, but not close enough—never close enough. A shameless response indeed . . .

Julie drew abruptly away. "I am not a Cyprian, Nick," she blurted out. It struck her as a very odd confession, but confession seemed the order of the day.

"Good God, I know that," the Captain said hoarsely. "We'll discuss the matter later; at this juncture I discover myself remarkably disinterested in the past."

He lowered his head again, but Julie squirmed to the far side of the seat.

"We shall discuss the matter *now*," she insisted. She had intended to sound very firm, but her throat was a trifle clogged as well, and she coughed to clear it. "How do you know? When did you know?"

"I *suspected* from the very beginning." Nick took her hand, traced one of the lines in her palm, and Julie shivered. "At the risk of offending you, love, I must say that you didn't *look* like a Fashionable Impure. I grew virtually certain on our last day in

London, but at that point I was trapped: I had already invested nearly two precious weeks in you. To say nothing of many hard-earned pounds. Had I admitted your respectability, even to myself, I should have been compelled to release you and start anew with someone else. So I convinced myself that you *were* a Cyprian, a fiction I managed to perpetuate until our—our 'rehearsal.' " He traced another line in her hand. "There is no other woman in the world I should prefer to kiss, Julie, but it was very clear that you are *not* an accomplished seductress."

"But you permitted me to go on with Sir Oliver's 'attack'!" Julie snatched her hand furiously away.

"As soon as I was persuaded of your respectability, I was at least *half*-persuaded that you wanted to marry Oliver. You were two babes in the woods, so to speak, and you'd spent a good deal of time alone while Oliver sat for his portrait. So I fancy I viewed the 'attack' as a test: if you were willing to compromise Oliver, you would prove—beyond doubt—that you didn't care for him."

"Odious," Julie said. "*Really* odious."

"The weather aborted the plot"—the Captain went on as though he hadn't heard her—"and I next found Oliver perched on your bed, holding your hand, murmuring who-knows-what tender endearments. You will remember my reaction."

"Yes," Julie snapped, "I *well* remember your unreasonable, unwarranted, unjustified . . ." She feared she was repeating herself, and she stopped. "And then?" she asked grimly.

"And then, on Saturday night, when you announced you wouldn't go to Norfolk, I realized I must be mistaken. I sought Emily's advice, and she informed me that *she* had discerned the situation from the start. Emily has a most irritating way of always being *right*."

And Aunt Emily always fulfills her promises, Julie thought. A grin teased the corners of her mouth, but it somehow got entangled with a burgeoning new lump in her throat, and she gazed down at her shoes.

"Emily further confessed that she had been plotting against *me*," Nick continued indignantly. "She abetted the original scheme with the hope that it would force me to recognize my feelings. She succeeded, of course, but I quite understand that it may be too late. I shouldn't be at all surprised if you refused to forgive me."

Julie willed herself not to look up; Aunt Emily would keep a *parti* guessing until the very last instant.

"Please, Julie, there's nothing more I can say."

She hurtled across the seat and nearly bowled him out the other side of the carriage. It was all very clumsy indeed—his lips were on her forehead, hers on his chin—but at last they managed a proper kiss. Several kisses actually, and Julie soon judged them most wonderfully *im*proper.

"I love you, Nick," she sighed, when he finally granted her pause for breath. "I had no opportunity to say so before—"

"It doesn't signify," the Captain interjected airily. "Emily gave me to understand that my suit would not be altogether unwelcome."

"You and Aunt Emily plotted against *me*!" Julie tried to sound highly vexed, but she could not repress a burst of laughter. Ah, Aunt Emily, you deserve to be a countess ... "What exactly are you offering?" she demanded aloud.

"I am offering you a very risky existence as Mrs. Nicholas Stafford, the wife of a moderately successful merchant. You will be compelled to travel to all manner of unhealthy, uncivilized places, and I venture to guess you'll bear at least one of our children in a ship's cabin. But I assure you, my dear love, that you will never be bored."

"I accept." Julie did not have to mull it over even

for a moment. "Where, specifically, do we proceed from here?"

"I propose we proceed to London. I've a number of friends there, and I daresay we can procure a special license and be wed within the week. Do you find my proposal satisfactory, love?"

In fact, Julie did *not* find his proposal satisfactory; she would have preferred to be wed within the hour. But she fancied his schedule was the best to which they could reasonably aspire, and she nodded.

"Unfortunately," Nick said, "I doubt we'll have time to procure a suitable ring. Perhaps we can purchase an interim ring, a simple band—"

"But I have an interim ring!" Julie dug in the pocket of her skirt and extracted the great, gaudy cluster of diamonds and emeralds. "A gift from Viscount Romney, via Louisa. I daresay if we use it, we shall ease Louisa's disappointment: she expected me to become the premier artist in all the Empire."

"But who is to say you won't? Anything is possible, Julie."

The Captain pulled her against him, she laid her head on his shoulder, and he clucked the horses to a start again. Julie was reminded of the night they'd met—so short a time ago, so infinitely long ago. A matter of weeks, but she hadn't known Lord Arlington or Miss Crane or Wyatt or Sir Oliver. Hadn't known Aunt Emily; dear, omnipotent Aunt Emily. Hadn't known Baxter or Lucy or Lord Carlon or Miss Vernon . . .

"Miss Vernon!" Julie gasped and bolted upright. "Miss Vernon is waiting for you; what is to happen to *her*?"

"If Georgina is clever," Nick drawled, "she will wait an hour or two, give up, and take the first coach to Norfolk. If she is *not* clever, she may well linger in Bath until she is sufficiently aged to profit from the waters. And if I may be perfectly candid, my love, I do not care a deuce one way or the other."

Julie wriggled against him again and watched the trees blur by. They were on their way to London, but after that ... After that, the whole world awaited them; as her own dear Captain had said, anything was possible.

About the Author

Though her college majors were history and French, Diana Campbell worked in the computer industry for a number of years and has written extensively about various aspects of data processing. She had published eighteen short stories and two mystery novels before undertaking her first Regency romance.

SIGNET Regency Romances You'll Enjoy

(0451)

- [ ] **THE KIDNAPPED BRIDE** by Amanda Scott.
  (122356—$2.25)*
- [ ] **THE DUKE'S WAGER** by Edith Layton.
  (120671—$2.25)*
- [ ] **A SUITABLE MATCH** by Joy Freeman.
  (117735—$2.25)*
- [ ] **LORD GREYWELL'S DILEMMA** by Laura Matthews.
  (123379—$2.25)*
- [ ] **A VERY PROPER WIDOW** by Laura Matthews.
  (119193—$2.25)*
- [ ] **THE DUKE'S MESSENGER** by Vanessa Gray.
  (118685—$2.25)*
- [ ] **THE RECKLESS ORPHAN** by Vanessa Gray.
  (112083—$2.25)*
- [ ] **THE DUTIFUL DAUGHTER** by Vanessa Gray.
  (090179—$1.75)*
- [ ] **THE WICKED GUARDIAN** by Vanessa Gray.   (083903—$1.75)
- [ ] **BROKEN VOWS** by Elizabeth Hewitt.   (115147—$2.25)*
- [ ] **LORD RIVINGTON'S LADY** by Eileen Jackson.
  (094085—$1.75)*
- [ ] **BORROWED PLUMES** by Roseleen Milne.   (098114—$1.75)†

*Prices slightly higher in Canada
†Not available in Canada

Buy them at your local bookstore or use this convenient coupon for ordering.

THE NEW AMERICAN LIBRARY, INC.,
P.O. Box 999, Bergenfield, New Jersey 07621

Please send me the books I have checked above. I am enclosing $_____
(please add $1.00 to this order to cover postage and handling). Send check
or money order—no cash or C.O.D.'s. Prices and numbers are subject to change
without notice.

Name_____

Address_____

City _____ State _____ Zip Code _____
Allow 4-6 weeks for delivery.
This offer is subject to withdrawal without notice.